1

Also by Victoria Heckman

K.O.'d in Hawai'i Series

K.O.'d in Honolulu
K.O.'d in the Volcano
K.O.'d in the Rift

Burn Out

Kapu
Sacred
A Coconut Man Mystery of Ancient Hawai`i

Victoria Heckman

2010 Revenge Publishing

Published in the United States by Revenge Publishing.

ISBN 978-0-9846098-0-2

Front Cover Liam Heckman
Back Cover Jason Crabtree
Original Art Eric Schofield
Author Photo Blue Moon Photography

For my husband
Dave Doust

Acknowledgements

This book was a long project in that for two years I researched on ancient Hawaiʻian culture, plants, animals, etc., before I started to write. Then came another problem. I didn't have a main character. I thought he would be a male who could access different caste levels and be able to move around the islands, but nothing came to mind, and nothing worked. Gratitude goes to a basket weaver at the top of Wailua Falls who told me stories and in part, inspired my "Coconut Man." Thanks also, to Blossom Sap at Puʻuhonua O Honaunau, who graciously answered many questions over the phone about the *heiau* (place of refuge). *Mahalo* to my mentor and *kahuna*, Alexandra Sherwood, who helped with *hoʻoponopono* and many other things.

As always, my special thanks and love to my husband Dave, and my sons, Zach and Liam who let me hide in my office and "kill people." I could not do it without you. Thank you also, to my 11th hour saviors, Jason Crabtree, Mark Frank and Liam Heckman.

To my editor, Margaret Searles, you have the magic touch.

This is a work of fiction. Because I have set the series before European contact, there was freedom as well as difficulty in its creation. I intentionally have not named a specific date or island. I also created my own ahupua`a, or village, and use those words interchangeably, although they are not truly the same in definition.

Commoners, or maka'ainana, probably would not have had a wedding. A formal ceremony would most likely have been only for the ali'i or chiefs, however, I am a romantic and wanted a wedding to bring the village together.

Ritual and prayer was the framework

of Hawai'ian life upon which all activities were built, so that is woven throughout. The rituals have been modified to maintain their sanctity, but the proper principles have been included.

Some aspects of the life or culture have been altered, such as the wedding, or the strict eating rules because of lack of written information. The basis of this book is oral tradition, which was later transcribed. That information is difficult to get and transcriptions and translations vary. Another reason is to continue the fictional plot. Things may not have happened this way, but they could have, and that is the premise of any story. Aloha and mahalo!

I `aina no ka `aina i ke ali `i,
a i waiwai no kai `aina i ke kanaka.

The land remains the land because of the chiefs, and prosperity comes to the land because of the common people.

Chapter 1

Coconut Man twisted the long olonā fibers around his feet and snugged against the coconut palm. The fibers kept his feet a set distance apart and allowed him to hop and scoot up the smooth trunk until he settled, comfortably squatting, at the base of the fronds. Sweat trickled down his brow. He inhaled deeply the salty ocean air and surveyed the clearing. All was quiet in the early morning. He preferred to collect his materials before the village was awake and bustling in its eagerness to start the day. The small rustlings of birds were all the accompaniment he wanted.

Although he could not see the nearby ocean through the jungle, he could see slivers of the green-brown Wai river rushing past, a hundred feet from the edge of the village.

His work-swollen hand pulled the shark-tooth knife from his *malo*-- loincloth--and he severed the longest and most beautiful fronds. Each lacy branch fell gracefully, with a shhhoooosh as it hit the ground. He was in no hurry. When the sun was above the trees and he felt he'd cut enough fronds to weave his customary number of baskets and hats, only then he freed a large coconut and carefully husked it, all the while clinging to the trunk with only the security of the twisted vine around his feet. He punctured one of the eyes and salivated at the sweet scent of the milk. He drank deeply, then cut out a wedge of shell and scraped at the meat with his strong teeth, made slightly jagged from years of using them as tools, or as a third hand in his daily work.

He slid to the ground and squatted by the branches, inspecting them carefully. He would spend the rest of the day weaving them into baskets of varying size and utility. Some he would weave into hats. He would trade them for food, *kapa* sleeping cloths, shark's teeth and other items he needed, but would not or could not make for himself. Only women made the fine *kapa* cloth for sleeping and clothing. He was not a skilled fisherman, although he could fish when pressed. He could not swim well, an oddity in this coastal community, and thus refused to enter water too deep to wade. He could tickle an octopus with a cowrie lure, or catch the delicious 'ōpae shrimp in the Wai river, but he preferred to trade for much of his food. Some foods, like bananas, poi, and anything red, the women were not allowed to handle, so he approached the elder men for those. He spent his days away from the village, unusually nomadic in this familial, but highly structured community. He traveled regularly among villages, another anomaly, but this was not widely known. He was just *niu kanaka,* a coconut man, who made baskets and hats, who came and went in silence and was the subject of speculation. Soon, it was his name as well as his occupation.

Voices approaching the clearing broke his concentration and he shoved the fronds back into the jungle and squatted, nearly invisible, in the foliage.

"Nuu! You are so lazy! I'm doing all the work and you're carrying one little bundle of *pili* grass!"

Coconut Man recognized the voice of 'Ehu, an ebullient, stocky man named

12

"Red," for the interesting color his skin turned when he was excited, angry, or exerting, like now.

Two men approached the clearing from the mountains to the north. Each was laden with huge bundles of long grasses, tied on, so he was nearly enveloped.

"'Ehu, if your face gets any redder, the women won't be able to touch you!" Nuu joked.

'Ehu turned even redder at the innuendo. "Lehua won't let anyone touch me, anyway. Even though our wedding isn't until next month, she's already bossing me around." 'Ehu said this with a smile.

"We'd better get this *pili* back and start building your marriage house. If we don't make the stone foundation solid, and this grass roof water-proof, you two will bring down the *hale* on your wedding night!"

Coconut Man watched 'Ehu struggle to chase Nuu out of the clearing and down the trail to the village. He smiled to think of how close the two friends were. Like brothers. And 'Ehu and Lehua. Married soon. Coconut Man had never married.

The thought made him a little wistful. He was half-way through his life, and happy enough, but lonely sometimes. 'Ehu and Lehua were a good match. So much in love, they were the objects of much teasing in the village. Everyone was excited about the ceremony and nearly everyone had some integral part in the wedding and post-wedding plans. Like the *hale*. A married couple moved out of the separated men's and women's sleeping quarters and lived together in a *hale* built for them by the villagers. Stones for the foundation were brought from the mountains, a tedious job for many small boys.

The men built the foundation, dry stone--no mortar--fit together one at a time and with many prayers. *Pili* grass, brought in large bundles, was woven together over wood ridge poles, tied and blessed against the weather.

Coconut Man sighed. Would a marriage house ever be made for him? He would attend 'Ehu's ceremony. He always attended such celebrations. Although he was not specifically invited, the villages he frequented were too polite to exclude him outright. This would be no different. He would be given a place to sit and eat. He would listen and pray with them. He would make the most beautiful and elaborate

14

basket for 'Ehu and Lehua. He would infuse each strand of coconut fiber with his strongest and most heart-felt prayers for the couple's happiness.

With that in mind, he again assessed the fronds. "'*Ae.*" Yes. He gathered the greens, his tools, and some food, and set off to the ocean, an hour's walk away, where he would begin his day of prayer and weaving.

Chapter 2

Once on the shore, Coconut Man found a level area on the lava rock strewn beach. The sky was clear and a pale, searing blue. He spread out the fronds and selected a long branch with lime-green leaves. In about a year of curing, even the greenest baskets and hats would dry to a dusty beige, and with care, would last for many years of hard use. He was proud of his baskets, their beauty and strength. For the wedding couple, he would weave frond-blossoms and twist them into the pattern. This storage basket would be a double-weave, with a looping cross pattern. He would make a set for them, he decided with satisfaction. His hands worked quickly and surely. Once in a while, he glanced at the rolling waves, but mostly

16

his attention was fixed on the basket. He prayed as he wove, imbuing the piece with good luck for the users.

Bless this work
Bless this work
May the strength
And bounty
Of the niu
From the root to the fruit
Stay with 'Ehu and Lehua
With 'Ehu and Lehua
And all their children
And na keiki

When the basket was finished, he carefully turned it in his large hands, tightening the weave here, tucking in the last edges there. He nodded, satisfied. He would begin the curing soon, but his growling stomach reminded him of the time.

He stood and stretched. His knees cracked. "Eh, not so young anymore." Coconut Man felt new aches in his hands and hips that he hadn't felt even last *Makahiki*-- harvest festival.

He opened a packet of *poke* wrapped in *kī* leaves. The bright green leaves spread like flower petals and juices

17

from the raw fish and vegetables dripped onto the sand. He used his fingers to scoop out the delicious mix. Salt tang puckered his cheeks and he sucked in.

He drank deeply from his calabash, a gourd filled with fresh water. He squinted down the beach and saw some of the children from the village playing in the waves and along the shore. As he watched, their faraway voices became clearer. Their laughter and banter lifted his heart and eased his tired fingers. Kaleo, so named for his incredibly strident cries at birth, was of course, the easiest to hear. He was aptly named, for even as he grew, he could always be heard, even when he insisted he *was* whispering.

Kaleo was holding something at arm's length and chasing Honu, a pretty little girl, who had been born the night the turtles hatched and made their way to the sea.

Coconut Man walked down the beach to watch. Many of the children were in the water, using an old canoe as a diving raft. Honu clearly enjoyed Kaleo's attention; although she shrieked and ran from whatever he had, she ran slowly enough that Kaleo didn't give up the chase.

Coconut Man moved away from the water to sit in the stand of trees lining the shore. He wasn't hiding, but didn't want to alarm the children. He knew he was an odd figure with his large-brimmed coconut frond hat, his hermit ways, and his nomadic life.

Kaleo held a baby octopus, or rather it held him. Honu saw Coconut Man sitting in the shade and stopped running long enough for Kaleo to thrust the baby *he'e* up to her face. She reared back but didn't run, and Kaleo turned to follow her gaze.

Coconut Man was surprised to see the boy immediately walk toward him, Honu following somewhat reluctantly. Patiently, he waited while the two approached. He smiled at them as they boldly studied him. He supposed he didn't fit the category of adults they were taught to address with respect and ritual. To his recollection, he had never spoken directly to any of the children in this village. Kaleo, arms dangling, still held the now limp octopus.

"Are you going to eat that?" Coconut Man asked.

"What?"

This clearly was not what Kaleo expected to hear. Coconut Man pointed to the *he'e.*

"That. Are you going to eat that? It's a little small. Better if you let it get big, get babies, before you eat it."

Kaleo lifted his hand and examined his prize. Honu's big brown eyes never left Coconut Man's face.

"I guess not." He dropped his hand once more. "What's your name?"

"I'm called Coconut Man."

"I know. Everybody calls you that. But what's your name?"

An interesting question. He had a name once. A real name. He truly didn't remember what it was.

"I'm just. . . Coconut Man."

Kaleo raised his eyebrows in the way that meant "yes," as if he, at the tender age of ten seasons, understood how that could be. "I'm Kaleo."

"I know." Coconut Man smiled.

Kaleo grinned. "Everybody knows me," he said with some pride. "This is Honu."

Honu ducked her head, her long hair hiding her eyes, but her wide smile shone through the strands. "Did you make that hat?"

"Yes. Do you like it?"

"Yes. I've never seen a hat like that."

20

Honu stepped closer.

"Me, neither," said Coconut Man.

"That's why I make them like this. I'm the only one who does. Maybe I'll make you one someday."

"Mahalo."

"You're welcome. What about you?" he asked Kaleo.

"I never wear hats. But, I might. If you made it." They smiled at each other, some agreement and kinship forming.

"Let's put your *he'e* back into the sea so he, or she," Coconut Man added to Honu, "can get big and strong and make more *he'e* for us to eat!"

As the threesome headed to the shallow reef, the children in the surf stopped their play to watch. One by one, they trailed until Coconut Man, Kaleo and Honu had a small band of followers.

* * * * *

Coconut Man left the children playing in the surf and headed back to his basket. He set it, weighted with a rock to begin the curing process. He said a brief prayer and returned to the pile of fronds. He fingered a few, but somehow, after creating the special basket for the wedding couple and spending time with the children, he was not in the mood to weave. He did not want to spoil this part of the curing process, which was time consuming. After the basket had absorbed salt water from the pool, he set it, still weighted, on the sun-warmed rocks to dry. When it had nearly dried, he set it back in the tide pool. He repeated this process, soaking and drying three times.

He pulled the palm branches into the shade of the *milo* trees and took the basket with him. He wasn't sure why he was restless, but decided he wanted to be near the bustle of the village. Walking back through the jungle with its scent of sweet-rotting foliage, through gulches between the hillsides, he surprised another man who also worked alone. Io, the net maker, whose sharp eyes missed nothing, stood at the base of a smooth-trunked *kukui* tree.

Slightly startled, Coconut Man called, "*Aloha*."

Io, working with his back to the trail, turned with a jerk, hands balled into fists.

"Oh, you. *Aloha*," he said uncertainly.

"I'm sorry to disturb you. I would have called out sooner to let you know I was here, but I was thinking of the coming

22

wedding."

"Oh, yes. Everyone is thinking of that!" Io laughed. "My Honu talks of nothing else. I think she has already picked out a groom for herself."

"I met Honu and her 'betrothed' today, I believe. What are you doing?"

"I am collecting *kukui* nuts for my nets."

"What do you do with them?" Coconut Man knew of many uses for *kukui* nuts. But, nets? Everyone used them for light, from small glows to large torches. The oil burned brightly. Also, eating too many of the raw nuts gave one diarrhea, as Coconut Man had experienced.

"I use the dye to darken my nets."

Since Coconut Man did not go out to sea, this failed to impress him. "If the nets are dark, they are harder for the fish to see. Catch more fish that way."

"Aah." Now he understood. Hmmm. Perhaps he could stain his baskets different colors, too. "Is that what is used to color *kapa* cloth?"

Io eyed him strangely. "That is women's work." Coconut Man waited. "Yes. They use *kukui* for that."

"Can you show me?"

Io looked startled. "Now?"

"No. But sometime?"

Io weighed this question. "I suppose. After the wedding. I am busy making nets for a wedding present. Also, everyone's nets seem to need mending. I am very busy," he repeated. Again, Coconut Man waited. Io sighed. "Yes."

"After the wedding. I will come to you." Coconut Man smiled. "*Mahalo.* I am an apt pupil. I will not take much of your time. Weaving nets is not unlike weaving baskets?"

"It is very different!" Io turned back to the tree. Coconut Man continued his walk toward the village, but not before he heard Io grumble, "Well, perhaps, a little."

Approaching the village, Coconut Man heard the ringing tones of *kapa* beaters hitting hollow logs. Some rang high, some rang low, and the rhythmic sound amid the talk and laughter of the women cheered him. He knew the drumming would announce the wedding as that day drew near, just as the drums announced his return to the village when he had gone afar to trade. At present, it was a merry accompaniment to the intermittent *mele* the women sang as they worked.

He paused by Lele who knelt before

her log. Her dark hair was piled on top of her head and pinned with a stick. Muscles in her arms, made sinewy by years of *kapa* beating, rippled as she worked. She pounded the pale *wauke* bark thin as cobweb, sprinkled it with water, folded it onto itself, then began again. She prayed softly to herself as she beat. Coconut Man understood the necessity to pray to the gods when performing some important task. Otherwise, how could one be sure the chore would turn out the best way it could? Lele folded the thin bark lengthwise and continued. When it was finished to her satisfaction, she squinted up at him.

"*Aloha*, Coconut Man."

"*Aloha*, Kapa Woman." He smiled at her. "That is beautiful. Is it for the wedding couple?"

"Yes. I must make it as soft and beautiful as I can to bless their union."

"'*Ae*," Coconut Man agreed. It was important to do things properly. To start married life and create harmony, everything must be done correctly.

"What do you do next?" asked Coconut Man.

"What do you mean?" Lele looked at him strangely, her straight brows angled down.

"With the *kapa.* When do you dye it? What do you use?"

"Ah." Lele looked as if this was not so odd a question from someone who was odd to begin with.

Coconut Man had felt a change in himself when Kaleo and Honu approached him so openly earlier at the beach. Ordinarily, he did not much care what others thought of him. He knew he was something of an outcast in the villages he visited, but that had never bothered him. Perhaps, he thought, he had never truly allowed himself to think about it before. A new feeling entered his heart, and he wished to explore it. At the moment, he wished to learn about *kapa.* Although it was women's work, he saw that he could use the knowledge for his work as well.

Lele fingered the thin cloth. "I must pound these strips into one big piece for the wedding bed. When that is finished, I must do a final beating with a beater carved with our family's designs, handeddown by my mother and the mothers before. It will leave a beautiful design in the cloth. I must pray and rest before I do that. If it is not done correctly, the design will not be even and could bring bad luck to the marriage bed."

"I understand." Coconut Man nodded gravely. Although he had a sleeping *kapa*, it was not beautiful with designs made especially for him. His was plain, a castoff piece from some village; a section deemed not perfect enough to complete with designs and dyes. It kept him warm, kept away the wet, but that was all. "Then do you dye it?"

"Yes." Lele smiled indulgently, as if to a child. "Then I dye it."

"What do you use? Can I watch?"

"We use many things. I will have to pray on what design and dye is best. I must think on it before I know if you can watch."

Coconut Man understood. Would a man watching change the luck of the users, if only women created *kapa*? Much to think about. Much to learn. Perhaps he could add color to his baskets. Or hats? Something he had never considered before. Perhaps he could add shells? He was filled with excitement at this new concept. People wore shells. Feathers. Necklaces made of hair. Why not his baskets?

"*Mahalo*, Lele. Many thanks. You have given me a great gift."

Lele looked surprised at his exuberance.

"You are welcome. But I have done nothing."

"No, you have been kind. You shared with me." Coconut Man decided to make Lele a hat. A special hat, to shade her while she pounded *kapa*. Beating *kapa* was hard work and must be done in order, at the right time, whether or not the woman felt like doing it! That much he knew. So, he would make Lele the first of his special hats.

He wandered farther into the village, cradling 'Ehu and L'Ehua's basket protectively. He needed a safe place to let it dry until the wedding. Perhaps he would move his sleeping mats closer to the village. He rarely slept in the men's sleeping house of any village he visited--only in times of the great storms that swirled and swept in from the sea, taking *hales*, uprooting trees, and some times, pulling people away, never to be seen again.

Chapter 3

Coconut Man found a place to lay his sleeping mat close behind the men's sleeping *hale*. He tucked the wedding basket into a tree, where it would continue to dry in the sun.

He heard the children returning from the beach and poked his head around the *hale* to see. Along with the usual treasures *keiki* tended to collect, they had brought seaweed to have with the evening meal. Elders praised the young ones on their helpfulness and generosity. *The village as a whole cares for everyone. Most of the time,* Coconut Man thought. He brushed that reservation away, not wanting bad feelings to mar this blessed event. He wandered to where the marriage *hale* was being constructed. Much work had been done this day. The rock foundation had been completed, and the framework of *kauila* wood poles of had been erected, ready for its *pili* grass cover. The men were completing their tasks for the day. Much grumbling over hunger, joking and laughter accompanied the slowing hands and trembling muscles. Coconut Man felt an urge to offer assistance, but was unsure how to proceed. He decided to wait until the next day to attempt it. "They are already finished for today," he told himself. "But," he admitted, "perhaps I am a little afraid. All they can do is say no." *Yes. They can say no.*

He returned to the children who were also helping ready the meal. Girls helped prepare the food, and boys helped with the fires and cleaning the village. The men's and women's eating houses were separate, so he entered the men's a little timidly, wondering how he could help. As he stood in the empty *hale,* he realized the women took care of the men at meals. He could not help, should not help, if he wanted to be part of a village. Did he want to? Perhaps. He left the *hale* and walked through the smoke of fires to the *imu,* the oven, where several men uncovered layers of leaves, sand, and hot rocks to pluck out hot *kī* leaf wrapped packets and toss them onto a *lau hala* mat. Coconut Man screwed up his courage.

"*Aloha.* Can I help?"

The laughing and tossing stopped. The two men crouched over the *imu* exchanged a glance and frowned. "Do you hear something, Lako?" one man asked.

"No, Manō, I don't hear anything."

The third man said, "I do. I hear a little squeak. Maybe an `ō `ō bird in a tree somewhere?" All three men made a great show of looking everywhere but at Coconut Man.

This rudeness was a new experience for Coconut Man. He had travelled many years to many villages. He had been welcomed and ignored, but never had anything like this happened. He was unsure what do to. So he did nothing.

"Perhaps if we feed the bird, it will go away," said Manō.

"Yes, let's feed it and see what happens," said the largest, and thus far unnamed man. Before Coconut Man had time to react, Manō picked up a hot *kī* leaf packet and threw it into his chest. The fire-roasted bundle struck him with force and the heat of it staggered him as he sought to escape the pain. A new emotion rose in Coconut Man. He lunged forward and pushed Manō into the *imu.* He noted with some satisfaction, the hiss of bare bottom on steaming rocks a moment before Manō screamed. Coconut Man watched calmly as Lako and Big Man pulled him from the pit. "Little bird has a sharp beak," he said. He noticed the pain in his chest had evened out to an unpleasant pulsing. *However,* he thought as he made his way to the Wai river to cool it, *it is nowhere near as uncomfortable as Manō's* 'ōkole *must be.*

He stood, his wiry body waist-deep in the Wai, and splashed his chest. He cupped water, poured it absently, thought about what had happened. He could only conclude that some people were kind, like Lele, and some were not. It was the same in the animal world. Some birds and fish were easy to catch, others fought and bit, or even killed people, like the tiger shark. Catching that one required great skill and caution. Although *manō* was sacred, and some families revered him as their `aumakua--family god--tiger shark was still hunted. And tiger shark hunted as well.

He examined his chest. The mahogany skin still held a tinge of red, but it no longer hurt. He waded to shore and

32

walked back to the village. Evening torches were lit and conversation and laughter indicated the meal was in progress. He hesitated outside the men's eating *hale,* however the smell of food compelled him to enter. He ducked through the long grass curtain and stopped once again. He saw his bullies and searched for a friendly face. Aah. Io the net maker sat against the far wall on the end. He could sit there.

"*Aloha,* Io," Coconut Man said as he quickly sat.

"*Aloha.*" Io looked a little startled, but good manners dictated that he make room. He scooted a little and Coconut Man folded his legs tightly. He rarely had the opportunity to join a community this way, so he intended to enjoy it fully. Dishes were passed and heartily enjoyed. Food was *kapu,* sacred, and thus a meal was filled with ritual and meaning, unlike most of Coconut Man's meals, which were mere survival. *How odd, this joking and laughter, sharing and passing. Comforting, but odd.*

The smoky smell of food cooked over an open fire competed with the oily smell of *kukui* nut lamps. The closeness of many men added another odor, not unpleasant. Most men spent time near the water, even if they were not fishermen. Cleanliness was sacred, from the skin and well-oiled hair to *malo*--loin cloths-- and shoulder capes.

Too soon the meal was *pau*. Gourds and calabashes were pushed aside, leaves covering the uneaten food. From the sides of the *hale*, *kōnane* boards made of stone were rolled into the center. Pebbles and shells of black and white spilled from *kapa* bags onto the boards. The men seemed to have partners already chosen, but a few remained seated and talked quietly. Coconut Man had played *kōnane* long ago but did not remember the details of play. He found himself across a large pock-marked stone from Io who expectantly held out two fists. Coconut Man tapped one and Io revealed a white stone. He returned the markers to the board and removed a dark piece from the center to create a 'jumping' space. Coconut Man removed one of his own, a white one. Io jumped his dark stone over a white and removed it from the playing space. Coconut Man jumped his white marker twice, removed Io's stones, but then became trapped. Similar games were played all around the *hale* with much laughter and teasing derision, alternated with extreme concentration as the games heated up. In the far corner, Lako and Manō played with quiet, fierce intent, while the large man watched. Between moves, Coconut Man noticed the large man nudging Lako, seeming to aid him in his play.

A burst of laughter called Coconut Man's attention to the stone where 'Ehu, soon to be married, played against his friend Nuu.

"If I wasn't so nervous, I would have won!" cried 'Ehu.

"If you were a better player, you would have won!" Nuu laughed. "What excuse are you going to use once you are married to that beautiful girl? Exhaustion?" The men near 'Ehu laughed. Coconut Man watched the faces surrounding the friends. Warm, open, *'ohana* --family. In contrast, Lako's game seemed to be reaching a different conclusion.

"Palani, you're helping Lako!" Manō shouted, sweeping the pieces off the board.

"He doesn't know how to play! It's only a game, Manō." Big Palani stood and made calming gestures. Lako still sat, stunned in front of the empty boulder. Manō stood and the two faced off over the board.

"Only a game? Only a *game*? Manō's fists clenched and in the torchlight his muscles bulged. "This *game* teaches us. Thinking. Plotting. Strategy. It is not a game. It prepares us for war."

"War? What are you talking about?" Lako asked, looking up.

"It is calm now. Peaceful. But it will not always be so."

Palani took a deep breath. "Manō. It is a time of peace. Our district chief is strong. He will not be overtaken. We are safe."

Coconut Man had stopped playing, as had all in the *hale*. Io rose to his feet. "Do not disturb the gods, now, Manō. I know you itch to throw a spear at something other than a coconut husk target, but it is Lono, god of games, not Ku, god of war, who blesses us now."

`Ehu also stood. "My coming union with Lehua is one of love and peace. Do not bring bad luck to my blessing day, Manō. Please."

`Umi, an older man, cleared his throat and many eyes turned his way. "This is not acceptable. If you cannot resolve this here and now, you must sit *ho`oponopono*," he said, referring to the problem-solving technique of sitting in a circle to discuss the issue.

"I know, old man." The men looked startled at this disrespect. Manō's hands balled into fists.

No one seemed to breathe as they all watched Manō. Lako still sat frozen, and Coconut Man wondered if all Lako's fruit was in one basket. After a tense moment, Palani gently slapped Manō on the shoulder. "Come. Let's make sure our canoes are above the tide."

Manō looked at each man in the *hale*, then nodded. He strode out without another word, Palani close behind. All eyes looked to Lako who rose uncertainly and followed.

"What was that?" Coconut Man whispered to Io. "A stand off?"

"'Umi is Headman--*konohiki*. He is in charge of this village. And he is head fisherman. The catch has been bountiful since he began, the *ahupua'a* prosperous. It was not always so." At Coconut Man's questioning look, Io shook his head and cleared the board.

The *kōnane* stones were rolled aside and markers returned to *kapa* bags, all in silence. Coconut Man decided this was not usual. Each man's face held thoughts unspoken. Coconut Man wondered what had really happened, and what he had missed. Even Io shook his head and would not speak.

The men dispersed to their sleeping *hales* and Coconut Man retired to his mat behind the single men's sleeping hut, after he reassured himself that the wedding basket was still safe.

Chapter 4

"Did you hear?" Kaleo shouted into Coconut Man's ear. Coconut Man jerked awake, heart slamming, ready to strike. "The district chief and his wife are coming for a visit!"

Fully alert, the pounding in his chest receding, Coconut Man sat up and assessed his visitor. Kaleo's shiny brown hair curtained his eyes, and with an excited flip every so often, cleared his vision. Bright eyes and wide smile urged Coconut Man to share in his joy. Kaleo fairly danced with happiness. Coconut Man held out a weathered hand.

"Help an old man up."

"You're not old!" Kaleo did as he was bid.

Coconut Man was stiff this morning. The tension in the men's *hale* at the end of the evening must have affected his sleep.

"What's this about the district chief?"

"To bless the wedding couple! They are coming! So now we must ready the village for the chief and chiefess *and* the wedding!" Words tumbled out and the boy hopped and jigged with his tale. "What should we do? Should we make a basket?"

Coconut Man smiled at the new partner he had apparently acquired. "Well, *we* will have to think about that." He looked beyond Kaleo. "Where is your sweetheart?"

Kaleo blushed and jumped back a bit. "She is not my sweetheart!" Coconut Man smiled again. Kaleo clearly knew to whom he referred. Kaleo scowled. "She is doing women's work," he said derisively. "We have men's work to do."

Coconut Man cocked his head. "Women's work, eh? Where would us men be without women's work? We are *'ohana*--family--and we cannot do without each other. Without all of us. You would do well to remember that." Coconut Man surprised himself with not only this revelation, but that he should feel so strongly about it. It was true. Although women were not *kapu*--sacred--like men were, he shuddered to think what life would be like without *kapa* and the food they prepared; *limu* gathered from the ocean to make the delicious seaweed salad that somehow never tasted as good when he made it. These thoughts skittered through his mind. Perhaps his solitary life made his thinking unique among men. In his travels to villages around this immense island, he had learned that women were there to bring forth babies, prepare most foods, and make life easier for men.

However, some women were special. *Kāhuna*--priests--were sometimes women. Why? He did not know, it was just so. Some women were born wise, with knowledge and talents for healing. Many *kāhuna* were needed to bless the village for: hula, harvest, healing, even battle. Often, the *moku*--district--had a single *kahuna* to serve all within its boundaries from the mountains to the sea.

"Are you awake? You're eyes are open. You must be. Come on." Kaleo grabbed Coconut Man's hand and pulled him to a *hale* on the far side of the village.

"My mother has food. I can take some with us, so we can plan."

"Your mother, eh?" Coconut Man stopped and eyed Kaleo. "Why not you? Don't you know how to cook yet? Aren't

41

you a man? She is only a woman."

Kaleo's eyes narrowed. He clearly understood this jibe. "She is my mother," he said with dignity. Coconut Man agreed.

A mother was *special.* He smiled and allowed himself to be pulled to an array of calabashes filled with fruit and *lomi* fish. Unbidden, thoughts of his long-forgotten mother danced behind his teasing words, as they collected the food. He did not remember her. He did not know her name or what she looked like. A surge of loneliness swept through him and he placed that thought, along with other strange ideas that had come upon him lately, aside for further contemplation. Perhaps he would seek out a *kahuna* to advise him. A woman *kahuna.*

"Come on!" Kaleo set off for the beach trail, arms swinging.

"Oh, well. I can weave another basket while this young one plans his life. And probably mine." Amused, Coconut Man followed more slowly, already planning a basket for the chief and his wife. *Perhaps, I can ask Io for help in dying this. It will be my first dyed basket, and that should be granted to the chief,* he thought.

At the edge of the forest, Coconut

Man freed his collection of fronds and assessed them. He decided to make a large basket--big enough to store *kapa,* or feathered cloaks, or anything bulky. He had never attempted to make a basket as big as the one he now envisioned. As big as a man squatting. Kaleo shrieked as a large wave splashed him in the morning chill. *Or to contain a small boy.* Coconut Man smiled at the thought of Kaleo inside such a basket.

He would ask for help. Another new idea. He had always created things alone, with only his prayers to the gods for guidance. He must have been taught by *someone.* At *sometime.* Why could he not remember these things? And why did these thoughts plague him now? He had visited this village before. Not often, but something was different. *Enough.* He would ask Lele and Io to aid him in the decoration of the largest, most beautiful basket the people had ever seen. The highest tribute to the district chief and his wife. This might take a while. The prayers alone would need to be even more heartfelt. . .

"Kaleo!" he called. The boy looked up and flipped his wet hair out of his eyes.

"When will the chief and chiefess

arrive?"

Kaleo squinted off into the middle distance. Coconut Man waited patiently. "Three days before the wedding."

Coconut Man nodded and began to pray as he pulled the fronds to him and started to weave.

The base of the basket was taking shape when the sun was blotted out and cold drops sprayed him. "*Aī*" Coconut Man looked up at Kaleo's sodden form . "You're blocking my light."

"Sorry." Kaleo moved just enough that the sun lit Coconut Man's dark hands as they effortlessly wove layer upon layer. "How do you do that?"

"What?"

"It just grows and grows. I'm watching, but I don't see how you do it. Is is magic?" Kaleo stepped back uncertainly. Magic was not a subject taken lightly. Much in this life could not be explained.

"No. It is practice." Kaleo looked unconvinced. "Sit. I will show you a basic weave."

Kaleo sat, mimicking Coconut Man's posture and position. *Is this what it would be like to have a son?* Coconut Man brushed that startling thought away, handed the boy a frond and took a new one for himself. He

44

sliced some of the leaves, making them thinner, on both of their fronds. "Hold it like this." He gently guided the boy's hands and slowly wove two basket bases--his own, and Kaleo's. Kaleo's sharp eyes followed the pattern but his short fingers and childish grip made the task difficult. Coconut Man saw his frustration grow.

"You know, weaving is difficult. It is not for everyone," he said casually. He continued to weave his own basket. "Io the net maker and I discussed it." Kaleo glanced up, stretching his fingers while trying to hold the weave in place. "Yes. Io thinks it is a difficult task. We agreed, net making and basket weaving are not unlike in skill." Coconut Man did not elaborate on the context of that conversation. However, he was right that the opinion of Honu's father had considerable weight with Kaleo. "I have a great deal of experience with baskets, and I must tell you, you have some weaving skill." Kaleo eyed his lop-sided basket with a skeptical quirk of his eyebrow, pointedly looked at Coconut Man's basket, and sighed.

"Of course, I have been doing this a very long time, but I can tell you, I have never taught anyone so young and seen such talent." Kaleo brightened. Coconut Man stopped weaving. *I have never taught anyone,*

45

young or old, so of course I have never seen such skill. . . Kaleo attacked his basket with new enthusiasm, tongue poking out of the corner of his mouth, chubby fingers straining.

This is not at all unpleasant. Coconut Man sighed contentedly and the two worked in companionable silence, broken only by short prayers or a quick correction, until the sun was high and hot.

Chapter 5

A sudden clamor up the beach drew their attention. *Keiki* hopping and pointing out to sea brought Kaleo and Coconut Man to their feet. Kaleo ran to join the children, basket forgotten, its weaving gently springing free. Coconut Man sighed and took the opportunity to stretch.

The noise increased and men poured from the forest, running for their canoes. Coconut Man jogged after Kaleo to the curve where sand turned to tide pools filled with children, who had paused in their play, to stare at the horizon.

Coconut Man could not see what everyone was looking at as he ran. When he reached the group on the beach, most of the men had hauled their outriggers into the surf and were paddling furiously. "What? What's going on?" he asked.

"Look!" A small boy pointed outward and at first, Coconut Man saw nothing to cause the furor. Then he noticed a roiling in the water and several large dorsal fins. As he watched, the dark and boiling water moved closer to just beyond the surf line. The men in canoes encircled an area, five or six canoes wide and twice again as long.

"What is it? Is someone hurt?" he asked. He saw that the canoes were stilled and the men communicated by gestures, and few of those. They gently slid nets into the water, ringing the thrashing sea.

"No." Kaleo appeared beside him. "Fish."

"Why are they doing that?" As they watched, scores of sea birds, attracted by the panicked fish circled and dived overhead, as though to mimic the circling and plunging of the fish below. The more Coconut Man watched, the more he saw. In the dark water he made out individual fish as they leapt and darted. The larger shapes of seals sped among them, taking advantage of the bounty. Herding the mass were dolphin, pushing, urging, spinning. Their silvery bodies propelled out of the water at intervals to cross the makeshift lagoon, apparently quite unconcerned at the canoes ringing them. The human hunters waited patiently, silently, their nets dropped below the canoes.

Coconut Man had never seen such a show and watched mesmerized by the interaction between hunter and hunted. The seals lost interest first, and when they departed, the water calmed noticeably and the men drew their net circle tighter. The dolphin were allowed to escape next. The birds continued to circle, but their strident cries and frenetic diving ceased. The men worked silently, closing the gaps. The group on the beach was also silent, understanding that the fish could hear and might elude capture. These fish represented many days of food for the village, and their presence was a gift from the gods and a good omen for the nuptials to come.

The children's sharp eyes spotted it first. A small sigh rippled through the crowd which had been swelled by women, elders, and most of the men not farming in the uplands. A huge, triangular dorsal fin sliced the water toward the nets.

This was unusual. Shark typically fed at dawn or dusk and were rarely seen this close to shore mid-day. This could be very bad. The fin sank out of sight, but the fishermen had spied it. The onshore group monitored its progress by watching the men in canoes. The older fishermen remained expressionless and immobile, but the younger men's eyes widened and they shifted in their canoes. Coconut Man felt this must be a very big shark. Probably a tiger shark. Large, aggressive, with a history of attacking people, the *manō* was sacred and respected. And feared. It was `*aumakua*--family god--to several in the village, but usually only hunted by chiefs, and their chosen fishermen. For the shark to appear at this hunt, was a sign he could be captured. The men watched the shark circle the net enclosure. A large shark could break through and scatter the harvest or even upset a canoe, throwing the occupants into the dark water. Coconut Man felt afraid. He bent to reassure Kaleo but the boy did not look fearful. He looked proud. Coconut Man checked others on the beach. They too, did not appear alarmed. Lips moved in silent prayer, but did not seem panicked. The energy on the beach had changed from excitement and exuberance to steady pulsing--like a fire ignited in a frenzy, then settled to long, hot burning. Coconut Man did not know what to think of this shift, but allowed the feeling to surround him and buoy him.

Intent, he watched the fishermen prepare not only to save this catch, but to capture *manō*, too. A fat noose, weighted with stones, appeared in the hands of the oldest man, 'Umi. His heavily muscled upper body spoke of years of wrestling nets, fishing lines and heavy catches into canoes. The noose was held open with a forked stick and deftly lowered over the side of the canoe. A man in the back of the canoe lowered a similar noose. No one moved. Eyes circled as one while the shark made its way around the boats. Suddenly 'Umi jerked his arms up and back, the other man jerked his own up and forward and a great thrashing and rocking ensued. None of the other canoes changed position. A man in the center of the canoe raised a spear and plunged it downward, then struck again. The water stilled. As if a *kapa* blanket had been lifted, all the fishermen cheered and quickly closed the net circle.

The group on the beach mirrored the actions of those in the sea. Coconut Man yelled too, surprising himself. He had never experienced such excitement, fear, pride, and relief all at once and it felt good, necessary, to shout.

The flotilla made its way to the beach and the catch was extraordinary, but the prize was tiger shark. *Manō* was longer than the head fisherman's canoe. He was beautiful and frightening; silver-gray skin gleamed in the sun. It looked smooth, but on closer inspection the stiff hairs that made sharkskin

51

useful for smoothing things glowed sharply. Black, solid eyes, fierce even in death, made Coconut Man keep his distance from the great mouth. Row upon row of jagged teeth pushed from the open jaw. Formidable weapons to be sure, the men would remove them and imbed them into war clubs.

Coconut Man could not imagine being in a boat while that thing circled him, much less falling into the water with it. He would die of fright, he was sure. It was clear the fishermen had encountered, even sought out this great hunter on previous exploits, and they respected it.

First fish was placed in the fishing shrine to give thanks for the catch. Special prayers would be said for *manō.* The families whose `aumakua* was tiger shark would give thanks also.

Coconut Man felt exhausted. His heart had raced from the moment the fish had begun their fateful run. He realized he was hungry and had nothing to eat with him.

"Come on!" Startled out of his musings, Coconut Man smiled as Kaleo dragged him into the fray of fish sorting.

The nets spread on the beach, laden with fish. The whole village sorted into baskets what would be cooked immediately, what would be dried, saved for bait, served raw, and myriad other uses. He allowed himself a brief glance at the community as it sang, danced and worked, ankle deep in the bounty from the sea, before he plunged in, happy to be included.

Chapter 6

Coconut Man was exhausted. He lay on his sleeping mat behind the men's *hale* and thought. The day's catch had been cleaned, cooked, preserved, stored and whatever all needed to be done to it. A novice at such large scale preparation, he had helped wherever he could, sometimes accepting slightly embarrassing instructions, as if the issuers, even women and children, could not believe one so ignorant could exist.

Every part of him ached from unfamiliar tasks, but pride would not let him quit while even the very old and very young kept working. It was a satisfying feeling, he decided. He was sure everyone else ached, too, and the sense of communal suffering, made him feel better. His mind rolled back over the day and he sat up with a lurch as he remembered his precious basket, the one for the chief and chiefess, left untended on the beach. After he and Kaleo had gone to the point, with all the frenzy of the catch, all other thoughts had escaped him. He could not even remember if they worked above the high tide line. He tried to picture the sand around them, straining to recall the seaweed line that marked high tide, and could not. He wanted to cry as he slowly sat up and the throbbing of his very skin reached new heights. He could not risk the *ali'i's* basket. Not only had he chosen perfect fronds, but to abandon it half-finished, half-prayed upon, because he was too tired, was unacceptable.

He struggled to his feet and shuffled like an old man through the silent village and down the forest path to the beach. The walk was not far on a bright, sunny day, when one was in good health, but in the shadowed night, when one was a thousand years old, the path was crooked and rife with hazards. Weak moonlight shone in patches and he walked evermore slowly, to avoid a fall. The thought of hitting the ground, or bruising his tired feet on a hidden root unnerved him more than he would have imagined.

At last he reached the beach and relief washed over him at the sight of the open sand and crash of unseen waves. He hobbled as quickly as he could to the spot he and the boy had worked.

The baskets were safe. The high tide had not reached them this day. He usually took care to work above the tide line, but sometimes when he was weaving and curing simultaneously, he preferred to work closer to the water. The fronds were cold and damp, but otherwise fine. Kaleo's forlorn little basket sat next to his own simple example, and Coconut Man smiled at the recollection of the boy working beside him, tongue poking out in concentration. The weave of the special basket had loosened, but was still perfect in its progress. He let out a breath he hadn't realized he was holding. So much to worry about with a visit from *ali'i*.

He carried the baskets back to the forest edge and sat to rest a little. The night was mild, the new moon gave thready light and the white sand glistened. Rhythmic surf relaxed him.

A shuffling sound on the path behind him roused him from his stupor. Someone was coming. He scooted further under the trees and watched as two men staggered out onto the sand.

One carried a gourd and stopped to drink from it. The other swiveled to say, "Save some for me."

Ah. The men were drinking '*awa*, the

fermented drink made from roots and normally used ceremonially. Their weaving and sloshing said too much '*awa* had been consumed. *What were they doing here? Now?*

Coconut Man was unsure of their identities, but their shapes seemed familiar. Their voices, slurred by the '*awa*, were loud and easy to hear as they wobbled toward the surf.

"I'm so hot," said the larger man.

"Me, too. Das why we come down here, stupid. Swim. Cool off." The second man toppled onto the sand and laughed. Big Man continued to stagger toward the water.

"I'm tired, too," said Big Man.

"Why don't you rest a little, first?" Second Man said from his prone position. "Sky looks pretty from here." They both found this very funny, and Big Man joined his companion. They lay flat, facing the sky and giggling. Coconut Man had tasted '*awa,* but had never consumed enough to create this effect.

He thought to gather his baskets and leave when Big Man's next words stilled his hand.

"When are we going to leave our little 'present'? How we gonna do it?"

"I dunno yet. Ssssh, stupid." This last was almost an afterthought.

"What? No one here. We should finish our plans so we know what to do."

"I know." They both spoke loudly, despite Second Man's admonishment to ssshh.

"Well? I got the stuff. When do I do it?"

"What did braddah say?"

"Nothing yet. He say he doesn't want to know, then he can be surprised with everyone else."

"Well, then. Now you know."

"Know what? I don't know anything."

"I know." This last was met by a moment of silence and then ringing laughter. Coconut Man hoped it was just drunken boasting, but somehow he didn't think so. The familiarity of the men grew until he was sure they were the three from the *imu* and the *kōnane* game.

They were planning something. But what? It didn't sound good, despite the word 'present.' And how? What 'stuff' did Big Man have?

"Listen, listen," Second Man said. "We can't do it right away. We have to let things get going first."

"Yes. But should I do it at the first dinner? Or the during the hula? I don't want to wait until the ceremony itself. That doesn't feel right."

"How do you know what feels right?" Second Man asked. More laughter.

"You know what I mean."

"Yes. Let me think." Silence. Coconut Man's already stiff body began to protest in earnest. He would have to move soon. He wanted to find out what was going on. Was someone truly in danger? And who? Furthermore, what could he do about it? Go up against three younger, stronger men of some repute and status in the village? *I don't think so.*

"Okay," Second Man continued, "do it the day after they come. We have the games and hula and everybody is together for that. It's slow, so he just feel sick. It's important for the village. If you don't give him too much, he won't die."

"Die? He could die?"

"No, no, no. Jus' listen. Jus' feel sick. He old, things gotta change for the better around here." Both men sighed heavily.

"Okay. Then what?"

"What what?"

"I mean, for Manō, what does he do next?"

"I don't know. He'll tell us." He lurched to his feet and weaved into the sea with a sharp exclamation. Big Man laughed and also waded in.

Coconut Man did not want to be caught and decided he'd heard all he was going to. He made sure his baskets were hidden and safe, then walked as quickly as he could back to his sleeping place, aches and pains taking second place in his thoughts.

Although he hurt and was exhausted from the day's events, he could not sleep. The men's plot revolved in his brain like the circling seabirds. They were going to do something to someone--make him sick, with the possibility he could die. That possibility did not seem to trouble them, and Manō had set it up. Manō would benefit from this illness and potential death somehow. It wasn't someone currently in the village. That meant, most likely, it was someone arriving for the wedding. He had seen weddings where many people came from other villages to celebrate. Relatives married to members of other villages returned to participate. The ceremony was only a few days away. People could begin to arrive as early as tomorrow. Today! Morning was near and he bemoaned his inability to sleep. He rolled onto his side, determined to let go these thoughts until morning. He would ask around the village and see who expected friends or relations. If he could discover who might be the target, perhaps he could warn or prevent it. With that plan in mind, he was able to fall asleep.

Coconut Man awoke tired and stiff. The morning sun was high, but he had been shaded by the *hale* and so the bustle of the village roused him. He staggered slightly as he stood and was reminded of the drunken men and the plot he'd overheard. A weight settled on him as he made his way to the privacy of the forest to relieve himself. Thirst prodded him to continue to the *Wai*. He waded in to his knees and scooped cool water.

His recent desire to be part of the village had lessened, he discovered, as he reluctantly made his way back. The responsibility of protecting the unknown victim squatted heavily on his shoulders.

The village's usual activity was even more enthusiastic and he noted a shifting of belongings, to make room for guests. He spoke to no one, and was grateful for his invisible status while he walked to the marriage *hale* under construction. It had been nearly completed in his absence, and he marveled at that. He had thought the entire village had turned out yesterday for the fishing. *Perhaps he had lost a day somewhere,* he thought grumpily. He stood at the front of the *hale* and admired the tightly woven thatch and sound foundation. The thought of the happy couple spending many years here, raising *keiki* and enjoying the bounty of the island cheered him a little.

I'd better get on with my prying, he thought wryly. A private person himself, he did not relish the thought of probing into the spirits of others. *However, someone's life was at stake, and that had to take precedence.* The cloak of responsibility was so tangible he glanced at his shoulders to make sure nothing covered them. Strange. *Perhaps this burden is too much for one alone such as I am.* Who could he ask to share it? Kaleo was the one he knew the best, but this was not a task for a child. Lele the *kapa* maker? No. Io the net maker? Perhaps. He would think on it while he asked his questions.

He met a band of rather sullen *keiki*, headed by Kaleo. "What's wrong?" Coconut Man asked.

"We have to work," grumbled a boy with hair sun-faded to honey-brown.

"It's not fair," Honu added.

"Why is it not fair? What are you to do?" Coconut Man hid a smile, but immediately his heart rose a little in his chest.

Kaleo put chubby fists on his hips. "We have to gather enough firewood to last until the wedding is over and all the visitors have left!" Coconut Man opened his mouth to respond but was cut off by exclamations of outrage from the children.

"Do you know *how* much wood that is?"

"Do you know how far we have to go?"

"It's not on the beach, either."

"We have to go into the uplands to get it!"

Each child had a calabash encased in a net bag tied to his or her waist, and more nets and vine ropes festooned them like jewelry.

"Ah. I see you have provisions."

"We might not even come back!" said a small boy, barely old enough to be included.

"I'm sure you'll come back safely. I will watch for you." This time Coconut Man could not help his smile. "Tell me where to look for you, just in case."

Kaleo scowled. "We are going to the upland *kalo* patch, where they, *we*," he corrected with some pride, "cleared the trees for the plants."

"I have never been there. Could you tell me how to find it? Just in case," he added solemnly.

"Follow the path behind the *imu* up the hill. The first turning takes you back to the village the loooong way. Stay on the main path. It goes to the ridge and follow that path for a while."

63

"It is a hard walk," added the small boy.

"You can see the *kalo* patch before you reach it. Just watch." Kaleo turned to his charges. "Come on," he said heavily. They trudged away in silence.

Coconut Man felt immeasurably better and greeted Lele enthusiastically as she pounded her *kapa*.

"*Aloha*, Lele!"

Lele squinted up at him and he remembered his plan to make her a hat. "*Aloha*. You seem happy today."

"Yes, well. I am," he said with some surprise. *I am*. "Your cloth is beautiful. The pattern is very even." He did not have to feign admiration. Lele's wood pattern-block made precise designs as she carefully imprinted each section with a brisk tap of her mallet.

"*Mahalo*. I prayed upon the design and now I am almost finished."

"And the dyeing?" He could not disguise the hope in his voice.

"Yes, Curious Man, the dyeing. You may watch. But," she stopped her tapping to point the mallet at him. "You may not talk while I do it. I will need to concentrate."

"Can I ask questions before?" Lele nodded. "And after?"

Lele let out a snort of laughter that seemed to catch her by surprise. "Yes."

"When will you do this?"

"Later today I will choose the dyes and mix them. I will start if I am not too tired. Tomorrow at the latest. It must dry before I can present my gift."

"*Ae. Mahalo.* I will look for you." Coconut Man rose and stretched. "Do you have any relatives coming for the ceremony?"

Lele shook her head and continued to work. "All my family is here. Now go and leave me in peace."

Coconut Man accepted his dismissal. He turned and walked to an old woman cutting fruit into a large calabash. His stomach growled. It was almost time for the midday meal and he had not even had his early meal.

"Good day, *Tutu.*" He used the familiar word for grandmother.

She craned to look up at him and he squatted so she wouldn't have to strain. Her nut brown skin, wrinkled from years in the sun, shone with health. Although her chin bobbed with age, her hands were sure as she deftly peeled and sliced bananas and mountain apples.

"I am Coconut Man. I weave baskets."

"I know who you are."

Coconut Man realized he had no idea what to say to this woman. "Would you like help?" As soon as the words were out of his mouth he wished he could take them back. The woman stopped slicing, juice dripping from her gnarled hands into the calabash.

"You are a strange one." She smiled and showed gaps where several teeth were missing. "Kind, I think. But strange."

Coconut Man smiled, too. "Do you need a basket? I would make you a lovely one."

"I don't need anything from you." The words were harsh, but she said them kindly. "You need something from *me*, I think." Her hands went back to her task.

Coconut Man, surprised out of his squat, dropped onto the ground. The woman placidly continued to slice her fruit, but there was something about her.

"Yes. I have a question." She raised her eyebrows, *yes, go on.* "Do you have any relatives, or friends," he stumbled over the words, "who are coming for the ceremony?"

"That is all? That is your question?" Once more her hands stopped their work. He held his breath. "Yes. Someone I know is coming." She smiled, closed-lipped now, and he knew she wanted him to *ask* who. If he did not ask, she would not tell. A twinkle in her eye confirmed this as she met his gaze.

"Who is coming?" he whispered.

"Why do you want to know?" she

whispered back.

He laughed out loud, surprised. This *tutu* had been around for many more years than he, and had not kept her sense of humor or her wits by simply watching the island go by. He decided to tell her.

"I overheard a conversation. Someone's life may be in danger sometime during the wedding celebration. I think it is someone arriving for the wedding, rather than someone who lives here in the village. I am trying to find out who is coming. Perhaps I can prevent this. . ." He hesitated to use the word 'death,' but that is what he feared. It sounded weak even to his own ears, but he did not want to endanger the woman by giving her the names of those he suspected.

"Do these persons know you heard their talk?" She gave him her full attention. All humor and twinkle were gone. Death was a serious crime, although it was a common punishment for breaking a variety of laws.

"I don't think so."

"You must be very careful. Do you know who it is or why this person is in danger?"

"No. The talk did not progress that far. It involves three. . ." the weight of the burden pressed down again and he sighed heavily. "I just do not know what to do. I cannot openly accuse them. I have no proof. I am a stranger here with no status. Not only would I lose face, but those criminals would know I knew. They would just change their plan and succeed another way." He had kept his voice down, but the strain of emotion made his fists clench and jaw ache. Tutu patted his hand with her sticky one and finished her task.

"Do you know who these men are? And I assume these are men?"

"Yes."

"Will you tell me?" Coconut Man shook his head. He would not tell her. A small part of him warned him she might not be the innocent, helpless old lady she seemed. She might even be allied with those men! He looked at her open, wizened face; the withered but strong hands now empty; the mound of fruit neatly sliced in its bowl and shook his head again. This time at himself. Suspicious of a grandmother!

"I know I am old, but I might be able to help. If you need it." Once more she stickily patted his hand and then stiffly rose to her feet, waving off his silent offer of assistance. She picked up the calabash of cut fruit, its tantalizing scent pinching his nostrils and roiling his empty stomach. She handed him a small, filled bowl.

She took two slow steps and turned back. "By the way, the person I know who is coming? She is my daughter and her name is Kehaulani--Dew of Heaven."

That name was familiar. But why? Wasn't that the name of the District Chief's wife? Could it be? Coconut Man stood open-mouthed, and watched her march slowly but steadily toward the eating *hale*. The sweet scent of banana drifted up from his bowl.

Chapter 7

Coconut Man returned to the Wai to wash his hands. He could have washed with water from one of the many calabashes around the village for that purpose, but he chose the Wai. He had spent much time at the river of late. There was something healing and cleansing about the Wai rushing past him to the sea.

Although the afternoon had not fully arrived, the air was still and hot. Water swirled around his knees and cooled him while he was lost in thought about Tutu, the chief and chiefess arriving, and his problem.

He did not know the intended victim, but he knew who was involved in the plot, and he thought he knew their method--poison during the second day's hula exhibition. He did not know what kind of poison, and even if he knew the name of the victim, what could he do? He was still an unknown in the village. He would be scorned, cast out of the village, or perhaps even accused himself. He did not know which would be worse: to be banned from the village, or have to flee to a *heiau*, a place of refuge, until his 'crime' was deemed erased. How long would that take? Assuming he could outrun or outswim the warriors or *kāhuna* sent to execute him.

He sighed unhappily and sat on the river bank. What a tangle. Another option, one he had not realistically considered, was to do nothing. Let the murder plot unfold and matters fall into place as they might. He shook his head.

That would never do. Although he was a loner, or *had been,* he was a just man. To do nothing was tantamount to assisting in this crime, and that he could not do.

These maunderings circled in his brain until he could stand it no longer. "Enough!" He clapped his hands and startled the birds above him. He would do his best to discover the victim and the why of it all.

Back in the village he found more uproar than before. Upon observation, he learned it was excitement at the chief and chiefess's arrival the next day. While he had been complaining to himself, a runner had arrived from the chief's village to announce their plans.

Now everyone was abuzz with activity, preparing food and gifts. Guest *hale* for the couple and their attendants were cleaned and decorated. The *ali'i's hale* were laden with succulent treats, the softest *kapa,* lei of shells, seeds, flowers and sharks' teeth. Human hair necklaces with beautiful shell and stone pendants were displayed for the royal couple's pleasure. The ruling *ali'i* had not been blessed with children who had lived, and now they were past the age of childbearing, so the villagers took extra pains to show how much they loved their chief and chiefess.

Truly, the *moku*--district--was blessed with health, good crops, children and especially the gods' good will was evident, and that was largely attributed to the kind and just rule of the chief. This rare, personal visit was looked upon as an opportunity to show fealty and joy.

The first feast would be tomorrow evening, after the *ali'i* had arrived and settled in. A celebration of their rule and of the coming wedding promised to be lavish. However, that would pale in comparison with the second day's feast, games, and hula. The third day, the wedding itself. The *kahuna*--priest--would bless and perform this ceremony.

The second day celebration brought the tang of fear to Coconut Man. How would the poison be distributed and to whom? It would look like an accident, or illness, he supposed. But why? He had seen much in his life, and figuring out the motives of others had never been his strong point. As an outsider, he had honed his observation skills, and they would be his best assets now.

He had only a day to finish weaving and to cure his greatest basket. Well, maybe two days, if he presented his gift on the second day. If he wanted to add dyes and other special items to the design, he had no time to lose.

He returned to the beach with his work and with his curious single-mindedness, shut out the island and its problems and began to weave.

By the day's end, the basket was complete. It stood as high as his waist and was sturdy. The sun was low, but he decided to begin curing. The sun's heat would remain long enough to dry his basket between dunkings.

He soaked it in the sea and set it to dry. He drank deeply from his water calabash. His stomach rumbled. Had he eaten? He didn't think so. He returned to the forest trail, following the circuitous route that avoided the village. He did not want to become distracted from his curing process. He envisioned the bustle of preparing the evening meal, the delicious smells wafting among the *hale*. . . *stop it!*

Off the trail and down a slope, a mountain apple tree still held ripe fruit. He picked up a strong vine and slithered down until he was just above the tree. Because of the steep grade he was able to stand close and toss one end of the vine around the fruit-laden branches. Holding both ends of the vine, he pulled them. He cut off several apples using his shark's tooth knife and ate one, legs splayed for balance against the hill, the setting sun making fire against the mountain.

He carried several more back toward the beach, and considered the next step in his basket-making. Should he decorate it? Shells? Feathers? Dyes? Perhaps a basket for the royal couple was not the time to experiment with untried techniques. As he neared the beach he spied Io, the net maker. Io trudged wearily, head lowered, a mound of nets slung over one shoulder.

"*Aloha,* Io," Coconut Man called from a distance, not wanting to startle the man.
Io raised his head. "*Aloha.*" He did not make eye contact or slow his stride.

Coconut Man took the net maker's appearance as a sign to pursue dyes for his basket. "What brings you to the beach?"

"'Umi needs nets mended by tomorrow. The chief arrives soon and these nets," he wearily indicated the mass on his shoulder, "need repair. I had intended to sew them on the beach, but they also needed re-dyeing, and I brought no materials for that. So. . ." Io trailed off, hands at his sides.

"I have apples. Would you like some?" Coconut Man recognized one who was exhausted and hungry.

"Well, it is late. I should be going." Io made no move.

"Come. Just have an apple and a rest. Then perhaps I can help you carry those back. They look heavy."

"*Mahalo.* Yes, perhaps just for a moment."

Coconut Man led Io back the few steps to the beach and gave him some apples. Then he retrieved his basket and stored it under the trees, safe from the tide and passers-by.
Io had consumed all his apples when Coconut Man settled next to him. He gave Io some more, then cleared his throat.

"I have decided I want to dye my basket. Can you show me how to make dye?"
Io did not answer, but nodded yes. He

seemed weighted by more than nets. "I do not have time to show you before the *ali'i* arrive, but I can give you some dye to try. If you like it, I will show you how I make it." There was some emphasis on "I."

"*Mahalo.*" They sat in silence for a few moments, watching the final fingers of scarlet over the sea. A green flash of sunset, then nothing.

Coconut Man cleared his throat again. Hunger made him shift uneasily and he sensed the other man was troubled. "Can I help you carry those?" He pointed at the nets pooled around them.

"I suppose. Yes." Io struggled to his feet and Coconut Man pretended not to notice, putting away his basket making effects.

Coconut Man did not know how to ask Io what was wrong. They were not friends. Were they? Io did not offer to tell him on the walk to the village. Once there, he thanked Coconut Man for his help and food. He handed him a packet of dye, then excused himself to the eating *hale*. Coconut Man followed slowly, understanding Io did not want him near, but not understanding why.

Coconut Man stored the dye near his sleeping mat, then entered the eating *hale*. His eyebrows raised in surprise when he saw Io, now laughing and boisterous, regaling several men with a humorous tale of becoming tangled in his own nets. Obviously, Io had something to hide from the others. Coconut Man didn't know whether to be annoyed or flattered that Io had chosen to show him a little of his true feelings.

Coconut Man settled at a separate eating mat and ate his fill. The conversation swirled around him as his own mixed and mottled thoughts swirled in his brain.

After the meal, the *kōnane* boards were rolled out and the games began. This time, Coconut Man had no partner, so he watched for a while, but felt left out and ducked under the frond curtain and out into the dark village. Cook fires had been banked, and he heard low-voiced conversations. Evidently the children had returned safely while he worked, and he smiled at their anxiety over this adventure.

The evening was quiet after the rush and preparation of the day. *Perhaps*, he thought, *everyone is tired of being excited. I know I am very tired.* The weight of village membership was heavy. Nothing new had occurred to him while he worked, his mind blank with concentration on the basket. His prayers and images of the completed gift had been all-consuming in his mind. Now, although fatigue had caught him, he lay on his sleeping mat with nothing but worry to occupy him. He needed a plan. Tutu offered to help, but what help could a frail old woman give? Kaleo was too young. Io had been a possibility, but after today, Coconut Man decided not to burden him further. Clearly, Io had his own troubles. *Alone.* He sighed.

I have always been alone. That has never bothered me before. But it does now.

He tried to still his mind for sleep. He pictured his body at rest, peacefully regenerating for the big day ahead. He saw himself in the crowd of well-wishers when the chief and chiefess arrived. Pictured giving them his basket. A bump under him announced itself and forced him to adjust his mat. He pulled his *kapa* closer, more for comfort than warmth. He tried to still his mind once more. Images of someone dying, a scream and thump as a faceless person, hit the earth, lifeless. Or worse, the poison striking many, at random, like the time the gods were angry and the island heaved and shook, felling all who stood and tumbling trees and *hale* at a single blow. He saw his villagers crumble and fall, still and cold, one by one, and he powerless to save them. *His* villagers. *When did that decision happen?* His eyes opened and he sighed again. A sliver of black sky gleamed through the trees. Tutu's smiling face came before him and he blinked, it seemed so real. "'*Ae*," he said aloud. "I will speak with her. You. '*Ae,*" he repeated in some exasperation.

He rolled onto his side, Tutu's face nodding complacently, and slid into sleep.

Chapter 8

Coconut Man awoke tired, but inspired. He remembered his promise to speak to Tutu and rose immediately. He made sure his basket was in the sun, yet protected from passers-by or rascally children. It was a tempting morsel, he was sure. Big enough to hold a child, and he remember enough of his own child-self to know a child would want to be inside it. He smiled, thinking he might even be able to fit in it now. Although he was grown, he was thin. And crouched down . . . he shook his head and picked up the packet of powdered dye. He was about to tuck the dye into his *malo* when he eyed the basket once more. Why not? Just see what it looks like.

He opened the dye and dipped a thin stick into it, and drew a line along the ridge of the top weave. There. That looked nice! He extended the line along the rim, carefully dipping the stick and scratching laboriously. It was not easy and the line became uneven where his grip wobbled. His hands were large and strong, used to weaving and grasping, not delicate work like this. He wondered if he could remove the line and redraw it. He rubbed gently with this thumb, and to his dismay the line crumbled into nothing. Discouraged, he easily erased it. That was no good. That obviously was not the way. The dye would never withstand daily use, much less dampness.

He would have to speak to Io again. He rewrapped the dye packet and set out to look for Tutu, his spirits dimmed from his failed endeavor.

He heard the *kapa* beaters at the far side of the village and headed that way. Perhaps Lele would be there. He saw Io and Io saw him, but ducked quickly out of sight into the forest, the tangle of nets on his shoulders swinging in his haste.

The village had awakened when he reached the clearing where the beaters worked. Today was the day the chief and chiefess would arrive! He heard the chanting and singing of prayers for many chores. Each worker asked for guidance in the task at hand: leis to be strung; fires to stay lit; fish to be caught, all things required harmony of the three internal spirits, *Kū, Lono,* and *Kāne,* and the help of the external spirits, to whom each person prayed.

More chanting. . . food to be delicious and give nourishment. . . *food! Poison.* The murder plot came rushing back. He had become distracted with his basket and nearly forgotten his promise. Tutu. Perhaps this entwining of thoughts meant the entwining of his work and preventing a wrong? A heavy task for a man. A task for a god, yes. *But,* he sighed. *I am not a god, and I seem to be the only one who can help. 'Ae. What a sticky place to be!*

He would speak to Lele about his dye project *after* he had spoken to Tutu. That seemed only right. However, that was not to be. Lele and Tutu sat together, a *kapa* spread before them. Gray and brown heads close, they conferred.

"Yellow is a chiefly color, Tutu," Lele said.

"Yes. That is nice," Tutu agreed.

"How much *noni* root should I use? If I don't have enough, I might have to mix more and then the color might not match."

"This is a big *kapa.* It is lovely." The gnarled hands fingered the cloth.

"Mahalo, Tutu. Here are the roots--how

much?" She offered a calabash of pounded roots.

Coconut Man sat quietly, close enough to listen, but not seem rude. Tutu closed her eyes.

"This is enough." Tutu opened her eyes and swirled a small amount of water into the calabash. Water! That's what Coconut Man had forgotten. He had only scratched on powder. He had not mixed it with water. *Lōlō! Idiot!* Of course.

The women carefully dipped sections of *kapa* into the yellow–orange water, chanting a request for blessing

> *O Gods*
> *Bless this kapa*
> *Make the color*
> *Even and Beautiful*
> *O Gods*
> *O Gods*
> *For our Beloved*
> *Chief and Chiefess*
> *Even and Beautiful*
> *Even and Beautiful*

Long after Coconut Man would have stopped dipping and praying, the women continued until the cloth was an eye–burning sun–yellow. Satisfied, they smiled and reverently laid it to dry. They both looked up and noticed him.

"*Aloha*, Coconut Man," Lele greeted him.

"Well?" was Tutu's greeting.

"*Aloha*, Lele. Tutu." He cleared his throat. "Why did you make the kapa so. . ." he searched for a polite word, "dark?"

"The dye fades as it dries," Lele answered.

"Well? What have you decided?" Tutu asked him.

"About what?"

"Your problem."

Which one? Coconut Man did not want to discuss it in front of Lele. And how did that old woman know he wanted to talk to her? Lele was cleaning up her supplies with the air of one who knew she should not listen but couldn't help it.

"Your baskets, of course. What did you think?" Tutu's eyes crinkled and Coconut Man knew she was teasing him. He expelled a breath. "Isn't that why you came to Lele? Because she is the best *kapa* maker anywhere?"

"Yes. That is why." She was the only *kapa* maker he had ever spoken to, so she was the best. Perhaps she was. He admired the uniform yellow color and even thickness.

"Lele? Will *kukui* nut charcoal stay on my baskets?"

84

"I don't know." Lele gazed into the middle distance. Had he offended her in some way? He knew *kapa* was women's work, but Io the netmaker used dye, so. . .

"I think it might. Perhaps not when the basket is green. I think it must be dry? I am only guessing of course, but if you could soak the whole basket in dye, like we do with *kapa*." She stopped moving and talking again. This time Coconut Man waited, understanding that she pictured the process, much as he did when he was working. "*Kukui* charcoal may not be the best choice, either. I will give you other dyes to try."

"That is most generous. Thank you." Coconut Man was touched. Gathering roots for dyes was hard work. So was pounding the roots. He had heard the women complain when they pounded roots all day. Their necks and backs ached from the strain. He had never given it much thought before, but now he imagined doing it himself, and a wave of gratitude washed over him. He decided to make Lele a beautiful hat, once the wedding was over. Wedding. That reminded him once more of his greater task. "You are very kind."

Lele must have seen something of the affection in his face for she blushed a dark red and waved him away. "Just let me clean up. I will ready some colors for you. Go now."

Tutu nodded that he should come with her. They walked slowly along the path out of the clearing, away from the village.

"You have decided something. I can see that."

"Yes, Tutu. I want to talk to you. I have no one else to turn to. I did not want to burden you, but I find this weight too much for me. You are wise and my problem already concerns you, I think." She raised her eyebrows. *Yes, go on.* "Someone is going to be poisoned at one of the feasts for the wedding. He or she is not of this village, but will come, probably today. The poison will be given and someone will become ill and perhaps die. Why?" He sighed heavily. "Do you see, Tutu? I don't know who, and I don't know why."

"Yes, I see. It is a problem. How can I help? Besides a pair of ears?" They had come to the Wai. They sat on a fallen tree and looked out at the green-brown water.

"I don't know, Tutu. Perhaps words of wisdom? A path I might choose?"

"I think I must know whom you heard speaking if I am to be of more help."

"I did not want to tell you that. I thought. . . I thought it might endanger you." He looked at her on this last.

Her firm gaze met his. "I can protect

myself. But that is kind of you." She patted his hand. "You are a kind man, I think." Her hand lay warm on his. He felt calmer now. Better for telling her.

"It is those three men who always seem to make trouble. I have only been here a little while, but it seems they have gone beyond childish pranks and rudeness. Manō, Lako and Palani. It was Lako and Palani I overheard. It seems to me that Manō is the head of the spear and Lako and Palani are the shaft. They will do all they can to see that the point pierces in a death blow."

"Aaaah." Tutu nodded. "This makes sense now."

Coconut Man raised his eyebrows.

"You are new to this village and do not understand the people or our ways. You are correct, however. There is much danger in this plan. It is more serious than I thought."

"What? What is it?"

"You are sure they do not know you overheard them?"

"Yes. They were very drunk and I was quiet. What is going to happen?"

"It is my turn to protect you, I think. I must give this some thought. I must take steps. I see that now."

She rose and slowly shuffled back the way they had come. He followed, but she did not acknowledge him. "I knew this might happen," she muttered. "I am sad to know that my dark dream could come true. All the *mele,* all the healing, creating, with no effect on that boy. Some spirits you cannot change." She entered her *hale,* and its *kapa* curtain fell closed.

He was dismissed. He returned to his basket, placed it in the direct sun and studied it. He had been distracted from the wedding basket by the basket for the chief and chiefess. He would finish the wedding basket and cure them properly.

He turned the giant basket. It was well-made and even. He did not want to dye the whole thing, he decided. He might experiment with dying coconut fibers some day, but not now. It would be terrible if the basket broke or deteriorated because of the dye. He would be responsible for anything that happened afterward, should that occur. He did weave flower buds out of more fronds and tuck them into the sides. Perhaps a shell. It was such a big basket, it would need a big shell, he thought. A *leho*--cowrie--perhaps? He had time to find the perfect shell. He wanted to present his gift at the second-day feast, and the wedding basket at the wedding on the third day, two days from now.

Hunger turned him to the cook fires

and he followed the scents of the midday meal.

Kaleo and Honu led a pack of children past him in some game. Coconut Man smiled and waved. Kaleo jumped into a mock-warrior stance for a moment, waved a stick at Coconut Man, and was off again. A blink and he would have missed it. *Was I ever that fast? That wild? Probably.* Honu's curtain of bangs hid her face, but he was almost sure she smiled, too.

Without meaning to, he had seated himself near Tutu's *hale*, and under the hum of the village and shouts from the *keiki*'s game, he heard the even tones of prayer coming from her hut.

Chapter 9

Drowsing with a full stomach, Coconut Man was startled out of his doze by the return of the children. Their excited cries were echoed by the pounding of message drums. The *ali'i* were near. The village roused from languor in the mid-day heat to a hive of activity. Not knowing what to do, Coconut Man remained seated at the hub of the swirl of activity. He felt invisible. Even Tutu popped out of her *hale* but did not speak to him, just hobbled off.

A messenger jogged into view, his body slick with sweat, long muscles straining. *It must be time.* Coconut Man rose to his feet and joined others in line to welcome their leaders. Women wore their finest *kapa* and men's shoulder cloaks showed a rainbow.

Kāhili bearers,--men carrying feathered standards--preceded the chief and chiefess.

Because they were lesser royalty, their advance party was small. A few guards and servants, but then the *ali'i* came into view.

The chief wore a shoulder cape made of thousands of tiny feathers that glistened and shone in the afternoon sun. His silver hair, shot with dark streaks, was bound for travel. He was still a large, powerful man, and Coconut Man could tell he would once have been a formidable adversary. His *malo* was of *kapa* bleached nearly white, undyed and unadorned except for his knife.

A large nose with flaring nostrils dominated his face. His smile of greeting was warm and his glance took in every detail. Never having been this close to royalty, Coconut Man realized belatedly that he was openly staring, which was against the law. He noted the people stayed out of range, behind an invisible line, and they all bowed low. Although it was only a bit after midday so shadows were small, care was taken that no shadow should overlap the shadow of any in the party.

This chief was kind, and the fealty genuine. Many offerings were placed along his route: fruit, *kī* leaf packets, calabashes. His wife was more striking than beautiful, but she had a quality of beauty. Her gaze was as warm and welcoming as her husband's.

Strong white teeth split her brown face when she smiled, which was often. Both spoke to the people, not a general greeting, but something for each person. It was clear the couple knew the village well, and although all propriety and ceremony was met, he felt an intimacy among them.

"Where is this groom?" the chief called.

'Ehu stepped forward hesitantly.

"Where is the beautiful bride?"

Lehua joined 'Ehu.

"Aha! This is the rascal who only a few years ago, left me a rotten banana on my last visit." The chief's booming voice carried to all in the clearing.

'Ehu shifted and blushed a deep mahogany. "It was an accident, Highness. I was only a boy. I meant it as an offering and. . ."

The chief included the people in his tale, eyes crinkled in suppressed laughter. "This boy wrapped a *mai'a* in a *kī* leaf and snuck it into a calabash. No one knew until we were on our way home and all these disgusting bugs followed us. It made a terrible smell and leaked all over the other things in the calabash!" The chief did not seem troubled by this.

'Ehu tried to shrink back, but Lehua held his hand and kept him from retreating.

"I'm sorry about that. I meant well."

The chief and chiefess laughed and the villagers joined in. It was kind laughter, and 'Ehu's high color faded. He smiled, too. "I can assure you, no rotten bananas will go home with you this journey!"

'Umi, the headman, and the man who provided fresh fish for the *ali'i*, stepped forward. 'Umi was the oldest male who still worked for the village. He acted as the elder in times of dissent. He called for *ho'oponopono*-- group problem solving-- and called upon others in the village when a decision was needed. Most deferred to his status and seniority. Additionally, he relied on the village elder women who also policed the community. He was also very big. No one really wanted to tangle with him. *Except maybe Manō, Lako and Palani,* mused Coconut Man.

'Umi said, "You must want rest and refreshment. We will show you to your *hale* and provide for your needs."

"*Mahalo*, 'Umi. My lovely bride would like a rest." Indeed, the chiefess' smile was a bit thin and she leaned on her husband. "Kehau, let us go. We have much time here and a little refreshment will do us both good." The words were whispered, but Coconut Man was close to them and had spent a lifetime alone, just listening to surf, jungle, and sometimes, interesting conversations.

Kehau. Interesting. No Kehaus lived in this village. Was Kehau Kehaulani, the daughter of Tutu? If so, that meant a great deal. Tutu was related to the royal family. What was she doing cutting fruit for meals? Shouldn't she be sitting on woven mats lined with kapa *with a palm-leaf fan waving away the heat?* She was not jesting when she said he knew little of this village.

'Umi escorted the chief and chiefess to their *hale.* Guards remained at the ready, but the servants moved about the village with familiarity, greeting and hugging as they readied food and comforts for their sovereigns.

I have a few things to ask Tutu. Hands on hips, shaking his head, he turned to her but she was already at her *hale.* Just before the *kapa* swung shut, she winked at him. *Winked!*

He would find her later. In the meantime, he needed to finish those wedding baskets and find a shell for the big one. And what about Manō? The excitement of the day wore off as he donned the heavy cloak of frustration and worry. With leaden steps he returned to the beach and retrieved the wedding basket, woven with joy only

94

yesterday. So long ago.

Chapter 10

The day was late when the wedding basket was finished to Coconut Man's satisfaction. He had not been able to concentrate and initially the details had not been up to his standards. Ordinarily, he would have stopped work, deciding the gods were too busy to bless him. Since he did not have the luxury of time, he forced his hands to continue. Now, he stretched his aching fingers and rose stiffly, bending and leaning to wake his cramped muscles.

A shell. He must find one. At some point, *not* adorning the royal basket with a shell had ceased to be an option. Now it was important, vital even. *Why?* He did not know, but was wise enough to listen to his *kū*--lower self--in these matters.

He still had several hours until sunset which marked the beginning of the feasting and dancing. He wandered slowly at the surf line, eyes sweeping the sand. Just beyond where the village had watched the fishing were the tide pools. He heard echoes of the *keiki* laughter of the day when he met Kaleo and Honu. *That was the beginning*, he decided. *The beginning of what? A change. Birth. Something.*

He stepped carefully over seaweed-coated rock looking for *something*. A shell. *A sign, really.* Much life lay in these small pools separated by rock barriers and controlled by the tide. If the tide was low, or too long in coming, this life would die. Just like that.

A tiny crab struggled to stuff itself into a hole when Coconut Man's shadow fell over the water. He clearly saw its panic. He carefully trapped it and placed it in a larger pool. *Odd behavior for me. Well, I've been thinking a lot of odd things, lately.*

The sea was filled with beauty. Perhaps, someday, he would venture out on it. In the past, that thought would have filled him with panic, but not now. Not today. He squinted against the glare. Perhaps Io or 'Umi would take him out. He would feel safe with them. Their knowledge of the ocean was as great as his of weaving. *But weaving won't kill you if you make a mistake*, he mused. The tide was going out, isolating the pools filled with life. He hopped to a deeper pool and squatted. A lovely shell lay at the bottom, out of reach unless he got wet to the waist. Brown and white, large and smooth, its spray of sun-like rays spreading from one side, beckoned to him. There was nothing for it but to slide in. He checked the surf and the waves were still far out. He would be safe enough for the moments it would take to reach the shell.

He eased into the water, surprised at the chill. Starfish and *wana,* the round spiky creatures that could give a nasty sting when stepped on, lined the pool. He did not want to get stabbed by a *wana* spire as his hands searched for safe holds. That would certainly put a damper on finishing his baskets and the wedding as well. As a child, he had stepped on a *wana* and his foot had swelled and burned. He had hopped uncomfortably for two days and learned his lesson.

When his feet touched the sandy bottom, silt churned and he lost sight of the shell. He waited for it to settle. As it did, myriad small fish darted about, alarmed at this presence. When he did not move, the pool resumed its life cycle.

He studied the intricate crevices. Eyes peered from every crack. Mostly crabs, but he thought he spied an eel. Normally he would catch everything that was food. But today. . . not today. Odd. The fish resumed their circling and he marveled at their variety and color. At last he realized he was numb from the waist down and crisping in the sun above. He bent to retrieve his treasure, startling a large-eyed fish. The fish instantly rounded itself like a little breadfruit, covered in small spikes. He had heard of these funny fish but never seen one alive. People in the villages used them for decoration. They dried them in their rounded state and hung them from *hale* beams.

He reached his prize and brought it to the surface. It was smaller than it had looked under water, however it was lovely and perfect. Best of all, no animal lived inside. It was abandoned and ready for Coconut Man to use.

Despite his enthusiasm, he was careful leaving the pool too, the memory of the *wana* sting still ripe in his mind. His lower half was gray and wrinkled from the soaking but he emerged unharmed. A good sign. *Several good signs*, he amended.

Returning to his basket, he attached the shell securely with fine fibers and sat back, content. He carried the basket to the village, hungry, ready to join in the festivities. He was nearly to his sleeping place when he remembered the horror he was sure would occur tomorrow and felt powerless to stop. The joy drained out of him. Tutu's wrinkled face appeared in his mind and he vowed to follow up her mysterious comments. Perhaps at tonight's feast and dancing. Men and women ate together, but at separate mats during a feast. He was determined to find her before it was too late.

Chapter 11

Newly lit torches, smoking slightly, transitioned the day to evening. No *hale* was big enough to hold the entire village, so mats had been laid in the clearing near the *imu* where a large boar had been steaming all day for the celebration. The clearing was decorated with flowers and fruit. *Kāhili* --the royal standards, lined the area. The tufts of bright feathers looked like torches themselves.

Excited chatter greeted him as he inhaled the mixed aromas of food and forest. Large, green kī leaves stretched along the center of each eating mat, some already laden with *lomi* fish, poi, cut fruit
and other succulent treats.

Women brought out dish after dish as the men seated themselves. The chief and his wife, already seated at separate mats, close to each other, greeted villagers with a familiarity that spoke of great love and great respect.

Coconut Man found this most interesting. He had never been close to royalty. In fact, the high chief, the *ali'i nui,* of the *mokupuni*--all the districts--was something of a legend, spoken of in hushed tones and with more than a little fear. This chief, the *ali'i moku* of the district, seemed, well, almost like others in the village. Hmmm. There was greatness, yes, a god-like quality about him, but the way the people spoke and laughed told him something else.

Tutu sat on a mat close to the chiefess, listening to something the chiefess was saying. Tutu was well-respected in this village, he knew, and it appeared she was known to the wife of the chief. *Well, she had said as much, hadn't she?*

Coconut Man knew so few men in the village, and he could not sit with the women. Sitting with the children was also not possible. 'Umi, as village headman and head fisherman, sat close to the chief's mat. Io was the only man he knew well enough to approach.

He made his way toward Io's mat. A burst of raucous laughter drew his attention to another mat close to the royal couple. Manō laughed loudly and clapped Palani on the shoulder. Lako, head down and silent, seemed to be the focus of the joke. Coconut Man was close enough to see Tutu and the chiefess stop their talk and exchange a glance. The rest of the chatter ebbed and flowed, continuing around them. Coconut Man froze at this tableau and Tutu's glance flicked to him and was gone. He was sure she meant to include him somehow. What did it mean? He had to talk with her. His desperation rose like bile, his knees weakened and he sat abruptly. Fortunately, he was near Io so perhaps it did not look as odd as it felt.

Preoccupied with his problem, he barely acknowledged Io's greeting and introductions to those around the mat.

The welcome prayer, conducted by a *kahuna* from the chief's party was brief. Coconut Man ate and responded to queries, but could not have repeated what was said. His eyes constantly darted from the royal couple to Manō, waiting. *For what?* He wasn't sure. How would the deed be accomplished? And to whom? Other than the royal party, he didn't see any new faces in the crowd. Perhaps not too many had come from afar for the wedding. *How was he to know?* All his life, he had taken great pains to remain distant from human connection.

Manō and friends seemed to be waiting and watching, too. *Perhaps it is just my imagination.*

Musicians rose and moved toward the mats strewn with drums, sticks, rocks, and other manner of implements. The audience arranged themselves closer to the dance mats. Chief and chiefess were given the best seats, slightly to the side where they could see their people, the dancers and musicians. Servants scurried to bring their drinks and unfinished dishes so they would want for nothing during the performance.

Had he not been watching for something, anything, Coconut Man would have missed a curious thing. Palani, rising from his mat, picked up a small calabash and moved closer to the royal eating mats. As a servant rushed by, he handed it to her. Coconut Man watched the servant place it on the new mat in front of the chiefess. No one seemed to notice the bowl. Coconut Man moved as close to the royal mats as possible. Tutu was seated next to the chiefess so they could converse. Manō, Lako and Palani, were strangely far from the dance.

Two young men dressed in *malo* stood at the edges of the clearing and brought large shells to their lips. Their chests expanded as they inhaled, then blew clear, deep notes. A different *kahuna* stood in the center, back from the torchlight. She seemed to appear from the jungle as if the tones from the shells had summoned her. A calabash in one hand, and a *kī* leaf in the other, her *mele* of blessing rang out as she dipped the leaf, shook it, and moved around the clearing. Even the *keiki* were silent. Coconut Man felt closed in, as if he were inside his own basket. He saw no stars and the moon, which should be near full, was hidden by clouds, clamping a dark lid over the village.

The blessing ended and drumming began--a slow throb of welcome. Soon the clearing filled with dancers--men with ferns strung around their heads and ankles. Loops of shells jangled as they simulated a battle with stomps and yells, spears crossing and bobbing in the torchlight. The music continued with songs of war, tributes to the owl and turtle, blessings for crops and good wishes for 'Ehu and Lehua.

Captivated and enraptured, it was not until the festivities were over for the night that Coconut Man realized two things. The sky had cleared to reveal a wedge of stars above the ridge line behind the *ahupua `a* and a white, burning moon that lit the clearing. And, he had been lost in the song and dance and had failed to watch. Failed to watch

Manō, Lako and Palani. Failed to watch the royal couple, and failed to watch the bowl. The bowl that had been so strangely passed and prominently placed. Failed.

Isolated in his despair, he trudged toward his sleeping mat, then stopped. Could his ears have deceived him? He waited. No, he had heard correctly. Tutu stood close to the chiefess after embracing her. *Good-night mother*. That was what he had heard. His jaw slightly open, he was digesting this when the next phrase confirmed it.

"Good-night *makuahunōwai wahine*," said the chief. *Good-night mother-in-law.* The couple and Tutu headed to their respective sleeping *hale.*

Coconut Man crossed to the royal couple's eating mat, still strewn with dishes, bits of food and drink. The small calabash was empty.

Chapter 12

A disturbance in the village woke Coconut Man. The moon had not set in its dark canopy, but he was unsure how long he had slept. The noise was not that of a bustling village but more an insistent rustling of many hands and feet, hushed voices, indistinct words. He rose from his mat to investigate.

The guest *hale* was lit from within. Wavering light from *kukui* nut lamps threw grotesque shadows as the curtain-door was opened and shut. Coconut Man crept closer, behind the *hale,* knowing that to be caught there would likely mean death or at the very least, banishment.

To his surprise, he heard Tutu's voice. "It is nothing, daughter. You were excited and exhausted from travel. You are feeling better now?"

"Yes," came a quiet response.

A deeper voice Coconut Man thought to be the chief's. "Kehau, let us sleep. You will wake refreshed. We will go to the sea and find a *honu* to bless you." The words were loving and gentle. "*Mahalo,* Mother," he continued, "for coming in the night, although it was nothing."

"I'm not so sure of that." Tutu sounded as if she were standing next to Coconut Man, and speaking directly to him. He was startled until he realized she must be just on the other side of the thatch. He heard rustlings and decided she was putting something away or looking for something.

"I would always come," said Tutu. "Not only are you my chief and she my chiefess, but she is my daughter," she added gently. "And, I am the healer."

"I have a healer, Tutu," the chief admonished.

"I know."

Coconut Man smiled at the barely disguised disdain. So like Tutu. Undoubtedly the other healer was exceptionally skilled, to be attending *ali`i,* but Tutu obviously felt something lacking. *Well, a parent and child. That is a certain bond.* A bond not experienced by Coconut Man but he understood its power.

The new information sank in. Tutu was

a *kahuna*. A healer *kahuna*. He understood she was a *kahuna* of craft, but a healer? He heard her move toward the doorway and he hurried to meet her.

"What happened?" he whispered loudly.

"Come. Not here." She guided him behind the *hale* toward the refuse area. Not pleasant, but they should be undisturbed here.

"My daughter felt ill," Tutu said. "She has been unwell for a long while and tonight she felt worse. She fell asleep and woke unable to move her feet and legs normally. She felt pain, like small *wana* spines in her flesh, and when she wanted to move them, she felt a great weight inside." Tutu's eyes stared into his. "What do you know? Why were you outside the *hale*?"

"I woke and heard noises. I have been watching them, waiting for something." Tutu opened her mouth to speak but Coconut Man cut her short. "I don't know for what! I failed. Perhaps that is why your daughter fell ill."

Tutu's eyebrows raised. "Something happened?" He told her about the passing of the calabash at the feast.

Tutu's mouth formed a grim line. "Stay here." And she was gone, moving faster than he had ever seen her move. The smell from the refuse area was strong and he moved

109

around it to where the slight breeze carried the odors away. The moon had begun its descent when Tutu returned. Without preamble she said, "She knows the calabash of which you speak. She ate a little of the *lomi* fish but the bowl was spilled before she finished. She said it tasted all right, but she does not care for *lomi* much and only tried it to be polite. Puna loves *lomi,* however."

"Puna?"

"The chief."

"I see." Coconut Man paced. "It is suspicious, but we cannot be sure."

Tutu remained still. "I have thought of nothing else ever since you brought this matter to my attention. All you have repeated can also mean absolutely nothing. All we have are guesses."

"What about the men talking of illness and death?"

"Drunken maunderings, nothing more."

"I came to you for help!" He stood over her, panting.

She stood serenely, eyes warm and unwavering. "Yes, you did. I do not say what you overheard is not the case. I do say, you have no proof. Do you not think I am concerned? It is my daughter who fell ill. However, she was already ailing."

Coconut Man backed off. "I am sorry. I

am worried. And unable to think of a way to prevent something I fear will be terrible."

"Kehau is weak. This is probably her last sojourn. No one knows of her true condition but myself, her husband and perhaps a few of the closest retainers."

"But why?" Coconut Man was confused. "She is the beloved monarch. Shouldn't all know of her illness? So they can perhaps help? Or say thank you or . . . ." He realized he had backed himself in a corner and stumbled to a halt. He had thought to say, *good-bye.*

"I understand your concern. And perhaps, in some ways you are right. I am going to confide in you. You brought this plot to me, and I feel I must reciprocate. Come." Tutu shuffled out of the grove and to the beach path. Coconut Man followed, not speaking, until they were on the wide white sand, far from trees and possible eavesdroppers. Tutu grunted as she sat on the rocky ledge where the village had watched the fishing frenzy.

"'*Ae,*" she began. Coconut Man studied her and, for the first time, she appeared frail.

"'*Ae,*" she repeated. "It is like this. Many years ago, Puna was chief of a neighboring district. Before Kehau, before many things. The island was in an uproar, many district chiefs fighting for control. The *ali'i* --high

111

chief--of the island was weak, and unable to stop his warring lesser *ali'i*. His reign had faltered under his loose hand. He was corrupt and allied himself with dangerous companions, not unlike those who seek to stir up this village." She turned to him and he nodded his understanding.

"The high chief was eventually killed and the younger, stronger *ali'i* fought for control. Much blood was shed. Spirits from those battles still walk these island paths." She sighed. "Puna was wise. He gathered warriors and many trusted advisors and eventually achieved peace, but not for himself. For another chief he felt was most fit to run the entire island. His brother, Ahukini."

Coconut Man inhaled. Ahukini was still the *ali'i nui*--high chief--of the island. He was very old, but very strong. Puna was much younger than his brother.

"Ahukini ruled, Puna ruled, other lesser chiefs ruled for a number of years. Both brothers married, had children, though none survived for Puna and my Kehau." Tutu gazed fiercely out to sea and Coconut Man turned away from her glistening eyes and trembling mouth.

"My brother was a good man. We were born together, though I was first by a few minutes." Coconut Man was instantly lost at

112

this turn of topic. He was about to speak, but chose to wait, to let her story unfold. As impatient as he was, Tutu was telling him something important.

"Many brothers and sisters fought, but not us. We both chose the path of the *kāhuna*. I became a healer, but he was a seer. There were exceptions to his gift. I do not know if he could not see his own future, or he refused to believe it. However, that ability became a problem because often he was unable to keep what he saw to himself." Her voice deepened as she fought back tears.

"During this time, after the battles, my brother also married and had a child. A boy." Coconut Man sensed that the point of the story was coming. She faced him. "This child was--infused with evil. He wore a cloak of camouflage so perfect that even his own father did not see. But I did. I tried to warn Kai and Hoku, my brother and his wife, but they did not believe. There was no proof, as we are finding here as well. What mother, what father, wants to think ill of their child?"

Tutu shifted on the rock, perhaps uncomfortable sitting so long. Coconut Man was definitely uncomfortable. A chill breeze had sprung up, and his hindquarters were numb from lack of movement.

"It was a big village. So, when things

disappeared, small at first, no one noticed. I watched and waited. Then birds and animals were found near the *hale*. Heads missing, bodies damaged. These animals had not been killed for food, but for sport. Again, I went to Kai. He was deaf to me. Hoku was pregnant again, and I was newly married. Things became busy. Puna approached Kai about becoming *ali'i* of a neighboring district.--this one. Puna would approach Ahukini on behalf of Kai, about the old district *ali'i* who was ill. When he passed, Kai would make an excellent *ali'i moku*. Manō," she glanced sharply at Coconut Man, "for that was his son and my nephew, was fast becoming a man. Strong and intelligent, he seemed the perfect son, and a likely candidate to inherit a *moku,* should something happen.

Something did happen. Hoku died. The baby was lost and for Kai, his sun and moon were taken. I had my suspicions from the beginning. I was sisters with Hoku. We spent every day together and she was never ill a day with this baby. I gathered water with her the evening before. She was happy, excited by the turn of events. The next day, she was no more. The *ahupua`a* went into mourning. Kai withered and weakened daily. Manō made a great show of caring for his father, but I knew. I knew!" Tutu's fist pounded her leg.

Coconut Man felt she was no longer speaking to him. To herself, perhaps? Her brother?

"I could do nothing but wait. I was banned from Kai's *hale.* Manō watched me. He became a big man almost overnight. I learned I was pregnant the day Kai's body was discovered. I was afraid for my baby.

"My husband was offered the position of *konohiki*--headman--of this *ahupua`a* and I urged him to accept. He was a good man-- a good second to help the village as its *ali`i* exited this world. I wanted to be as far from Manō as possible. No good could come from him and I knew his plan. With no brothers or sisters to compete with him, with no father in the way, and only a shiny skin of good behavior showing, he was the next in line for a position of power. He expected to become chief. But he got too bold. Of course, he was terribly smart. Cunning. Again, no proof, only suspicions, but enough had happened and Puna listened to me. Yes, he did."

Coconut Man, caught up in the story, spoke at last. "What! What did he do?"

"He was smart enough to let some years go by, yes he was." Her voice had become a higher pitched sing-song and Coconut Man wondered if this recollecting was too much for her.

115

"My Kehau was lovely. She was growing into a lovely girl. My husband was an excellent *konohiki*. A specialist in fishponds for the *ali`i*. He built and maintained them and as Kehau grew, coincidentally, Puna came to view these ponds more and more often on the pretext of having his own maintained similarly." Tutu winked at Coconut Man and he again was lost at the change of story and tone. "It soon was clear that Kehau and Puna loved each other deeply. Manō began to visit this *moku* as well, ingratiating himself to the dying *ali`i* hoping to be named next. I had the ear of the wife and warned her not to let Manō alone with the chief. She had at least that much control," Tutu said bitterly. "It soon became apparent that my husband would be named chief, not Manō. So, my husband had to die, too."

"Just like that?" Coconut Man exclaimed. "It sounds insane!"

"Yes. It does. I did not see it until it was too late. I thought we were safe, far from Manō's home *moku*--that Manō would not dare to harm him. I told my husband to be careful, but there was so much I could not control over a man's, even my own husband's, life. An accident at the fish ponds one day. They are as you see them now, to the far side of the shore, protected from the surf and intruders. Isolated. They tell me he slipped on a wet rock, hit his head, and drowned. Manō's mistake was being the one to inform the village. I finally spoke. I became crazed with grief and anger and although I don't believe Puna truly thought Manō had anything to do with it, my husband was of higher status and my words were heeded. That opportunity was lost for Manō. 'Umi was named *konohiki.* Puna married Kehau and when the older *ali`i* finally died, Puna asked to rule this district, the *moku* of his wife's remaining family. Ahukini consented." Tutu's gaze had returned to the sea. She seemed depleted and exhausted.

"What happened to the district that Puna ruled?"

"Ahukini gave it to Kona. A good man. It is also a prosperous district, though drier than ours. They are strong in canoe building and fishing and we often trade our *kalo* and sweet potatoes for their skills."

Her gaze shifted out to sea. "I am tired, Coconut Man."

"I am as well."

"I am tired of all of this. It is my whole life, it seems. I am tired of Manō. You are right. He is cunning and evil. I will stop him this time. Before he kills the last person I care about. My daughter will not die by his hand."

"No. She won't. I will help."

"I know. Help an old woman up." She held out her hand and he raised her to her feet. She linked her arm with his and they walked, silently, for all the words had been spoken, back to the waiting village.

Chapter 13

Morning found Coconut Man too early. Up late into the night with Tutu, he slept restlessly; dark forms and misshapen creatures loomed in his dreams. He rose and went blearily to the Wai to wash. Coming to the Wai was a habit now. He liked the solitude, the rush of the water and the physical and spiritual cleansing he gained.

The sun was a low smear in a gray sky. The birds twittered, subdued at their perches. A storm was gathering. Coconut Man studied the sky. Unlike the daily rains that showered the uplands and the valleys, this promised to be a drenching storm. Perhaps not like the rainy season, still several months off, but a formidable rain, probably inconvenient for the second day of festivities. He moved down the path to the beach.

At least his baskets were finished. He

would have to find a dry, protected place for them. Where would the hula and music be today? The feasting? The village had no lodge large enough to hold them all. In the storm season, people stayed inside their *hale,* or just went about their business. With a large gathering such as this, postponing it was not an option. The wedding ceremony must be held tomorrow, after today's events and blessings. This day had been chosen by *kahuna* and was therefore sacred. He had heard no mention of the coming storm. Was it unexpected? Or perhaps the *kāhuna* knew, and planned for it. He was ignorant of such things. He sighed. He had lived on this island his whole life, traveling from village to village, *moku* to *moku*, and yet was pitifully ignorant of its history and customs.

Another thing I must change. I must pay more attention. What if I marry someday? Have a child? The image of Lele flashed before him and he snorted. *I must be able to tell my wife and child the news. The history. The story. Yes, well. That is far away.* This *story is the one I must finish.*

He stood on the beach. The ocean was pewter like the sky. The horizon blurred where they met. Although it was early, he was not the only one to realize the severity of the coming storm. Many men were at the canoe shed up the beach, hauling the big canoes far above the water, securing them against wind and waves. The canoe *hale* itself was huge with giant tree trunks driven far into the sand and ridgepoles bent to support the woven roof. The ends were open to allow the heavy canoes, some seating as many as sixty, to be stored easily. Smaller fishing boats fit here too, as well as in a smaller *hale* a bit farther on.

Coconut Man felt isolated from the bustle and retreated down the beach. In the distance he spied Kaleo and quickened his step. He neared the royal fishpond where two men talked in the shallows and another worked on the far side, tending to the seawall. The child had disappeared by the time he reached the pond.

The royal fishponds had stone walls built to form a shallow lagoon. Small holes were left in the walls and the tide brought fish and food inside. The pond-tender also fed the small fish, encouraging them to stay where life was easy. In time, they grew too big to exit the small holes and were a ready source of food for the *ali `i*.

As he approached, Coconut Man saw one of the men was Manō and heard him say something harshly to 'Umi, who was in the water, strengthening the stone wall against the tide. He could not understand the words but the tone was angry. Manō splashed from the shallow water and strode up the beach into the forest. 'Umi's mouth was drawn down in a frown and he breathed heavily, although his labors did not seem very strenuous.

"Aloha, 'Umi," Coconut Man hailed.

'Umi looked up, startled. "Aloha."

"What are you doing? And may I join you?"

'Umi's hands stilled and he stood upright. "I am. . ." he searched for words. Coconut Man's bold inquiry had apparently surprised him. "I am reinforcing this boundary before the storm. I suppose you could help. If you like." This last was clearly in the vein of *I can't imagine why you would want to, but I will humor you.*

"Mahalo." Coconut Man splashed noisily toward 'Umi.

"Shhh. The fish are trapped, but I would not be surprised to see them jump out to get away from you."

"Oh, yes. I'm sorry."

"Move slowly. Shuffle your feet like this." 'Umi demonstrated. "If there is anything sharp or dangerous, you will push it away and not step on it."

Coconut Man stopped. "Dangerous?" His unfamiliarity with sea life was fast becoming a problem.

'Umi smiled. "There are many small creatures here that will cause you pain. A few might do worse than that, but still, pain is enough."

"*Wana?*"

"Yes, that. And shells with poisonous animals inside. And sea snakes, but they prefer deeper water and I rarely see them inside the pond." At Coconut Man's growing alarm, 'Umi stopped. "Yes, well. As in all things, as long as you know about the dangers, you can protect yourself."

Coconut Man froze. "Anything else?"

"For now, why don't you help me with this wall. See, look for weak spots under water. If it shifts when you touch it, push the rocks around to tighten the gaps. Water must flow in with the tide, but food fish must not get out. I will check the sluice gate."

'Umi shuffled to a wooden gate set into the water. "When the tide comes in, we raise it to allow more fish to enter. When the tide turns, we lower it to trap the fish."

"Ah. Very clever. I am learning much. *Mahalo*, 'Umi. I did not know you also tended the ponds. I thought you were head fisherman?"

"I am. Sometimes I help Kaiki, who is head of the fishponds." He gestured to a man as large as himself who worked on the far barrier. "With a storm coming, sometimes all need to help in a village such as ours." Coconut Man nodded in agreement. "If the wall is destroyed, many months of work will flow out with the fish. Yes. Well. The gate looks fine. Kaleo was to lift the gate today, but of course, he was too busy." 'Umi lifted the gate, sounding more resigned than angry. "I will lower it when I am finished," he explained. "I don't want the storm to take the fish if I can help it."

Coconut Man shuffled behind 'Umi as they checked the wall. Conversation had stopped. Kaiki worked toward them from the opposite side.

Coconut Man noted the similarity of the two men as they conferred over the project. Kaiki was large and muscled like 'Umi, but soft-spoken. Not a leader, just a hard-working man who undertook his tasks with utmost gravity. After they met in the middle and agreed the pond was as secure as they could make it, 'Umi straightened at last and stretched. "Come. Let's eat." Kaiki shook his head and shuffled away, up the beach.

"He will not join us?" Coconut Man followed as 'Umi led the way over the rocks to a shady spot and plopped on the sand, letting out a tired grunt.

"No. He will see to his own *hale* now. His wife may need him." Clouds had gathered in the sky, darker and more ominous. Coconut Man felt he could scoop a great handful of cloud, so low and dense was the cover.

Wind whipped around them as ʻUmi passed packets of *lomi* fish--raw fish and seaweed--to Coconut Man. Two bananas nestled in the sand near a gourd of fresh water. They ate in companionable silence, watching the sea build its cresting waves.

"That Manō," Umi began. Coconut Man was startled and stopped chewing, like a frightened animal. "He is. . ." ʻUmi searched the horizon for a word. "He is up to something," he finished at last.

"Oh?" Coconut Man didn't know how to respond.

"He came to me this morning and complained that I am not performing my duties as *konohiki* properly." ʻUmi's voice was gravelly with outrage. "He suggested among other things, that I should be preparing the village for war."

"War? With whom?"

"He would not say. He feels we are lax in our plenty and just asking to be overtaken."

"Is that reasonable?"

"I have heard nothing. Puna and Kona

125

are united in their protection of this side of the island. Together they are stronger than the other *ali `i*. Who would attack us?"

Coconut Man thought about what he knew. "Perhaps he is stirring up trouble because he wishes to gain a higher position?" he said cautiously.

'Umi snorted. "I have always wondered about that one. But who would chose him over me? I am *konohiki* now. Puna is strong. He has Kona for support. Our spirits are united. All *kāhuna*, well those I know, feel we are strong. What can he do?"

Coconut Man did not want to speculate. "Perhaps he is just an angry man."

"That is certainly true. I might be angry too if my father and mother passed when I was young like he was." 'Umi rose.

Coconut Man decided 'Umi was not aware of Tutu's theory that Manō had killed his own parents. "And do you know what else?" 'Umi puffed his chest out again. He stood over Coconut Man holding the remnants of the bananas. "He suggested Kaiki was not tending the *ali `i's* ponds correctly! That I should watch him closely! He *said*," 'Umi threw the peels into the forest. "That we had allowed dangerous things into the ponds! That I was endangering my beloved *ali `i*!"

"What kinds of dangerous things?"

126

"He would not say. He just told me he would report it."

"To whom?"

"I don't know. But it is not true. Kaiki would never!" He looked down at Coconut Man, his manner bleak and despairing. "What if the *ali`i* doubt me? What could I say? Words are spears that can wound. That wound can fester and cause death. Perhaps my own. Truth becomes an elusive prey."

Coconut Man rose. "I believe you. I do not trust Manō either. I will help any way I can."

Varying expressions flitted across 'Umi's features. Perhaps he regretted revealing so much.

"I know I am a newcomer to this place, but perhaps that is an advantage. I truly know none of you, your histories or relationships. I can perhaps be an impartial judge based on what I see."

'Umi did not look reassured. "So, you will judge us will you?"

"No! I did not mean that. I meant that. . ." his words dried in his throat at 'Umi's look of disdain. Once again, the village headman had returned and was in charge. Gone was the unsure man who might be accused of treason.

"What *did* you mean?" 'Umi's muscled chest rippled as he folded his arms. He was slightly shorter than Coconut Man, but much stronger. His *mana* was also more powerful, that sense of control and leadership that made him *konohiki*. In the approaching storm's odd atmosphere, 'Umi appeared like yellow light, his tatoos accentuating his handsome but scarred features.

Is this what a god would look like? Coconut Man's thoughts veered away from 'Umi's question.

"What did you mean?" 'Umi repeated.

Humbled, Coconut Man bowed his head. "Only that I believe you. If I can help, I will."

"If." 'Umi snorted and strode away. Coconut Man watched him go and prayed that another good man would not be destroyed by Manō. He vowed to dedicate himself to Tutu and to the village in this matter. He turned and entered the forest, nearly running with his need to be back among the people--the innocent people he now felt it his duty to protect, along with his *ali`i.* The festivities awaited.

Chapter 14

Despite the heaviness in the air and the gloomy sky, the village bustled with excitement and preparation. Coconut Man burst into the clearing out of breath. Kaleo, dogged by his assistant Honu, ran up to him.

"Where have you been?" Kaleo demanded. "I looked all over for you."

"I was on the beach. I saw you near the ponds, but by the time I got there, you were gone." Coconut Man could not help but smile at this boy whose world so clearly revolved around himself.

"Oh. Well, it is good you are here. The elders have decided to hold the second day's festivities in the large canoe *hale*."

"The storm is said to be great, but we must continue or the wedding might be. . ." Honu looked up at Kaleo through her curtain of bangs.

"Cursed," Kaleo finished for her. Honu shook her head. Coconut Man worked even harder to hide his smile.

Kaleo heaved a sigh. "Well, not cursed perhaps. What was the word?" He scanned the sky as he thought. Honu whispered something Coconut Man could not catch. "Yes. That is it. Tainted." Kaleo nodded with satisfaction.

"So," he continued, "we are helping to ready the *hale*. The men have moved the canoes up the beach and we are bringing the *hala* mats to line it." He walked on into the village, Coconut Man and Honu following dutifully. "Of course, all the village will not fit into the *hale*, but most of us will." He said this with the assurance that he, and his friends and family would be included among those inside.

In this society the *maka`ainana*--the working people and the largest caste-- would be included with the *ali`i* and *kahuna*. The lowest caste of *kaua*, lived apart. Defeated warriors, other outcasts, used as human sacrifices should the need arise, were not excluded from society so much as they were not included. Coconut Man did not know how this caste was specifically determined. At times he felt he walked the line of *kaua*. This status had not bothered him much, until now.

He did not want to be an outcast. He wanted very much to be inside the *hale,* inside the `ohana`--family. He felt that his presence in this *ahupua`a* at this time was ordained for the purpose of pulling the village, and perhaps even the *moku* together, before it knew it was being torn apart.

In this, Tutu was his partner and companion, odd as that might seem. These thoughts flitted through his mind as he followed Kaleo's sturdy little body through the village and back to the beach.

The large *hale* was quickly taking on an appearance far different from canoe storage. The *mauka*, mountainside, opening had been sealed with *hala* mats quickly stitched together. Floor mats curved up the sides from the base, protecting the openings against the wind. *Kapa*, calabashes, flowers, fruit, drums--all manner of celebratory items had appeared inside as if by magic. Kaleo stood importantly, arms akimbo, and surveyed the scene.

"Come," Kaleo said imperiously. He entered and sat along the side, close to where the musicians were setting up. While Coconut Man's thoughts had been occupied with his social status, the *hale* had filled with excited villagers. The *ali`i,* with much ceremony and respect, were installed in the place of honor near the dance mats and music.

From his position, Coconut Man saw a ring of brown faces outside the *hale.* The *kaua,* here to show respect for the event and *ali`i.* Not close enough to 'taint' the ceremony, as Kaleo would say, but close enough to see and hear.

Shell blowers, *malo* clad, stepped forward and raised instruments to their lips. The mournful sound announced the importance of the ceremony. The king's *kahuna* rose slowly and with a calabash in one hand and a *kī* leaf in the other, walked the length and breadth of the *hale*, sprinkling, chanting and blessing.

Caught up in the beauty and solemnity, Coconut Man had almost forgotten his real mission: Watching. He had no idea what to watch for, but his skin tingled with anticipation sprinkled with fear. He could protect no one since he had no idea of the method or time. He studied the populace. Manō. . . ah. Manō sat close to the *ali`i's* mat. Tutu was also close. Perhaps she had stationed herself there intentionally, between her daughter and Manō's threat. With her wispy silver hair and thekīleaves and fruit around her on the mat, she resembled a nesting hawk guarding her young.

Lako and Palani sat near Manō. 'Ehu

and Lehua sat at separate mats, but close together and near the entertainment, opposite the *ali `i*.

Coconut Man did not hear the *kahuna's* blessing of the upcoming marriage at all. He did not see the gestures of cleansing or the graceful transition to the music and dance. He looked up again when a burst of laughter drew his focus. Several of the *tutus*--old women--of the village were performing a rather lascivious hula, much to the discomfort of 'Ehu and Lehua who blushed on their mats. The entire hula was directed at them, to the enjoyment of the audience. It was all in fun and ended with much laughter and clapping, both from the couple and the visiting *ali `i*.

Next came the warriors. The men picked up their spears and stood with legs spread, backs to the crowd.

Several beats from the *ipu*--gourds--and the *mele* began. The chant told of a battle, how the men prepared and trained and then went forth. Coconut Man was surprised to see Manō, Lako and Palani dancing. They were as graceful as the others, but Manō wore a fiercer expression. His brown eyes bored into those watching and his bronze skin glistened in the light from *kukui* nut candles. His forceful spear jabs came too near those seated closest. Sideways stomping took him near the *ali'i* and Coconut Man watched closely. It appeared Manō looked directly at them, but that could not be right. Could it? The spears crashed together as the warriors turned. Airborne spears changed hands and the dance concluded.

The people enjoyed the feast. The large *pua'a* had been roasting in the *imu* all day and it fed many. Coconut Man had heard the stories of boar-hunting and this one in particular had been fearsome. He recalled the day he first encountered Manō. Manō had been close to the *imu* then, too. He wondered if Manō had helped prepare this meal. It was possible.

A commotion at the *ali'i's* mat caused a hush throughout the *hale*. The *kahuna,* Tutu, and the royal retainers rushed the chief and chiefess from the *hale*. It was hard to be certain, but Coconut Man thought the queen was supported and guided away.

As soon as the group departed, the silence erupted in chatter. Coconut Man rose to his feet and along with the crowd, left the *hale*. He overheard much speculation.

"That is a bad sign."

"Not so. The festivities were over for the day."

"Yes, even the final blessing was given."

"All is well for the couple."

"Our *ali`i*. They must be well, too."

"If something were to happen to them while visiting here, it could be interpreted. . ."

"Hostile? No! Everyone knows we love our *ali`i*."

"Wars have been started for less."

"We must pray."

The group broke up as it entered the forest and dispersed. Night had fallen during the ceremony. The heaviness of the air was a weight on Coconut Man's lungs as he breathed.

The village was subdued when he returned after a lengthy but unproductive walk along the beach. He considered waiting outside the *ali`i's hale* again, but was not inclined to push his luck on remaining undiscovered. He would hear what had happened in the morning along with everyone else. He sighed, discouraged with his progress. Or lack of it. Just as he reached his sleeping mat, big fat drops of rain began to fall. He pulled a second mat over himself and fell into a restless, uncomfortable sleep.

Chapter 15

"Did you hear?" Kaleo shook Coconut Man awake after a long, restless night.

"The chiefess ate stinging *limu*!"

Coconut Man rolled over, squinting at the boy. "What?" Heavy rain had fallen while he slept and his *hala* mats were sodden. The gray sky hung low and although the rain had slackened, it still fell.

"Her dish of seaweed had threads of stinging *limu*! It made her sick."

Coconut Man sat up, the events of the previous night rushing back. "That was why they left the *hale* at the end of the ceremony?"

"Yes. She is very sensitive, you know. She had barely put it in her mouth when her lips and tongue swelled like a breadfruit!"

"How do you know so much?"

"I am an excellent listener."

"I imagine you are." Coconut Man

136

creaked upright. "Tell me while we walk."

They made their way to the Wai, as was his habit. "Did she swallow it?" Coconut Man knew the stinging seaweed. It was distinctive, if one knew what to look for. It caused red skin and rashes, and extreme pain in the private areas, he recalled wryly. He remembered the time he was curing baskets in the sea and the wind whipped up, hurling threads of seaweed into the air. Several had brushed his skin. *Aī* the pain! He could only imagine the effects of the poison on the delicate tissues in the mouth.

"No. She spit it out right away, but it was enough to cause her to have difficulty breathing." Kaleo sat on the log by the water while Coconut Man splashed in knee-deep to wash.

"Ah." With his back to Kaleo, he asked. "What are they saying? How could such an accident occur?"

"I am not sure. I, uh, had to leave." Coconut Man turned and saw Kaleo eyes downcast. Had he been caught eavesdropping?

"I see." Coconut Man could think of no reasonable way this could be an accident. However, he did not want to alarm the boy. He joined Kaleo on the log and they watched the current.

"Do you think she could have died?" Kaleo's voice was thin and small, unlike his usual booming, cocksure proclamations.

"It is possible," Coconut Man said carefully. "Our chiefess does not look strong. Perhaps it would not take much to make her ill." He did not reveal his suspicions regarding the village politics. He recalled Tutu's tale of her brother's death, perhaps due to a broken heart after his wife died. He knew the love between Puna and Kehau was great, an unusual occurrence when unitings of convenience, prestige or power were the norm. If the chief were worried about his wife, he would not be attentive to his own health and safety, or perhaps the safety of the *moku* or the island. Then he would be vulnerable. To what, Coconut Man could only speculate. And if Kehau were to die. . . well, that was unthinkable. And yet, not only possible, but probable, given what Tutu had told him about Manō.

He sighed heavily.

"What?" Kaleo asked, his foot drawing a *honu* in the sand.

"I did not sleep much last night. So, when is the wedding? Today, is it not?"

"Yes. Tonight. The *ho'au* ceremony will last all night! 'To stay until daylight', that is the custom!" Kaleo scrubbed out the sand

138

honu with an excited swish of his feet. "I heard," he glanced sharply at Coconut Man. "I heard the chiefess is well and all will go as planned."

Thunder rolled and both instinctively looked up. The wind suddenly whipped up, sending sharp palm fronds dancing across the water into their clearing.

"We should go." Coconut Man rose.

"Yes, I have work to do." Kaleo was back to his old self.

Coconut Man smiled and led the way. *I could learn a lot from this boy. He hears everything, and is so sure of himself. Smart, too. Ah, to be so young.*

Although the day had darkened as though night approached, he felt the sun that was Kaleo at his back and was comforted.

The rain began in earnest until the paths of the village ran like the Wai. The *kūpuna*--elders--griped of aches, the *keiki*, trapped indoors by whipping branches and dangerous conditions were conscripted to tedious chores by the women who tired of their chatter and complaints.

Men, fearing familiar destruction, tethered, bound, reinforced and worried, keeping a wary eye on the sea as it pulsed ever higher, closer to the lower crops, sheds, and *hale*.

The sky was black as night yet the day was only half past by Coconut Man's reckoning. The sun god La, in his chariot, had not been seen since the storm's fierce upsurge, so none could be sure of the day.

Kaleo had left Coconut Man to join his mother, saying nervously, "She will be worried about the storm, so I will comfort her." Coconut Man longed for a mother to comfort him. This storm was like none he had experienced in many seasons. It isolated the people, made them feel the wrath of the gods and the fragility of their existence.

He yearned for companionship. He had ducked into the men's eating *hale* when the storm became too fierce for him to shelter in the trees or against the *hale* wall. Alone and cold, Coconut Man was unsure how to make himself feel less, well, vulnerable. When the storm's fury waned occasionally, he heard shouted commands and calls. He knew the men struggled to protect the village from the storm and chided himself for not helping. He was not part of the village yet, as much as he desired to be. He had no real skills to offer.

He wanted to be alone no longer. He wrapped his sleeping *kapa* around his head and shoulders, inhaled deeply, and ducked into the storm. It was worse than he imagined, attesting to the building skills of

140

the men who had built the *hale*. He now saw his world in flight. Green palm fronds, ripped from healthy trees, flew like giant birds. The black sky was broken by shafts of fire, yellow-white spears thrusting to earth and sea. The air, saturated and nearly unbreatheable, wrapped around him like cordage and tried to prevent him from moving. He was instantly drenched.

The center of the village was a sea of mud, undulating and writhing with waves of its own. Again Coconut Man marveled at the stability of the *hale,* the poles driven deeply into the ground. Now, outside, he saw the skeletons of *hale* appear as the coverings of fronds and grasses ripped away in the false night.

Sadness gripped him as he realized there would be no wedding this night. Even if the storm ended in time, the damage would be considerable, and to start a union with this omen would doom it.

He heard shrieking and saw figures struggle from one damaged *hale* to another, seeking protection. A group staggered past him, toward the upland path. Despairing voices call out "to the caves." This group sheltered the *keiki,* and urged them out of the village. It was a large group, mostly women, children and elderly, with several strong men to accompany them. He had been waiting to hear the children were safe, and this encouraged him to move. His feet stuck with every step and he threw off the *kapa* since it impeded his progress and the sopping cloth had lost all ability to keep him warm. Shedding the *kapa* also freed the blinders on his eyes and he truly saw what was happening to his village. His village. He wanted to be with the other men, to help, to perhaps seek comfort, if he was honest with himself. No paths, fire pits, small plants or other guides were left to mark the usual routes to and from the sea. He made his way as best he could toward the guest *hale* and was dismayed to find them denuded of covering, poles bared, the few personal belongings remaining soaked and muddied. Where had the rulers gone? Had they left the village before the worst of the storm hit?

He forced each breath into his lungs through the dense rainfall. *I am a fish,* he commanded himself. He ducked his head and rested, exposed and exhausted, against a corner pole. The wedding *hale*! What had become of that? And the beach. Where are the men? Could they all be dead? And the rest of the village in an upland cave somewhere? What if they never came back? What if the *ahupua`a* was so damaged they relocated and

142

he never found them? Panic set in and he shoved off from the pole, aiming for what he remembered as the marriage *hale* and the beach.

The storm, if not lessened, had not worsened, and for that, Coconut Man was grateful. Panic had spurred him from the pitiful shelter of the pole, and he was met by flying debris and deeper mud as he neared the sea. The forest near the beach was a collection of upright sticks, nearly bared by the fierce winds. Obstacles forced him to slow and bring a small portion of reason. Of the marriage *hale*, he had seen nothing. He prayed he had taken a wrong turn, disoriented by the disappearance of every known landmark.

The open beach was almost non-existent as the waves now crested at the forest edge. He saw with great relief the dim outline of the massive canoe *hale*. His relief vanished when he looked down the beach and saw no sign of the fishponds. All the work of years under the care of Kaiki and 'Umi was washed away as if it never existed. That portion of beach was unrecognizable and that vulnerable part of the shore was likely lost forever from a storm like this.

With a heavy heart he turned toward the canoe *hale* and hugged the tree line, one eye always on the roiling surf. The rain lessened as he stepped through the shallows, pulling each foot from the sucking earth with greater effort than the last. Head down, he finally reached the *hale*. The hanging matting had been torn to strands by the gale, but the structure was sound and offered some protection to the men inside. Coconut Man recognized only one, Io, who lay against a torn wall. His skin was gray and he breathed shallowly. Coconut Man noted two things. The rain had ceased. And Io's thigh had been pierced. The bleeding was slight, perhaps because the segment of razor sharp bamboo that had caused the wound, now served as a plug and kept him from bleeding to death. In the dim light, Coconut Man saw that all the men here were hurt. Healthy men had brought them to shelter and given them such aid as they could, then left to fight the storm. Manō had spoken of readying for battle. No one could prepare for this battle, and Coconut Man prayed for few losses. He sat next to Io, his hand resting on the Io's shoulder, offering what comfort he could.

Chapter 16

Although the rain had stopped, the wind and surf were still high. Coconut Man heard the small moans and breaths from the injured. He did not know the others in the *hale*, but he offered what comfort he could. They were all cold to the touch so he decided to make a fire. He left the *hale* and stopped in his tracks. The sea was beginning to recede. The waves were still high and filled with unidentifiable objects. The sand, littered with refuse, rose in large hills, or plunged into craters, making walking difficult. He gathered the coconuts that lay in profusion. The husks would be fuel for his fire and the meat and juice would encourage the wounded. He dragged as much burnable material into the *hale* as he could. He dropped, exhausted onto the sandy floor and began stripping the husks. His fire-making tools had remained dry in the oiled *kapa* he kept tucked inside his *malo*. His hands shook from cold and strain as he lit the fire, but the gods lit it quickly and he thanked them. He built the fire as large as he felt was safe. The damp fuel smoked and burned feebly, but it would increase as it dried. By the time the fire was established, the wind had calmed and blew down the beach, not from sea to mountain, as was often the case. He chipped open several coconuts and began to feed the men, assessing their injuries. Several who had been hit by flying objects were recovered sufficiently to leave, after expressing their gratitude. One had a broken arm and Coconut Man, although not a healer, had watched the splinting process and could wrap the damaged limb. That man too, wanted to be on his way. Coconut Man had the presence of mind to make a request. "Send some men to carry Io to a safer place. I don't know what is left of the village, but he needs more care than I can provide, and more shelter than this *hale*." The man nodded and was gone.

"Well Io, it is you and me, now."

Io opened his eyes and nodded.

Coconut Man knelt and offered a section of coconut shell filled with the rich milk. "Drink a little of this. It will give you strength." The fire had warmed the *hale* and

146

helped Io's gray color.

"*Mahalo.*" Io lay back.

Coconut Man felt alone and worried and *responsible* for Io. "Well, Io, I see you are a little better, so I will fill some of these holes in the *hale*. Perhaps that will make it warmer, too." Coconut Man talked to Io constantly as he worked, returning frequently to offer more coconut.

When he had repaired the walls as high as he could reach, and was almost accustomed to the frightening view outside, he heard voices.

Lele was the first person to enter, followed by four older men. "*Aloha*, Coconut Man, I see you have been busy."

Joy and relief filled Coconut Man and he happily relinquished all care of Io. "Yes, I have been keeping Io company."

Lele and the others prepared Io for travel. "What?" Lele bent to Io. Coconut Man stepped closer to hear.

"He never stopped talking. I almost died just so I wouldn't have to listen to him."

They burst into laughter, a release of the terrible tension. Coconut Man wondered if he should be offended. Lele shot him a look of such warmth that he let the kinship of the moment fill him. The men lifted Io onto a makeshift pallet of poles.

As they passed Coconut Man, Io grasped his hand. "*Mahalo*." Io's eyes were wet and Coconut Man felt the unfamiliar tingling that began in his nose that signified tears. He fought them until his glance turned to the bloodied *kapa* that had been under Io. Despite the bamboo plug, much blood had flowed from the wound. His tears spilled as he realized that Io, his first friend, could die.

Now that he was no longer responsible for Io's care, he was unsure of his next task, but he did not want to be alone. He followed Lele's group through unfamiliar terrain to an upper section of village he had never seen. Sheltered by the mountains, it appeared to be a temporary camp.

"Where are we?" he asked the last puffing man as they entered the clearing.

"Upland *kalo* patch," he managed between gasps.

Coconut Man nodded his thanks and the group took Io to a *hale* that was still being thatched. Coconut Man's heart lifted as he heard the excited chatter of *keiki,* most predominantly, Kaleo. The storm had not dampened Kaleo's spirit or his voice. He hurried toward them on the far side of the new village. He was amazed at the speed at which the old foundations were resurrected. This upland setting had been protected by many trees and the *mauka* --mountainside-- shelter. He assumed the caves the villagers had sought were somewhere nearby as well. He was gratified to see that this village was being constructed much like the *makai*--sea--village. Although the area for this village was much smaller, he was comforted to think that everyone would be that much closer.

He had so many questions. Who was injured? Where were Tutu, the *ali`i*, the wedding couple? Well, they were not wed yet. He prayed all were safe in his new-found family. These flashes were as quick and fleeting as a school of fish racing from a tuna. One question was immediately answered as he saw Tutu sitting surrounded by bubbly-spirited children. Their barely contained energy reminded him of a volcano he had seen on his travels. The terrible smelling earth had bubbled and popped, roiling with energy. He felt this in the children, a boiling of nervous energy, contained only by the power of Tutu's story, which he overheard as he approached. He recognized the story of the timid *kalo* and settled to hear the end. Kaleo noticed him and smiled, even as he asked another question.

"Why did the chief continue to pursue the *kalo*?"

"A chief sometimes does not know when to let go, even of his own subjects. Now, back to the tale. The chief had made the cooking *imu* ready for the two plants, but because they had been warned, they were able to use the wings they had made, and escape once again."

"*Kalo* do *not* have wings," Kaleo stated.

"Were you there?" Tutu asked.

"No." Kaleo's mouth was a flat, hard line.

"Besides, little one, who knows what magic occurs when two spirits love each other, like these two *kalo* plants and their love is threatened?"

Kaleo made a mmmph sound, but did not interrupt again. "The wind helped them escape to a neighboring district with a kind chief who did not want to eat them. They settled here happily for many years and a large family grew up around them."

Kaleo rose and came to Coconut Man.

"Where have you been?"

"Where have *you* been?"

Tutu clapped her hands. "I'm sure there are chores to do, so find one. If you need one, come back to me." Her eyes met Coconut Man's and she winked, both of them knowing no child would reappear for an assignment. Lele hurried to Tutu and helped the old woman to her feet. They went off toward the *hale* where Io had been taken.

"I have been here, helping," Kaleo said to Coconut Man.

"Ah. I, too, was helping." Kaleo looked skeptical. "I was on the beach in the storm, aiding the injured in the canoe *hale*." Kaleo raised his eyebrows, *yes? Go on.* "I cared for Io through the storm and he will make a full recovery." He was guessing, of course, but his words had weight with Kaleo.

"Honu was worried. She and her mother waited through the storm with us, but Io did not come back. She cried."

"He is being attended to now. I supervised his transport to this place," Coconut Man said. That was a sticky stretch of the truth, like the gum of the *papala kepau* tree.

"Where are the *ali`i?*" Coconut Man changed the subject.

"They are safe. We all came to the caves last night. It was very exciting. Early this morning, everyone started to rebuild the *hale.* We use this area when we are working the upland fields, so the workers can stay close to the crops. We already had everything we need."

"Where do you get water?"

"The Wai is not far from here. There is a

falls for swimming and jumping. Let's go see!" Kaleo pulled at Coconut Man's hand. He felt he should be doing something more constructive. At the moment, he could not think of what that might be. All would be revealed in time, but for now, this little boy was the moment.

Kaleo led him up a steep but short path to another that traversed the spine of the ridge. He heard the falls, a great rushing that filled his head. Even Kaleo was stilled when the cascade came into view. Impossibly wide, the blood-red water overran its banks on the way down the mountain. Kaleo's gentle falls and swimming pool were a violent crash of surging waves. Coconut Man had heard of the red waters that sometimes ran after storms, but had never seen them. It was the earth's blood, and the intensity of it made his heart pound. His rooted feet had lost the power to move and he was comforted by Kaleo's sweaty hand clasping his own.

"I have never seen this." Kaleo's trembling transmitted through their clasped hands.

"It is the earth bleeding after the violent battle she fought to keep us safe." Coconut Man was not sure if he believed they were safe, but he *needed* to believe. "All will be well. Her wounds will heal quickly and your

152

water will be gentle again. Look, even now, the wound must be sealing above the falls--see? It is less red, now." He pointed, and it did seem that the water ran less red than before.

"Yes, I see."

"Let us go back. I'm sure there are things we can do to help. You should attend to Honu, should you not?"

"Yes. I must." Kaleo set off down the path, his sturdy legs marching, once again in command of his feelings.

He is much like me in that way, Coconut Man mused. It occurred to him that he had not heard of a father for Kaleo. *Perhaps he is dead. That would explain a lot.*

They reached the village to find it in an uproar. A woman was screaming, supported by several others. Facing her was someone Coconut Man had hoped not to see again. Manō.

Chapter 17

Coconut Man approached the nearest man, who stared at the woman, mouth agape. "What happened? Who is that?"

"Kauila. Wife of 'Umi. He is dead. Manō told her. He just. . . told her." The man licked his lips and swallowed. "He was so abrupt. She was smiling when he approached, but. . ." His words fell away.

Manō stood over the swaying woman, an impatient expression on his tattooed features.

Coconut Man felt a surge of fear and sadness. 'Umi. He had spoken with him, helped him reinforce the fishponds along with Kaiki, the head of the fishponds. They had shared food, discussed their concerns. 'Umi was dead?

So, it has started. The deaths. Then, in a day or so, the injured will choose to live or

154

die as well. His joy at the end of the storm drained away.

Kaleo ran across the clearing to his mother, who was one of those holding Kauila. Her lips moved, words of comfort no doubt, but Kauila's face said nothing could comfort her now.

"How did he die?"

Coconut Man's question was overheard by Manō who stepped toward the shocked group. "He drowned. He must have gone to check the ponds during the storm and slipped on the rocks, hitting his head. Remember, those of you outside in it, how you could not see to put your foot to a path?" Several, Coconut Man included, nodded in agreement. The power of the storm flooded back to him and he shuddered. *It must have been terrible for all.*

"Where is he now?"

"I did not move him. He is still at the ponds. Where the ponds were," he amended. "Out of respect for the family, I did not move him."

Kauila's keening grew more intense.
Manō's voice rose above it. "We need a *konohiki* now. A headman. I will volunteer to take 'Umi's place. If our *ali`i* agrees." His eyes bored into each in the clearing, and many heads bowed in assent, whether in true

155

agreement or exhaustion, Coconut Man could not tell.

A figure pushed into the opening next to Manō, clearing the group. "What is this? A new headman?" 'Umi's short, muscled figure pressed forward. "Who will take my place and why?" He looked around at the faces, now absolutely vacant. Coconut Man's legs did not want to hold him. 'Umi was *not* dead. The combination of the storm, the joy of survival, the despair of loss, comprehension of new leadership, was too much. Kauila tore herself away from the women and threw herself at 'Umi, tears flying and hands clutching. He held and reassured her, eyeing Manō speculatively.

"As you can see, I am here. Is there some reason I should not retain my post as headman and perform my duties?" He glared at Manō.

For the first time, Manō looked unsure of himself. "You are dead. I found your body at the ponds."

"You are mistaken."

"Then who?" As one, the group streamed out of the upland village, exhausted feet pounding a panicked rush to the beach, Manō and 'Umi in the lead.

Shock once again ran through Coconut Man as he and the others reached the former site of the *ali`i's* fishponds. The landscape was completely altered: rock walls immersed or scattered; trees uprooted and strewn like sticks forgotten by a child. There, in the receding surf a body, rolled face down.

It did look like 'Umi. From the back. As 'Umi and Manō rolled the man over, Coconut Man watched Manō's face. While the villagers wanted to know who they had lost, Coconut Man was more interested in Manō's reaction. If he had not been watching carefully, or had been distracted by the piercing scream of grief from the true widow, he would have missed the rapid sequence of emotions that flitted across Manō's face: surprise, anger, frustration. As they pulled the man higher onto the sand, Coconut Man quickly lowered his eyes. He did not want Manō to know he had been observed. Coconut Man was positive something had gone wrong in Manō's plan, but was not sure what or how.

Coconut Man heard the name Kaiki and realized the dead man was the head of the *ali`i's* fishpond. Someone he did not know, but nonetheless had been with just before he died. His thoughts raced around his brain and dampened the screams of Kaiki's wife, who was comforted by Kauila, 'Umi's wife. From bereaved to caregiver in moments. From offering succor, to being unable to accept it.

157

How fleeting this life is, how it spins and dances like sunlight on waves. How things can seem to be one way, but by looking in a different way, or in a different place, are totally different.

Kaiki's wife collapsed near his body. The others let her, knowing this was the first step of her long grieving. Coconut Man focused completely on her, shutting out all other sights and sounds on the shore. He allowed himself to see inside her, to feel what she felt. He had never experienced this before, but it felt natural and he let it happen. Let himself go to her, and she, come to him.

She scrabbled in the dirt, tearing a fingernail, without feeling it. Her heart pounded, crushing in upon itself as she refused to absorb the realization that he was gone. Would not come back to their hale, *would not wrap her in his arms when she was cold.*

Gutteral moaning pulsed from her throat and she scratched at her skin, not seeing the rents in the flesh and the blood that beaded. Her legs had collapsed at the first news, and she chanted "no no no no" as her hands grasped hanks of her hair, jerking them from her scalp.

Then her hand found another target, a large, sharp rock. She clasped it and felt its rough edges, slashing palm and fingertips as she did so. Tears had blinded her from the outset, so she guided the rock to her mouth and smashed it sharply into a dogtooth. Did not feel the pain. A chip fell to her kapa wrap. She struck again, this time missing the tooth, but striking gum and lip and starting a fresh flow of bright blood. She adjusted her grip on the rock, now stained red and slick with tears, and through her keening, pounded the tooth free. Shattered it fell to the earth.

She was lost inside herself, and her mind began to wander as she felt her husband's spirit leave her. She had never been alone before and was terrified. I want to follow you! Don't leave me! Take me with you. *She allowed her heart to wrest itself from its place in her chest. She wanted to die.*

Coconut Man had never experienced such depth of emotion and felt himself drowning in it, like drowning in the ocean. He could not breathe. He had never loved like this, had never been loved, had never lost like this. He felt swept along with her desire to join her husband, but fought against it. He wanted to pull away from such grief, but did not. Instead, he knelt and placed his hand upon her heart. While their spirits were joined, he gave her his strength. He felt her spirit register surprise that someone was

159

there with her. That was enough.

Kaiki was gone, and Coconut Man made a promise to him, and to her, and to himself that he would discover the truth, if there was something to discover. His spirit slowly came back into him as he supported the new widow, walking back toward the upland village. The others followed silently. Her head hung, chin bouncing on her chest, remaining hair, lank and bloodied. Coconut Man's arms felt as though they cradled a dead thing.

When he entered the upland village, he had no idea what to do next, or where to take her. He stopped. Gentle hands pried his grip from her, and Lele and Kauila guided her to a *hale.*

He felt physically weak, and he needed to lie down, but his mind and spirit spun with questions. He stood alone in the village clearing, and people avoided him, though not as they had on earlier visits. They met his glance, smiled or nodded, but with some respect now. A kind of reverence.

He had no idea what had happened back on the beach, but one person could tell him.

He must find out. He needed Tutu. She had not been there when Kaiki's body was discovered, but he had no doubt she would be able to help.

160

She would be with her daughter. He began to search.

Chapter 18

"Where are the *ali'i?*" Coconut Man asked a woman carrying fruit.

She ducked her head and pointed to a small opening in the trees he had not noticed.

"*Mahalo.*" The entrance to the path was deceptive, for the narrow opening led to a well-traveled way that quickly brought him to a group of *hale* buzzing with domestic sounds. He smiled. *How much he had missed this!* He had found the children. A few of the younger ones were chewing sweet *ko*, then hurling the stalks like spears at a bush target. Chubby brown bodies tense with concentration, some still with *ko* hanging out of their mouths as they absently chewed and eyed their prey, the shrub. It was so pleasantly normal that Coconut Man felt lighter, safer, and more capable. He let that feeling carry him to the far *hale* where the *ali ʻiʻs* retainers and servants were working.

He stopped a respectful distance and said, "Aloha." A woman with a calabash looked up at him. "I am looking for Tutu. Is she here?"

The woman nodded and pointed to the *hale* before ducking inside with the calabash.

"Hmmm." *Aliʻi* etiquette escaped him. Would the woman tell Tutu someone waited for her? He sat. The day was beautiful, no sign of the storm infected this upland haven. The children's laughter and games, along with the warm sun beating on his head, birdsong and buzz of insects, lulled and relaxed him.

He dozed until he felt a sharp poke to the top of his head and saw two dusty brown feet before him. He looked up into Tutu's bright eyes.

"Good morning, Coconut Man."

"Yes, it is good. Is it good for you and your family?" Coconut Man struggled to his feet, still a bit stiff.

"Let us walk." Tutu led him around the *hale*, past her daughter's and son in law's. "Yes, my family is well. Now."

"Tutu, I have so much to ask you."

"I know. That is why we must keep moving. Let us see what has happened."

Coconut Man didn't know if she meant physically to the village, or in terms of Kaiki.

163

Tutu could be so exasperating! He was about to tell her as much, but he caught her glance and she winked. Even in desperate times, she kept her head. Coconut Man had to admire that.

"I don't know where to begin," he confessed. "What of the injured? Any more dead?" He knew he was blunt, perhaps insensitive, but now more than ever, he felt the danger mounting. The wedding was postponed, but the plot was far from over.

"I have seen to the injured. Most are already recovered. Io's leg will heal, but that will take time. We must watch for infection that could cost him his limb. But that is. . ." she waved her hand in dismissal. "Old Koa, he is ill. He was near his time anyway, but we shall see."

"Kaiki." They had reached the *makai* village from the upland path. Every able hand was at work. The stone foundations of the *hale* had already been repaired and some children had been assigned the task of collecting the scattered ridge poles and stacking them. Several men checked to see if they could still be used. Another group of children gathered thatching material, while still other men sat high on frame skeletons weaving roofs. Women had rebuilt cook fires and begun to prepare a meal, collecting lost gourds, replenishing food stores.

Coconut Man was surprised at how urgently he needed the village life to resume. *Probably all feel as I do. It is just new for me to feel this way.*

Tutu stopped here and there to offer a word of comfort, or to answer a question. *She moves with a security above her mere female-ness,* Coconut Man thought. She was well respected here. He felt a heightening of his own senses when he was around her, like she gave him some unseen energy or insight. As new as that sensation was, he liked it. As he trailed in her wake through the reconstruction, he felt a warmth emanate from her, like a beam of sunlight. *Odd. Everyone must feel that. That is why she is so revered beyond her gender. She protects them in some way.* A startling thought occurred. *If we all feel the protection, and we are all, well,* good *people, what do* bad *people feel?* In particular, he thought of Manō. *He, too, must be aware of Tutu's power. Is he afraid of her? He certainly seems to avoid her. Too much thinking! When had he thought this much in his entire life?* "Aī!"

Tutu heard him and raised an inquisitive brow. "Let us see to the beach." Once more they walked side by side.

"What of Kaiki?"

165

"What of Kaiki?" she repeated.

"He drowned."

"Yes, during the storm, I hear."

"I don't know. Something is wrong."

"Tell me what you are thinking. Even if it seems unimportant."

"Yes, well. It is nothing, each thing, in and of itself. But I feel, all together, these things are tied to what we spoke of yesterday." *Was it only yesterday?*

She only nodded in understanding. Reassured, he recounted his meeting with Kaiki and 'Umi at the fishpond, and seeing Manō talking or perhaps arguing there as well. He told of his whereabouts during and after the storm. "You?"

"I was at the caves with my daughter and many others. Go on."

"After the storm, I tended to some injured in the canoe *hale,* and then followed to the upland village. Kaleo and I went to see the falls--why were they red?"

"The earth is red. When the storms are bad, the earth bleeds. Go on."

"When we returned to the upland clearing, Manō had told everyone that 'Umi was dead, and he would now be *konohiki.*"

"Yes, he would be the logical leader. However ill advised. But 'Umi is *not* dead. Tell me exactly what Manō said and did." She

166

gestured to a palm log, one of many thrown about the shore. They sat. The sun warmed them and the surf appeared to fall within its proper boundaries. If one faced the ocean, as they did now, no storm might have ravaged their lives.

Coconut Man closed his eyes and let his mind retreat to the moments Manō stood over Kauila. He reported what he saw.

"So. 'Umi drowned by hitting his head at the fishponds? Is that what he said?"

Coconut Man nodded.

"Do you remember what I told you happened to my husband? He too, 'slipped on a wet rock, hit his head and drowned.' In these same ponds. And Manō was the bearer of the news then, too. I am sure, with so many years between, and the fury of the storm, he thought he could succeed this time."

"But he killed the wrong man. An innocent man. Again, his plan is damaged, another kind spirit is lost, and the evil one still walks."

Tutu turned to him. "We have no proof."

"I will get proof! All heard his pronouncement to Kauila! It was most cruel. How could he know it was 'Umi? He admitted he did not touch the body in the surf. He cannot explain that away. And then, to discover it was Kaiki. I was there. I watched his face when he and 'Umi, yes, 'Umi, turned the body over. He was angry! He was shocked yes, but the shock of seeing 'Umi in the clearing had prepared him for that. I saw no sign of loss or regret. Only frustration and anger at his failure."

"He is clever. He lusts for power. I am beginning to see the end to his road. He wants to rule this *moku*, but he is far from that. I will say, he has shown patience all these years. Waiting for the *ali`i* to come to him. Formulating this plot, a ladder to control. I am sure he desires to be high chief. There is no war, so he will make one."

"What would happen if the *ali`i* died while visiting our village?"
"Probably war. Puna is brother to Ahukini, the high *ali`i*. Ahukini would avenge his brother's death. If Ahukini died as well, Manō would be free to step into the breach."

"What of Kona? And the other district chiefs? Would they not unite against Manō?"
"That I am unsure of. I think Ahukini still rules only because there are no threats from the outside islands. He is a good chief, but he is old. These are prosperous times, and both Kona and Puna are strong chiefs, supporting Ahukini. If something happened to them, this island would be vulnerable to attack, and that

we, none of us, would allow. I think Manō is building a war and dreams of presiding over this island one bloodied district at a time. Starting with this one."

"What can we do?"

"I do not know. Wait and watch. I can assure you of one thing, however. No one will get to my daughter again. She and Puna have a love that transcends most conventions. My daughter and I are sisters of the spirit. She will listen to me, and he will listen to her. That is how I can protect them. However, I cannot stop Manō's plan. That is your part."

"I will do my best. Would 'Umi listen to me?"

"Perhaps. He is most revered in this village next to the *ali'i,* and now his suspicions must be alerted and he might listen to an outsider." She rose. "I am cold. Let us go back. I wish to see my Kehau."

As they slowly returned, Coconut Man gathered his courage to question her about his experience with the widow. "I stood over her, I suddenly found myself, I am not sure how to say this, *with* her? Inside her, but not as a man lies with a woman, but in her heart and her thoughts? I am not explaining this well, but I know no words for it. You are the only person I could think of who might understand."

"Yes, I do understand. Actually, there are many with gifts like yours, as there are many without. And, many with other gifts, too."

She smiled speculatively at him. "I am not surprised by this. I am surprised it happened so quickly. It must have been the shock of 'Umi's supposed death combined with your fear and knowledge of Manō that allowed you to stop blocking yourself."

"Blocking myself?"

"As I said, few share this gift. It often begins as compassion, for some, like you, an event can push past the barriers and allow you to enter the spirit in trouble. Usually, this is done for the benefit of the other, but it can be dangerous." She smiled her gap-toothed grin. "Not you. You are like the sun. So, kindness progresses to compassion, which can turn to this spirit-travel."

"You have done this?"

"Yes, since childhood. I am a healer of many forms. That is one."

"When I was with her, it seemed she knew I was there."

"That is a good sign. She was not entirely lost, then."

"I touched her heart with my hand."

"How did it feel?"

Coconut Man thought back. "Like a gift.

She loved Kaiki so thoroughly that when he died, she had nothing left." Their pace slowed to a crawl. "She let me touch her heart and bring her back. I cannot explain it better."

"What you did, is give her *your* heart. That allowed her to come back."

"My heart is gone?"

Tutu laughed. "Of course not. When you give your heart to someone, in love or healing, it is undiminished in you. You are unlimited. The more you give, the more you heal, the bigger and stronger you become."

Coconut Man looked at his familiar, wiry, slightly wrinkly frame, with its strong hands and feet, both swollen from work, now scarred by his efforts during the storm. He raised his eyebrows. He felt like Kaleo had when told his basket showed promise. Skeptical.

Tutu's chuckle became a belly laugh. *"Aī!* You are the funny one. I like you. I am going to like having you live in this village."

It was Coconut Man's turn to laugh. "Live here! I travel. I make baskets and hats for many villages!" Still, the thought was there. *Well, it had been there for a while,* if he truly admitted it.

"You grow bigger on the inside. Where it matters," Tutu said.

They had reached the *ali`i's hale* and

171

Tutu winked and chuckled once again, shaking her head. "You are a funny one." She ducked inside the *kapa*, leaving Coconut Man to ponder how one could grow bigger on the inside and not be fat. *Hmmmm.*

Chapter 19

Coconut Man wondered how he was to expose Manō. Some kind of trick. But what? Manō had already begun to sow seeds of doubt in the village, but how to compound that and convince the people and the *ali`i* of the danger? Perhaps the people might begin to question what they heard and saw, once Manō's persuasive powers and charm began to weave their spell. Fear. Manō would control by fear, that was clear. Coconut Man shuddered at the future of the village ruled by a monster who used fear as his first weapon.

He knew Manō was behind the chiefess's first illness. What had he used? Many plants and fish were used for healing, for illness, burns, every day. None of those was truly dangerous.

He walked toward the falls. The Wai, always a source of healing and strength for him, called him to its rushing waters. He followed the path Kaleo had showed him, and this time, when he reached the pool he found it as Kaleo knew it: a swirling, gentle, sheltered cove. The falls remained inside the rocky flume and only clear blue-green water spilled from above.

He wanted to be *in* the water. Strange. He *never* wanted to be *in* the water. He shuffled slowly down the gentle slope into the chill. He gasped when the water hit his crotch and sat, bringing the water level to his chin, another thing he had never done intentionally. He sat in a quiet eddy, far enough from the falls and the rush of water on its way to the village and the sea. The still air buzzed with insects and birds, warming as the day progressed. His body adjusted to the temperature until he was quite comfortable. He continued to turn his problem over in his mind like a bird turns a seed in its beak, looking for a weakness, a way into the delicious meat.

Tutu said the queen was already ill, weak. But she also said not many knew that. Manō was family, however in disgrace. It is possible he knew of his cousin's illness and could take advantage of it to advance himself toward the rank of chief. What had he used? All the hale *had washed away from the lower*

174

village. It was unlikely he had kept whatever it was in the mens' sleeping hale *anyway. Too many eyes. Most things took preparation. If he had to make something, he would probably keep it around in case he wanted to use it again.*

He ducked his head in exasperation, and came up spluttering. What had possessed him to do *that?* It didn't hurt. In fact, it was rather refreshing. He held his breath and slowly submerged. He pushed down a feeling of panic, letting his hands clutch at the sandy bottom, reminding him he was safe, on the earth, and could reach air at any time. When he had control of his pounding heart, he surfaced and blew out his breath. A victory! He laughed aloud to think what Kaleo would say to him. He pictured Kaleo's sturdy body on the shore, arms folded, lips pursed in superior concentration. *"So, you can now do what any child of two seasons can do."* Coconut Man laughed again and pulled himself out of the water to dry on the warm boulders lining the river.

Kaleo's statement reminded him of something else. A child of two. Well, Manō was smart--cunning and dangerous. But his companions were not. They were children of two, where this plot was concerned. They were the ones who carried out Manō's plan at the hula feast. They were the ones to poison the *ali`i*, and they were not smart at all. The one place known to all three and fairly safe from other villagers was the *imu.* They prepared the *imu,* cooked the food, always stayed near it. If something was hidden, it would be there. Too many people at the eating and sleeping *hale*, canoe *hale*, or anywhere else. Quick access and safe from discovery.

Coconut Man slithered down from his rock and walked quickly back to the upland village. He continued through it and down to the *makai*--sea--village. The *imu* had not been cleared of storm debris, but he could tell where it was. The area, on the *mauka*--mountain--side of the village, had been somewhat protected from the storm. The pile of stones used to heat the food was still intact. Leaves and fronds spilled into the hole. The mats had blown away. Water lay in the bottom, but not as much as Coconut Man expected. The trees surrounding the cooking area had survived, however stripped of their dead leaves and branches by the winds.

They would not put it, whatever it *is, inside the* imu. *Too hard to get when cooking. It would be accessible, and would be marked in such a way that Lako and Palani could find it, but no one else would suspect.* He slowly circled the area, eyes scanning the dirt and rocks. *Was one out of place? Larger? Smaller? Pointed or piled just so?* He cupped his hands to the sides of his eyes, shutting out all but what was directly in front of him, and repeated his slow scan of the clearing. *Perhaps a hole? Buried?* He bent nearly double to examine the ground the same way.

"What are you doing?" Kaleo's strident voice interrupted his search. He actually left the earth in a startled jump. Kaleo's laugh only accelerated his heart beat.

"Do *not* sneak up on people!"

"I did not sneak up! I walked up the path and saw you crawling like a *kahuli* snail!"

"Yes. Well. I am concentrating. I was looking for something."

"You cannot find it? What did you lose? I will help you." Kaleo dropped to all fours and began to crawl.

Coconut Man was so touched by Kaleo's immediate help, his anger vanished. "I have not lost. . ." He could not involve Kaleo. He might endanger him. However, his young sharp eyes might be of use. "I am looking for a calabash. Or a pouch."

Kaleo stopped crawling. "You lost something but you don't know what?" The eyebrow went up. Coconut Man was becoming familiar with the eyebrow.

"You see, I hid it before the storm and now it might have moved."

"You don't remember what you stored it in?"

Coconut Man shook his head. "I hid it when first I arrived, some time ago, and now with the storm, I just can't quite recall. . ." He hated to lie to the boy, but knew no other course.

Kaleo brushed off his knees and muttered something about "old people," as he scanned the clearing. He trotted to an `iliahi tree and climbed. He perched on a branch and searched the clearing from above.

I would never have thought of that. I don't know if I could climb a tree anymore.

Kaleo slithered down and crossed to another sandalwood tree, climbed that and scooted out on a branch. Sheltered by the foliage, Kaleo was hidden until he climbed down and approached Coconut Man, holding a small calabash wrapped in a *kapa* pouch tied with *olonā*.

"This was hanging, tied to the branch. It was hard to see because it is the same color as the tree. But, even you could have gotten it." Kaleo's eyes sparkled. "If you were the one who put it there."

So he knew. "*Mahalo.* You are a wonder." It was true, Coconut Man could have retrieved it, had he known where to look. "How did you know?"

"I just thought about where an *old* person could hide it. You had already looked on the ground," he giggled, "so up was the next place. If you had already looked in the trees, because you put it there, you would have stopped me."

Coconut Man shook his head. "You are right. I cannot tell you more," Kaleo's mouth took on the familiar flat, hard line, "right now. I promise, I will tell you everything when the time is right." Kaleo looked about to protest. "Come away from here. I will tell you what I can. It is not much, but it is not a game." Kaleo's little-old-man face evaporated and he was again a child at Coconut Man's severe tone.

Coconut Man led him to the section of the Wai where he normally came to wash, to drink, to think. The logs had been disturbed by the storm, so he and Kaleo rolled one to a satisfactory site near the water.

"You must listen to me, Kaleo. We are friends, are we not?" Kaleo nodded. "I think so, too. The most important thing about a friendship is trust. Do you know what that is?" Kaleo nodded again. "It means, that I cannot tell you everything right now. That you must trust me when I say this is for your own protection. I will tell you what I can, when I can. *You,* must not tell anyone. It is very important. Not your mother. Not Honu. Not anyone."

Kaleo's brown eyes studied him as the boy thought about his words. Finally he nodded. "I can do that."

"Yes. I think you can. When we are finished here, you will have an important job. Do you want that? Before you say yes, think on this. With information, with knowledge, comes responsibility. If you agree to safeguard this information, you must hold true to your word and keep my trust, even as I keep yours. This knowledge is part of keeping the village safe. There is a danger here. I am helping to repair that danger."

Kaleo dropped his head, hair hiding his face. "I have felt that danger. It comes from all sides and I did not know what to do. I thought it was just the storm."

"It is the storm. It is more than one kind of storm, though. Do you wish this information? This knowledge and the task I set before you?"

"I want to help." Kaleo looked up through his hair. The stubborn mouth was back. "I am *sure!*"

"Then, let us see what is in this wrap." Carefully, together, they opened the *olonā,* the *kapa* and then the calabash. A milky liquid covered the bottom. Coconut Man smelled it.

"Coconut."

"Let me smell." Kaleo inhaled. "Yes, and something else."

Coconut Man breathed again. "I am not sure, but my sense of smell is not as acute as a young one's. I will trust you." He smiled at Kaleo, who smiled back and reached a finger toward the bowl.

"Don't touch it." Coconut Man closed the calabash and began to rewrap it. "We don't know what it is. This is what I can tell you. This substance, I am sure, was added to the *lomi* at the hula feast. It was meant for the chief, but it made the chiefess sick instead. It might have killed her, had the bowl not spilled." Kaleo's eyebrows rose so high they were invisible under his hair. "Yes. It is serious, and dangerous. Not a game."

"Who would do that? Our *ali`i* are good!"

"I think I know who, and possibly why, but if you knew, you would be in danger. I must stop them before all is lost."

"*We* must stop them." Kaleo stood. "All what is lost?"

Coconut Man led the way back to the village. "Remember, you must speak of this to no one. I have your promise?"

"Yes, I know. I am not a baby."

"It is possible that someone wishes to bring war to this village."

Kaleo's shock was apparent on his face beneath the dirt. Coconut Man knew that war had not been near this village since long before Kaleo was born. An unusual and blessed thing. "Where are we going? What do we do?"

"First we find out what this is." He tucked the calabash in his *malo* and strode through the *makai* village to the upland path, Kaleo trotting behind.

"How?"

"Tutu. We will find Tutu."

Chapter 20

Once more Coconut Man waited outside the *ali'i's hale*, the calabash hidden inside his *malo*. At last Tutu emerged, head drooping, her customary quick step lagging.

Coconut Man jumped to his feet, as did Kaleo. "What is wrong? Our *ali'i*?"

"No, they are both fine. I am just tired." She eyed them, the tall and the small, both wearing similar expressions of entreaty. "What? You have news? I take it this little one is your assistant now?"

"I'm not that little," Kaleo grumbled.

How does she do that? "Yes, Kaleo has been invaluable and I have something to show you that I would not have found, except for his help."

"I am hungry. Let us eat."

"Together?"

"Why not. We are all outcast in some

way, are we not? The nomad, the *keiki*, and the *kupuna*. None of us much good, yes?" Her sparkling eyes belied the words. Kaleo's little chest inflated with importance and he fell in next to Tutu as she led them to her food storage, and then to a clearing past the upland village toward the falls.

Seated, they shared the contents of the gourds she had brought: dried fish, fruit, poi. Thick and delicious, she scooped up the purple mass with two fingers and sucked them noisily. Coconut Man shared his water and Kaleo insisted on sharing the breadfruit pudding his mother had made.

Coconut Man leaned back against a tree and patted his stomach. "That was delicious."

Kaleo leaned back and also patted his distended abdomen. "Yes, it was."

Tutu covered the poi bowl and closed her eyes. "Tell me now. Kaleo, you begin. Tell me your part and what Coconut Man has said. I must be sure he has his facts right."

Coconut Man knew what she was about. He had wondered how to tell her which parts of the story he felt were acceptable for Kaleo to know, without Kaleo feeling hurt.

Coconut Man closed his eyes, too. Better to think and listen.

Kaleo chuckled and told the story of finding the calabash. Silence fell over the clearing. Coconut Man opened his eyes. Had Tutu had fallen asleep? She was looking directly at him, hand outstretched. He felt the weight of the calabash in his *malo* and handed it to her.

She unwrapped it and inhaled deeply, swirling the contents within the small gourd. She poked a gnarled finger in and tasted it. "They have disguised its bitter taste with coconut, I see. *Akamai.* Smart."

"What is it?" Kaleo's words echoed Coconut Man's thoughts.

" `*Akia.*"

Coconut Man raised his eyebrows.

"It is very safe. Usually. The bark, roots and leaves contain a relaxant. It is bitter, but effective. It would be difficult to ingest a dangerous amount of it. A very important use is in fishing. 'Umi could tell you. Kaiki could have. I wonder. . ." Her voice faded and she gazed at a distance. Coconut Man knew she saw, but nothing that was within his own sight.

Kaleo was not patient. "What?"

She smiled at him. "You will learn quickly little one." Coconut Man had no idea what she meant, and apparently neither did Kaleo. "I wonder if this choice of weapon was chosen because it is something we use in fishing. Perhaps if 'Umi was held responsible for the queen's 'accident' and then found drowned, no one would look for the truth."

"How would 'Umi have been found responsible?" Kaleo frowned. "He is our *konohiki* and his word is--" he searched for something he could not express. "A rock. His word is like a rock. It is always there. It does not go away when the wind shifts."

"Well said." Coconut Man smiled.

"S*omeone* in the village would have come forward, pointing in that direction. And, with the fury of the storm and 'Umi unable to come to his own defense..." Tutu took another finger taste of the coconut liquid. "Hmmph. I was not sure, but yes, I think so."

"What?" Kaleo crawled nearly into her lap to peer into the calabash. Even Coconut Man scooted closer.

"This has been made into something very dangerous, I think." Her steady gaze encompassed them both and Coconut Man saw how troubled she was. "I have never tasted it this way. So strong. I think they intended to kill our chief. I think, had he, or my Kehau," her eyes became moist, "ingested the entire amount during the hula feast, one or both would be dead. Kehau is not well, and even the small amount she tasted made her sick and weak."

"Tutu! What did they do? Could it

186

happen again?" Coconut Man was close to panic and crouched close, his voice a hoarse whisper. Kaleo wriggled even closer between the two adults. All three were connected now, sitting in the hot, sunny clearing.

"They did what we all do. At times. When we make *kap*a." Coconut Man wanted to shout with frustration. *Not a home-making story! A murder plot!* At the last moment, common sense prevailed and he clamped his words inside.

"Some of the dyes are not strong enough alone. So, we gather many flowers or seeds or pieces of bark, and dry them. Then we pound them. Then we boil them. We boil them so long that the water goes away because of such heat, leaving the dye materials concentrated to make the color we wish. We repeat this until we have intense color." She looked at each. "Do you understand this process?" They both nodded. Coconut Man nodded to keep her talking, not because he grasped what she was saying. Perhaps Kaleo truly understood. He sighed.

"As a healer *kahuna*, I have done this process when I had need of strong medicine. I boil it until the water goes away. For some reason, although it makes less of a thing, it makes the thing strong. Do you see?" This time Coconut Man's nod was of comprehension.

"If they knew of this, they could boil down a healing tonic and make it deadly. Especially to one already fragile."

"I see!"

"Shhh." Tutu patted Kaleo to calm him. "Yes. You do."

"I see, too."

"Coconut Man. Hide this. You must keep it safe." She handed him the calabash. "We are going to need it."

"Where?"

"I don't know. I don't want to know. And this little one should not know either." Once again she patted Kaleo. "Help Tutu up."

Kaleo jumped to his feet and pulled Tutu to her feet.

"Me next." Coconut Man was hauled to his feet with surprising speed. "*Mahalo.*"

"I must be with my daughter. You be careful, Coconut Man. Kaleo. You, too." She shuffled off down the path.

"You must go back to the village, Kaleo. See to your mother and your chores." At his expression he explained. "All must appear normal. Follow your routine, but keep your eyes and ears open."

Kaleo nodded and raced off. *And I must hide this.* He turned the calabash over and over. *Such a small thing to contain death. Will*

I never understand the lusts of other men?

Chapter 21

Where to hide the calabash? He tucked it back into his *malo*, but now it weighed upon him heavy and hot like a stone from the *imu. The imu again. Well, that area is not possible.* He ambled toward the upland village.

As he neared, he heard children. Of course, Kaleo's voice was most prominent. He waved at them and noted Honu in the group. He had not seen her since her father had been hurt. He waved her over.

"How is Io?"

Her long hair swayed as she bobbed her head and smiled. "He is better. Getting better all the time. My mother says he is well enough to complain because he is not out mending his nets." Her face grew solemn. "When he first came back, he did not speak. He only slept, but it was not a good sleep."

"How is his leg?"

"Mother says he will be up and around soon. She hopes. I am just happy he is here. Even though he is grumpy!" She ran off to join her friends.

Coconut Man called out. "Where is his *hale*?"

Honu pointed to the nearest *hale*.

"Mahalo!" He was unsure which exact *hale,* but saw one had a *honu* shell near the *kapa* door. "Aloha?"

A woman ducked out. "Yes?"

"I am Coconut Man. I came to see Io."

"Ah, yes. He has said how you helped him during the storm. I am Mele, his wife. We are most grateful."

Coconut Man shifted, uncomfortable with praise. "Yes, well. How is he?"

"See for yourself. I'm going to get water. Please, stay as long as you like. He will be glad to see you."

I'm not so sure about that. He ducked into the *hale*. It was dark with the flap closed, and smelled of illness. Too hot. Io lay on mats, his leg resting on soft *kapa*. A poultice covered his thigh.

"*Aloha*, Io. It is Coconut Man."

"I know who you are. I've been stabbed, not made deaf." *Honu was right. Grumpy.*

"It is very close in here. Can I open the

kapa? We can talk."

"We have to see to talk? Do what you like. Help me up."

Coconut Man threw open the flap and helped Io sit up. He propped him against piles of belongings and arranged his injured leg accompanied by much griping from Io.

The fresh breeze from the open flap cooled the *hale* and cleared his head. Io's color began to improve as his nostrils flared, taking in the clean air.

"Are you hungry?"

"Stop fussing. Mele has done enough of that." Io's face softened. "She was very worried. I would have been, too, had I not been out of my head with fever. But," he clapped his hands, "I am ready to work on my nets, I think. I sent Honu to bring me my things." He looked expectantly at Coconut Man. "Did you see her?"

"Yes. I think in her joy at your recovery, she may have forgotten her task," Coconut Man hedged. To his surprise, Io laughed.

"That is as well. Playing is she?" Coconut Man nodded. "Plenty of time for nets. She was like a limpet, never leaving my side. Perhaps you can help me later?"

"Oh, yes. I would like that."

"So, what has been happening while I have been asleep? What is the damage?"

Coconut Man took a deep breath and began to relate the death of Kaiki and Manō's mistake of identity. He did not tell Io of his suspicions about a murder plot against the chief, and left out the poison calabash. If Io knew, and mentioned it to the wrong person, he was defenseless with his injury, trapped in his *hale* with only his wife and daughter.

Io's next words surprised him. "I do not believe my injury was an accident. True, many branches flew about in the storm, but I was hit as I walked the path from the beach to the village. I was actually seeking more men to help us tie down the canoes. I thought they would be helping in the village, so I headed there to get them. Where I was hit, no stands of bamboo grow, and the path is narrow and sheltered. I did not think of it before, but while I was feverish, my addled brain told me that the forest was the perfect place for someone to hide to do harm, and had the wind not been so strong, or the man so far away, I would have been hit in the chest. As it was, the shaft went clear through the meat of my leg. When I fell, the pointed tip broke off and was lost. You saw the remaining section in the canoe *hale*. What does not make sense is why someone might want to harm me."

Coconut Man's thoughts swirled like the tide. *Perhaps Manō knew Io had spent time with Coconut Man. That made no sense. Manō was not aware that I had overheard hit plot. Perhaps he just does not like me. That seems obvious.* He still did not want to name names, because Io would be an easy target. But was Io already a target. *What to do? Tell him, so he can at least know a potential enemy? Perhaps, like Kaiki, Io was a* mistake. The storm was fierce. The danger high. It could *have been an old shaft flung about in the tempest. Or not.*

His eyes met Io's. "How long before you can walk?"

"I am healing quickly. The greatest danger is infection, but Tutu thinks I am past that. I don't know, it seems soon."

"Can you move your leg on your own?"

"I have been a little afraid to try. Mele has been like a hen on an egg."

"It could not be because, you avoid the pain?" Coconut Man. smiled.

"Perhaps a bit. But the poultice has kept the wound clean and healing, and the potions Tutu and Mele concocted kept me sleepy while the fever was high. Let us see." He inhaled deeply and Coconut Man held his own breath while Io shifted his leg off the elevated rest.

"*Aī*," Io hissed through clenched teeth. "It is all right. Just a little stiff."

Beads of perspiration popped out along Io's hairline. "Perhaps that is enough for right now."

"Let us make sure you are not bleeding. It would not be wise to damage you more. I think Mele would banish me."

"Yes. After she smothered me with *kapa* for undoing all her care." Io smiled as he spoke of his wife and Coconut Man felt a pang, less intense, but a bit like the love Kauila felt for Kaiki. Together they unwrapped the leg. To their great relief, the herb packing inside the hole had not shifted, nor had the wound seeped or bled.

Coconut Man was curious. He knew wounds could be sewn shut but this one was not. It was open, but packed with material. It looked dry and clean. "Why has it not been sewn? Will it heal this way?"

"Tutu said this kind of wound, a puncture, is most dangerous. It must be open so she can check its progress. The herbs inside are to prevent infection and speed healing. She can look inside and make sure all is well. She explained to me that a wound of this nature must heal from the inside out, and if she were to close such a deep hole, infection could find its way deeply in and kill me. We would not know, because the outside would be sealed and hide the little death."

"Ah." Something new. Having never been in a battle, nor experienced life after a battle, he knew little of wound care. For small illnesses and hurts, everyone knew which plants to use—for diarrhea, stomachache, but for severe ailments and injuries, one sought a healer.

"Shall I find your net? And your tools?"

"Yes, let us work for a bit. My hands are restless."

Coconut Man had not thought about his weaving for a long time, and once Io mentioned it, his hands itched to work as well. His heart dropped a little at the thought of his baskets in the storm. Had they survived? He had not even thought of them, and now must postpone his own curiosity for a time. "Where shall I go?"

"My nets were outside the old *hale*, but I don't know where to look now. I hang them from the poles to dry and so I can see where they need work, but who knows? My tools, I managed to take the pouch with me, with *olonā* and needles. I think Mele took them. Look outside."

Coconut Man found the tools in the

shade of the *hale* and brought them in. Io immediately began to check them. "Yes, this is good."

"I will look for a net for you. I don't know how long it will take. I will go to the *makai* village first."

"*Mahalo*, Coconut Man."

Coconut Man waved to Mele who was returning from the Wai with full calabashes. He walked down to the village. In only a day, it appeared nearly as it had before the storm. All available hands had reconstructed with astonishing speed what the terrible storm had destroyed. He knew the crops would not recover quickly and the livestock would have to be rounded up after their pens were destroyed. The fishpond would have to be rebuilt. The fishpond. *Kaiki would not return. I will help 'Umi build the pond again. I can do that much.* This thought spelled his sadness a bit and spurred his determination to see Manō punished. Io's *hale* had been on the *mauka*--mountain--side and had been repaired comparatively quickly, as had the others in his section. The ocean facing *hale* required more work, and the noise and laughter of the men as they worked cheered him.

"*Aloha!*" he called to two men throwing pili grass to the roof poles of a *hale*. He recognized 'Ehu and Nuu.

"*Aloha,* Coconut Man!" called 'Ehu. "It is a beautiful day, is it not?"

They knew his name! "Yes, it is. You are doing wonderful work. And so fast."

"This one," Nuu pointed with his thumb, "does not work fast. But he does work." They both laughed, old friends with old banter. "He is still worried about his wedding night."

"Do you know when that will be?"

"No, but perhaps next moon. If all goes well." 'Ehu sobered a little.

Coconut Man knew many prayers and chants and sacrifices to the gods would take place to purify the village, and bless a wedding ceremony. Kaiki would have to be buried at night, as tradition demanded, the injured cared for and recovered, the village back in balance.

Coconut Man changed the subject. "I am helping Io. He wants his nets. Have your seen them?"

"Io!" Nuu smiled. "How is he? He is probably fine, yes? Just avoiding work."

"I should have thought of that!" 'Ehu flopped onto the dirt. "I am too sick to help."

Coconut Man laughed. "Yes, he is faking it. But doing it so well, I have to comply. His wound is deep, but clean. The pain is down. He is fussing."

"Ah!" 'Ehu elaborately crawled to his feet. "That is good. Yes, I saw his nets. The winds pushed them into the stone foundation of his *hale*, and when the poles of the next hale fell, they anchored his nets."

"That was most kind," added Nuu.

"I moved them inside after his *hale* was rebuilt."

"*Mahalo.* I'd better take them to him, before he decides I've gone off somewhere."

"You are a good man, Coconut Man." 'Ehu climbed up the frame and straddled the ridgepole. "Eat with us anytime."

"Yes, until this one is married, then we will never see him." Nuu threw a huge bundle of *pili* up to 'Ehu. The cord holding the bundle broke, spraying 'Ehu with long strands of grass.

"Hey!" came from inside the stack.

Coconut Man entered Io's *hale*, empty except for a large pile of netting. Coarse and dark, he could not carry all of it. He pulled out a large section of netting which had many tears. Lots for Io to work on. He poked his head back out the doorway.

"When are people coming back to this village?"

"Soon I think." Nuu stopped throwing *pili* to the roof. "When we finish these *hale*. That side is finished." He gestured to those near Io's. "This side will take longer. 'Ehu! 'Ehu!"

"What?"

"When will this side be finished? When will the people come back to live? "

'Ehu squinted along the *makai hale*. "Two days? Three? First they will bless the village and we will have a feast. Then they will move back."

"Mahalo!" Perfect. Coconut Man needed that time, or perhaps more, to set his trap for Manō. He hid the poison calabash deep in the pile of netting and shouldered the net he had selected for Io. He tried to wrap it and carry it as he remembered Io doing, but it was huge. And extremely heavy. Waves of netting slid off and he bounced them back on top. He did not want to stop and rearrange the whole bundle. It was so heavy! How did Io do it with such ease? By the time he reached Io's *hale* his arms ached and half the bundle was draped over his head, the rest trailing in the dust at his feet. Raucous laughter told him the children noticed his undignified approach.

Dropping the pile outside the *hale*, he took great gulps of air and let his sweat dry in the breeze. Inside, Mele put her hand over her mouth *ssshhh.* Io was asleep. She smiled, indicating all was well.

He left the net there, determined to

200

return and help Io mend it--and to continue his new friendship.

'Umi was his next stop. 'Umi would know if they had enough information to take to the *ali'i* and accuse Manō of treason. Before the worst happened. The village was vulnerable while Manō gathered strength to ruin them all.

Chapter 22

Coconut Man found 'Umi exactly where he thought he would, the fishpond. *Time to make good on my promise.* "*Aloha*, 'Umi. I have come to help."

'Umi glanced up from his pile of rocks. "*Mahalo*."

"What are you doing?"

"I am rebuilding the fishpond. For Kaiki." His firm mouth drooped and his skin hung loose on his strong features. "I am gathering the rocks that were dislodged in the storm. Fortunately, most of them were not carried away, just buried."

"How can I best assist you? I have never done this before."

"Check the boundary line of rocks in the pond. Do you remember what it looked like?"

Coconut Man remembered perfectly because it looked just like a basket. He

202

nodded. "Do you want me to put the rocks on the shore?"

"No, just find them and put them along the line of the old wall. We will rebuild it." 'Umi turned away and continued to pile his rocks. Dismissed, Coconut Man headed into the water. *I can't believe that I am going into water that I am not familiar with; but water that no one is familiar with since the storm changed the entire beach.* It was easier than he thought because the wall started in the shallows, and that was not so bad. He discovered the best way to find the wall underwater was to smash his toe into it. *Painful, but effective.* He was glad to feel the wall had not been damaged as much as he had feared. Built of two walls with a fill of smaller stones, it had a wide base and tapered near the top. The shifting sands had disturbed the base near the shore, but not in the deeper water. There, the pounding surf had destroyed the upper portion of the wall. Many of the fish had not discovered the escape route and remained in the pond. *That would save restocking.*

To really check it and do a good job for 'Umi, and Kaiki, he would have to go under water. *I don't swim.* Then he thought of the pool at the falls. *Maybe I do swim.* In an ocean of water, his mouth was dry. *I do not want to disappoint 'Umi. But I don't want to make more of a fool of myself than necessary.* The surf was nearly flat. *It is like the pool.* He glanced at the beach. *Good. 'Umi was not watching.* Something about 'Umi's posture stayed his plunge. He waded out to where 'Umi squatted.

"What is wrong?"

'Umi squinted up at him. "This." He pointed to a rock he had just dug out of the sand. It was round and smooth, unlike the rough, black rocks used for the wall. It was covered with a thick dark substance dusted with sand.

"What is it?"

'Umi lifted the rock carefully from its hole. He sniffed it. He scraped at the coating with a thick finger nail. "Blood." He held the rock for Coconut Man to see.

"It does look like blood. Why is it here?"

'Umi grunted. "This rock was brought here. There are no rocks like this near the beach."

Coconut Man had envisioned the *makai* village before the storm. Many rocks just like this, used for so many things. He had gathered some behind his sleeping place near the men's *hale* to anchor his baskets. "Anyone could have brought it. Even I use rocks like that in my work."

'Umi stood, knees popping, and eyed him speculatively. He still held the rock. "I think it means Kaiki did not slip and hit his head while examining the fishpond during the height of the storm. I think I must take this to the chief."

"Not yet." Coconut Man said. "I want to talk to you about this. I am worried. I did not know who to approach because I have no status. But now, I think you have discovered enough yourself to believe me."

"So, now you trust me?"

"I think I have to, because you might be in danger as well."

"So, you do not want to trust me, but you seek to protect the *konohiki?*" 'Umi wore the faintest of smiles. He was much stockier and stronger than Coconut Man, with rolls of sinewy muscle from years of hard work. Although Coconut Man was younger and taller, Coconut Man throwing himself between Manō and 'Umi made a ridiculous picture. Coconut Man smiled, too.

"What I have to tell you, may very well protect you. And help the *ahupua'a*. However, if I did have to protect you physically, I would do my best." He meant it, and 'Umi saw that and sobered.

"Let us sit and clear the air." 'Umi led them to the trees where several gourds

205

cooled in the shade. He poured fresh water and unwrapped kī leaf bundles of food to share.

Why do I never have anything to share? Why are others always providing for me? This too, will have to change.

'Umi said a short prayer and they ate in silence, looking out at the fishpond, each lost in his own thoughts.

"Begin." 'Umi still looked out to sea, his strong features in profile, silver hair pulled away, bundled and tied with *olonā.*

Where to begin? Coconut Man sighed. 'Umi misunderstood his hesitation.

"I know I am of higher rank than you. Please do not concern yourself. You have acted to help the people in all things. Yes, I have been watching you. I am headman. My people are in my care, for the chief. So, speak to me with complete confidence. Your words are safe."

"*Mahalo.* So much has happened. I do not know where to begin. Some of my thoughts are speculation, but when they are added together with the actions of others--I am very worried."

"I see. Sometimes our thoughts, our guesses, are the gods telling us things we need to know. You must listen to those thoughts."

206

"Then I will begin with my arrival on this visit." And he did. He even included Tutu and Kaleo, because he knew they would be safe in the headman's hands. While they ate, Coconut Man opened himself to 'Umi and was surprised at how much 'Umi had already guessed. He also confirmed that 'Umi was of the purest heart where the village was concerned. His history with his chief was unblemished and above suspicion. He would die for his *ali'i. But he should not be murdered for him.*

"I told Tutu about Manō's announcement that it was your body on the beach. Her daughter has the ear of the chief. Tutu said she would take this to the *ali'i.* But, Manō is family. It is possible that Puna will not believe he is in danger. Remember, that night on the beach I did not hear who was the target. I don't think they meant Kaiki. Or you. I think you were something else altogether."

'Umi nodded. "I am angry. Angry that the peace of this village is disrupted by one's greed. I am angry that my cousin, Kaiki, died for me. An innocent. And the chiefess endangered as well, another innocent. The *ahupua'a's* prosperity is because of our *ali'i,* and that is now in the balance. The storm told us that. A storm with no warning? That was a sign from Lono to show us something is

207

wrong. He who has brought us peace and prosperity wanted to tell us something is wrong in our *ahupua'a*. Something endangers our *ali'i* and he favors them. If we do nothing, much worse will befall this place." He strode off, leaving the calabashes, the rocks, everything.

"What of the wall?" Coconut Man struggled in the sand after him.

"The wall can wait. I call *ho'oponopono*."

Chapter 23

'Umi worked quickly, finding the elders of the scattered village, including Tutu. The circle did not include the lower caste, *kaua*.
Although Coconut Man followed him in his pursuits, he was unclear as to how 'Umi convinced the village of the necessity of *ho'oponopono,* or *to make things right* so quickly. He did understand that the elders were in agreement that the storm's suddenness and severity were a sign from the god Lono that all was not well in their world and to draw their attention to a problem. A village meeting, *ho'oponopono*, was the natural problem-solving method. The *ali`i* would not be present, but would be informed and make a decision after the outcome. If necessary. Coconut Man thought it would be necessary, after all was said and done.

All met in the newly repaired men's

eating *hale* in the *makai* village. It had been made larger and blessed. Perhaps to accommodate such gatherings? Manō, Palani and Lako were present, and Io had been helped to the gathering. The elder men, and some of the more respected women of the *ahupua `a* were there, including Lele, the *kapa* maker. *Keiki* were not allowed.

The day was waning by the time all were settled in a circle. Tutu conducted the session. *What had 'Umi said to Manō to get him here? Surely he must suspect he is the subject? Perhaps his ego is so great that he thinks he is safe.*

Bodies shifted in the *hale*, eyes closed, breathing became deep and regular. Tutu began a chant, a prayer asking for assistance from the ancestors, calling them to the *hale*. She asked for assistance from the gods, particularly Lono, in resolving the conflict. Coconut Man felt relaxed, comforted by the presence of others nearby. He was a bit surprised when Tutu finished the opening prayer that he could not see the spirits that had joined them, although he sensed a fullness in the *hale*, and the darkness outside. How long had that taken? *Perhaps the spirits travel from great distances to reach us.*

"We are ready. I, Tutu, ask for your help. *Mahalo* to the spirits who come to aid

210

us. We have a serious problem in our village. *Mahalo* Lono for telling us. I call upon 'Umi to begin."

'Umi began to untangle the first thread of the problem. He spoke of Kaiki's death and how Manō had told them it was 'Umi who lay dead.

Manō took up the thread. "I was upset. I made a mistake. Was it not natural that I thought it was 'Umi at the pond? Does he not help Kaiki at times? I do not see the issue here."

"It is odd, that is all, that you would make such a mistake, and in the same breath ask for my position as headman." 'Umi stared at Manō.

"Well, am I not of rank in this village? I am connected to the royal family. It is natural that I would step in to do my duty and help the *ahupua'a* through a terrible time." Manō glared back.

Tutu called for another thread. "Palani. Tell us of the calabash."

"What?" The big man's face was confused. "Calabash?"

"Did someone give you a calabash to place at the *ali'i's* mat during the feast?"

Worry creased his forehead. "Oh. That. Yes. I was told to give a gift to the servant to place on the *ali'i's* mat."

"Who told you?"

"I do not remember."

Coconut Man could not tell if Palani was lying. The big man was strong, and probably not a bad man on his own, but few thoughts entered his head unless put there by others. In this case, the perfect tool for Manō's use.

"Did you know this 'gift' made the queen ill?"

"I heard."

"Were you not concerned? Perhaps someone would find you to blame for this? What the cost to you might be?"

Coconut Man saw by Palani's face that this had not occurred to him.

"No! I. . ."

Tutu seemed to reach the same conclusion as Coconut Man. Palani was a follower, and had not really been informed. It did not excuse him, particularly when Coconut Man recalled the drunken conversation on the beach, but Tutu let go of that *aka*--thread.

"I call on Coconut Man to speak of a conversation he heard on the beach."

Coconut Man's throat suddenly went dry.

"He is an outsider." From Manō. "Why is he here at all?"

Nodding heads from the elders.

212

"He wishes to stay with us." Tutu's gaze was piercing, defying argument. "He has proved his dedication to the well-being of this village he seeks to call his home."

What? He had not decided that! Moreover, he had not told anyone of his changing desires.

"Spying on good people? What do you call that?" More nodding from the *kūpuna*.

"Hear his words."

Coconut Man repeated the gist of the conversation. "They were both drunk on '*awa*, and I was new, but I am sure it was Palani, and Lako. They also mentioned Manō."

"How did they mention me?" Manō asked.

"They said you would tell them what to do when the time came."

"What time?" Manō swelled visibly. His face grew dark with anger.

"I am not sure. As I say, they were drunk."

"You would take the words of this outsider, who spied on good people, who perhaps had also overindulged and said things that did not make any sense, over the actions of a high-ranking member of this village with connections to the *ali`i?*"

"Let us be clear Manō," Tutu said. "Your connection to the royal family is through me,

213

my daughter and my line. Not by any action you have done on your own. Now, we must get control of ourselves." Tutu led them in another prayer. Eyes closed, breathing deepened. Coconut Man peeked and saw Manō's stony countenance had returned to its normal color. He saw something else that startled him. The *aka* they had begun to unravel like *olonā* cord lay on the dirt floor like glowing worms. Perhaps they did not exist for all in the circle, but he knew Tutu saw them as well. The threads sprang from Tutu, the leader of this *ho`oponopono*, and they criss-crossed the *hale* to Manō, Palani, 'Umi, with a single bright line to himself. So far, to those who had spoken. *This is going to be a long night.* Coconut Man sighed and allowed himself to drift into the resting place he was beginning to find familiar.

Chapter 24

After the prayer, they paused to eat and Coconut Man realized how hungry he had become. It was still dark outside. *Perhaps it was not even the same night?* He was tired. He knew this *ho'oponopono* had been long in coming and would not be over until all the threads were untangled and forgiveness asked for and given.

Another prayer, and the untangling resumed. Tutu scanned the dirt. With his double-perception, Coconut Man saw she was following the lines of conversation that lay there. *Perhaps Tutu saw the actual words? Or thoughts?* Whereas he just saw the connections. "I wish to call upon 'Umi."

"Again?" Manō's rudeness met with several gasps from the *kūpuna*.

Tutu ignored him. "'Umi, tell them what you found when you went to repair Kaiki's wall."

"I found a rock. A round, smooth rock, in the sand. A rock that did not belong at that place on the shore. A rock like no other. It was covered with blood."

"'Umi, what does this rock say to you?'"

"Kaiki's death was not an accident. This rock that did not belong was used to hit him in the head, dropped in the sand, to be lost, covered by sand in the storm, or perhaps washed clean."

"I see. Does anyone have anything to add?"

"Where is this rock now?" Manō asked.

"Here." 'Umi opened a calabash and displayed the rock, covered with sand and dried blood.

Murmuring and muttering from the group.

"Who would do this, and why?" Manō took the thread with the right amount of indignant propriety--his village. Manō looked around the circle. Few met his gaze.

Coconut Man met Tutu's eyes. She would pull these threads together into a net Manō could not escape.

"You!" Manō pointed a finger at Coconut Man. "Nothing has been right since you arrived!" Coconut Man's mouth fell open. "Don't try to deny it! Think, my people. All was well when he arrived to trade his wares, was it not? The crops were good. Weather was fine. A wedding to bless us, and the *ali'i!* To make a visit and further bless our lives. He comes and stirs trouble, the village separates, like *kukui* oil on water. Have you seen him prowling the village? Prying into things that do not concern him?"

Why did Tutu not stop him? He looked at her and she shook her head, the merest twitch.

"Lele. Did this man not come to you and ask questions about your sacred *kapa*? The one you were making for our chief? About your methods?"

"Well, yes, but he only wanted--"

"Yes or no? Did he pry into your ways? Women's ways?"

"Yes."

"What man, what man who cares for this village would do that?"

Manō's glare pierced him. "Did you not also approach our children?"

"What?"

"You have tried to make friends with *keiki!* A grown man! That is not acceptable. And I know why. He is a spy. He is getting information to send back to his own chief."

Tutu interrupted. "Why would he do that? Who is his chief?"

"I have not found out yet. Ask him yourself."

"Coconut Man," her voice was gentle. "Are you a spy from another district?"

"No." He could barely get the word out. *What had happened? What had gone so horribly wrong?*

"As a protector of this village, and of my *ali'i*--my cousin," Manō stared at Coconut Man, "I decided to find out about her illness. It is true that she became ill after the feast. It is also true, that she is weak and ill. So, someone attempting to undermine this district would find it easy to push for an advantage."

The expression on the elders' faces said this was news to them.

"Further, I think the man behind this made a mistake." Coconut Man was sure Manō meant himself, but also, Coconut Man--*my mistake was going against Manō*. "I decided to look for this calabash. And I found it. Right where the guilty man hid it!" Again he pointed at Coconut Man. "I confirmed this with two workers on the *makai* village."

'Ehu and Nuu. Both men looked ashamed. 'Ehu spoke. "All we said was that Coconut Man had come to get Io's nets! He was helping Io!"

"That is not the whole truth, is it?"

218

"What do you mean?"

"When I asked you what he said, you told me he wanted to know which was Io's *hale*, yes?"

"Yes!" Nuu became indignant. "There is nothing terrible in that! He was helping an injured man!"

"You also told me he asked when the people would come back to the *makai* village. Is that not also true?"

'Ehu's face was fiery red. "Yes, but it was to preserve Io's work!"

"You cannot be sure of that. But I am sure of my reasoning. Because when I entered Io's hale, I found *this* buried in the netting there. This calabash is tainted. This is the calabash that poisoned our queen!"

He stood, his frame and voice filling the circle. "Did you put this in the netting?" His eyes blazed and his *mana*--power--was overwhelming.

"Yes."

"You see! He is a danger!"

"I found it. I wanted to save it, so I hid it."

"Why would you want to save this? A poison! So someone else could suffer as our queen has?"

"No. I wanted to protect them." *What was happening?*

219

"A falsehood! And a flawed one at that. Another thing. I saw him at the fish pond just before the storm. He was talking to 'Umi. Kaiki was there. You all know he has been everywhere in this village, talking to everyone." To his dismay, many heads nodded now. "That is what a spy does. Asks. Listens. Think on this, my people. If he thought he was killing 'Umi, our headman--well, everyone knows what a leader 'Umi is. He is loved, and strong. A leader of men for years, perhaps even a district leader in time. If something were to happen to him, well, our village would be shattered! A perfect opening for another *ali'i* to invade us. We have had peace for many years. Do you think the *ali'i* in other districts have had life so blessed? And are they sitting around in their *hale* enjoying it? No! They are waiting for an opportunity such as this. A village in turmoil, ripe for taking. But *he* made a mistake! He killed the wrong man. So instead of the village torn apart, it is more united than ever and more resistant to attack."

Coconut Man was astounded. Manō's entire plot, his confession, almost the entire truth, but shunted onto him. His bowels turned to water. The *kūpuna* eyed him. The rumblings turning ugly.

"And one more thing. Because I love

220

this village so much, I watched this stranger from the day he came. That rock," he pointed dramatically to the calabash centered in the circle, "is just like the kind he uses to weight his baskets!"

"But those rocks are everywhere in the village!" Coconut Man went unheard as the people moved toward him. He scrambled to his feet.

"Tutu!" The last thing he saw as he ran from the *hale* were the lines of *aka* on the floor. They glowed bright red under the feet of his pursuers. Manō stood still, hands on hips, laughing as Coconut Man ran for his life. The only thing that could save him now was refuge. Refuge and Tutu.

Chapter 25

Coconut Man ran, pursued by Manō's warrior friends. It did not help that he knew the *kūpuna*--elders--also thought him guilty and supported his capture, if not his death.

One good thing. My accusation and pronounced guilt took all night, so now I can see where to run. The sun god La in his chariot had just begun his ascent.

Because of his travels weaving baskets for every district, he was familiar with the location of the refuge. If he could just make it to the *heiau*, temple of refuge, he would be safe. The priests there could protect him. However, getting there ahead of angry, athletic, determined men under Manō's control, would be a considerable feat.

While years of walking from village to village had given him some stamina, he was not a warrior, and not trained in weapons of

222

defense or offense.

He jogged and realized he could not keep it up for long. Walking he could do forever, but running, his joints protested. Bouncing on the hard trail, the ascent and descent of the ridgeline, and the burning in his lungs told him that at his age--perhaps 30 summers-- running a great distance was not an option.

Time spent in the forests had not been wasted. Time spent in villages with people of every occupation from bird-catcher to *kāhuna* had given him knowledge, and that would have to substitute for athletic prowess. *It would have to, or it wouldn't matter very long.*

The sounds of immediate pursuit faded. The men would return to the village for weapons and supplies. He estimated the *heiau* was two days away. Two very long days. Shorter if he was to swim around the point, but did he have the courage or skill for an open ocean swim? Even with death in pursuit.

How did this happen? I was there, and I still don't know. Perhaps Manō did pray to dark gods. The ones who help to kill men. The ones who honor dark pursuits in exchange for blood and death. Tutu said he was born evil. I have never heard of that, but I have never heard of many things I have learned from Tutu.

He slowed to a walk, still on the ridge trail. He had no supplies, no food, no water, no weapons. Not even a knife--that had been lost sometime during the storm. His *malo* contained a pouch with a packet of dye and a coil of *olonā*. *That will be a big help. 'Don't kill me or I will throw this dye at you.' I must get off this dirt path. They will follow my footprints as easily as if they could see me making them.*

The ridge line had tall trees, so he climbed one. Off the trail, the breeze and a false sense of security calmed him. Actually, being up a tree was a common and happy condition, so he stayed until his breath resumed and his muscles stopped trembling. Far below him he saw a line gap in the forest that indicated a stream. If he could get there, he could walk on rocks and perhaps be harder to follow. The line continued in the direction La began his chariot ride, and that was the direction of the refuge. He slithered out of the tree and carefully tried to erase his trail backwards for a way. Then he stepped off the trail and started downhill toward the stream. He promptly slipped on scattered leaves and slid, rapidly, painfully, and quite noisily down the steep embankment, coming to rest, bloodied and bruised against an unforgiving rock. Even in his shocked state, he saw the huge trail he had left down the mountain and sighed.

It is just like the grass slide track for hōlua sleds. But bigger.

There was no way, and no time, to conceal his ride. So, instead of a sheltered rest, he staggered to his feet, and continued, placing each foot with exaggerated care, not only to disguise his passage, but because he hurt. *It is all the same. They know where I am going. I just must get there first.* Tears pricked his eyes as he broke into a careful jog. The blow to his head had swollen and bloomed into a throbbing lump. Blood trickled from the break in his scalp and dripped onto his back, a small but persistent distraction.

Hot sun directly overhead congealed his head wound and he slowed to a walk. His stomach rumbled. *I must eat.* He looked up into the trees for fruit. A mistake. He whirled and fell as his brain reminded him of its injury. He did not move.

His eyes would not open. *They had found him and sealed his eyes as punishment for what he had seen!* He lay absolutely still and listened carefully for his enemies. If he overheard any plans, perhaps he could get away. Silence. *Maybe they are hiding, waiting for me to wake up and then they will jump out and kill me!* Nothing.

He knew they had bound him. His arms lay stiff and immobile. Perhaps he could wriggle and loosen his bonds somehow. He wriggled. *Aī, the pain.* He pulled his arms from under his prone body. No *olonā*. No binding. He rubbed his eyes. He was able to open them. His fingers came away with blood and eye glue from his injuries. He lay exactly where he remembered looking up to the trees for food. *As long as I am here, I might as well.* Above him was a canopy of green spotted with blue. Without moving his head too much, he looked for something to eat. There was much food, but he could not reach it. `*Ulu*--breadfruit trees, surrounded him. Two problems. He had no way to cook it, since he was afraid to start a fire, and the trees were five men tall. He was too exhausted to climb one.

He rolled to his side, paused for another assessment. Not too bad. He sat up. No noises of pursuit, or stealthy approach. *Just another result of hitting my head.* No dizziness. He slowly craned his neck, testing. He smiled. From this direction, several several *mai`a*. The rich, crescent-shaped fruit hung in groups from the feathery branches. Although his hunger seemed to have chewed through his entire stomach, he arose slowly, still waiting for his head to fly off his neck. He grabbed several and peeled them, the slightly green skins meant the fruit was not ripe, but that did not stop him. He ate two, scanned the ground and found two more, these yellow and brown, ripe and bruised. He didn't care. Their sweetness overrode the slight tang and unpleasant texture of the unripe bananas, and he felt better.

What he could see of himself was filthy, and severe thirst accompanied this discovery. *Water. Which way to the stream? I must not have been asleep long, the sun is still high.* He could see the sun's direction and that was all he needed to guide him toward the refuge. He moved slowly now, afraid of another fall. The sound of rushing water was such a relief that he almost went limp. His fear of capture had overridden his physical distress. With the proximity of water, his injuries came rushing back. He collapsed on his knees and fell forward, drinking and dunking his head. He rested his face on his arms and let the sound of the stream sooth him. Chill and refreshing, the water filled him with the moisture he lacked and the calmness he had not experienced since the last time he had stepped into the Wai.

He was about to pull himself into the

water when he noticed an abundance of red fruit along the banks. Squinting into the dappled sunlight, he saw trees filled with mountain apples. He still had no strength to climb, but walked along the bank until he found a tree with low fruit. He picked several and relished in the crispy texture and sweet-tart flavor. Lacking a carrying pouch, he stuffed some into his *malo*. It felt strange and probably looked worse, but he did not care. He would not starve now.

Sufficiently, if temporarily refueled, he scanned the area and was dismayed at how clearly he had marked his presence. He did his best to scatter leaves and brush away where he had lain. Then he carefully stepped into the stream and washed thoroughly. His head ached, so he did not scrub his hair, but floated with the injury in the water. Soon, the cool water numbed the swelling and he felt his hair loosen from the bloody mesh that held it. As he lay in the stream, the current pulled at him. He released his hold on the edge and let it carry him headfirst, downstream, his long, brown toes bobbing in the water. *Not an unpleasant sensation, floating. It is restful, cleansing, and leaves no trace. Why can't I float all the way to the--* His back hit a submerged log. Painful in his vulnerable state, but not deadly. *But, something deadly could come along and I would not see it. So. . .* he swiveled around in the shallow water and continued downstream. The stream bed varied in depth, sometimes so shallow his *'ōkole* scraped the bottom, sometimes deeper where the current slowed and the banks spread, making his journey like a dream.

He began to feel cold and tired and looked for a place to get out. The banks had become very steep here, with dense foliage to the water's edge. No hope.

This is fine. I can float like this for a long time. One reason he was cold was that La was finishing his ride for the day. The sky was clear, but La was gone, too low to see through the trees. La's warmth was gone as well, and Coconut Man feared remaining in the stream at night.

The fear contained a worm of panic that writhed in his stomach, as the sky grew dark over him and the canopy more dense. The chill, once refreshing now drained him of strength.

He could not see well at all, and sensed rather than saw a change in the stream. The water ran much faster than before. He felt out to his sides for the bank which suddenly seemed far away. As he struggled across the current to find it, he heard a terrifying sound.

The river was approaching a falls.

Unfamiliar with this river, he had no idea what the falls were like. It sounded huge. He flailed through the water, his lack of swimming skill compounded by panic. His feet sought purchase on a bottom too far out of reach. Every moment he sped downstream, the sky darkened. The moon had not risen, or if it had, the trees obscured it. Blackness and sound. Blindness and deafness created by the enormous rush of water. Numbness from cold. His body not listening to his commands to swim, to fight the water.

He slid under the ripples, water filling his mouth. He sank, unable to stop himself. His lungs had no chance to prepare for this dunking, and slowly closed on him. His feet hit a stony barrier. He pushed up and shot out of the water. His momentum took him into some boulders. He banged his knee but did not care. He used his last strength to pull himself up on the rock, grateful for the remaining heat left there by La.

He had no idea where he was. It was too dark to see if he was on the shore or stranded mid-river. The rock was large. He could not feel the edges of it. It was also above the water line, and unlike the ocean, tides would not submerge it.

His cheek was warm against the rough

stone and he lay on his stomach. He *could* lie on his stomach. That meant he had lost his food. Mahalo *to the gods for helping me, but, why is this so difficult? You do not want me to die? Or you do not want me to die right now? Is there something I should do? I have listened to your tales and to Tutu's words. Please tell me what to do. You cannot mean for Manō to rule the* ahupua'a. His thoughts flew to the dark gods. *Perhaps this is a battle between Manō's gods and ours. Perhaps I am just in the middle of a war. War again. When the gods war, does that cause war for us?* Another new thought. It somehow made him feel better to think he was not a direct target of the gods, but just caught in the middle of some higher conflict.

Where is the moon? I am so lost. I want to keep moving, but I cannot see where to go. He felt safe here from Manō's men because he had been in the stream so long. *They know where I am going. They know the fastest route to get there. My only chance is to arrive first. As soon as the moon rises, I will continue. Well, perhaps after more food. I have had all the water I'm going to need for a long time.*

The river had taken the last of his strength. His battered body could not take more. The warmth of the rock on his front, the chill and splash of water on his back mirrored the division in his thoughts. *Too tired to go on. Too risky to stay here. If they come for me now, I might just lie here and let them take me. Bleeding again. Knee. Where aren't I bleeding?*

The terrific noise of the river masked the approach of the search party. Coconut Man startled out of his doze to hear them right next to him, or so he thought. He still could not see. The night was that black. *Where are the stars to help me?* He barely breathed, realizing that the cloud cover that kept the stars from him, also kept him from being seen.

He heard men's voices, but could not understand the words over the water. He carefully turned his head, lying as flat as possible on his rock, his anchor. He couldn't identify any of the men, but was sure Manō, Lako, and Palani were among them to be sure he would die before he reached the *heiau.*

Gods! What are you doing? Toying with me for your amusement? Perhaps it was Manō's dark gods that cleared the sky, and made the moon rise. From his rock, Coconut Man faced the shore where his executioners stood. *Six. Perhaps more. I am lost. I will not move. I will not breathe.* He closed his eyes in prayer. Their voices became clearer and he opened his eyes. He now saw his rock was at the edge of a tumble of stone ten men long from the beach. A continuous trail led straight to him should they notice.

The breeze whipped across his back. The heat from the rock was gone now and iciness enveloped him. *Where could he escape? How to hide?* They were so close that if he moved, they could not help but see him. Then what? They looked well-rested, well-fed. They had probably not fallen down a steep embankment, hitting their heads becoming insensible.

Escape across the river was impossible. His only hope was that they move away, allowing him to cross the rocks to the safety of the forest. Then he could go around the falls and back into the icy water. It seemed they heard his wish, for they moved off, following a path Coconut Man could not see.

Slowly he rose from the rock and examined the forest edge. He listened. He prayed for assistance. Tutu's face popped into his brain, and he felt a little comforted. Abstractly wondered what was happening back at the village. He moved off his sanctuary and onto the next boulder. An easy route took him downstream as he moved to the shore. His legs were shaky, but he felt he could make it if he went slowly, resting along the way.

Approaching the falls, the rocks were wet and slick. He stepped even more carefully, grateful for the moonlight that guided him.

A man's shout and a laugh brought his head up abruptly. A figure on the beach called to others to join him. Coconut Man had been spotted.

Panic spread quickly down his body, from the crown of his head to his toes. It weakened him even as it spurred him to escape. Trapped.

The laughing man looked for a way to where Coconut Man perched. He found it. One by one, the man and his group hopped from rock to rock toward him. Frozen, Coconut Man could only watch as his forest escape was cut off. He turned to go back to his large rock, and realized that the rock would not help him. It led nowhere but the deep of the river.

To stay here was to die. There was no other place to go.

Jump.

"What?"

Jump. Tutu's voice. How could he hear her over the river, when he could barely hear the men?

You do not have time for this. Jump. Impatient now.

Coconut Man faced the falls. They were huge. Horrible. Mist billowed up obscuring his landing. Rocks, round, jagged, large, small, protruded from every angle. *I don't have to worry about hitting the bottom and dying. I won't make it that far.*

Jump! Tutu screamed. He glanced back and jumped.

Chapter 26

Manō had been right behind him. *The look on his face! If I am not dead, I hope I remember his expression as I jumped.*

Feet! Tutu's shout made him pull his feet to his chest like a perched bird as he hurtled past a rock protrusion.

He hit the water and made himself as small as possible. To be splattered on the rocks after coming this far would not do. He brushed a rock. Hit something, the bottom? with his feet. He had no air. *How do I do this every time?*

You have plenty of air, Tutu admonished. *Do not surface. Follow my voice. Swim. You are a turtle. Swim!*

He swam. He pushed until he felt his lungs would burst like a ripe banana. He surfaced and gasped, taking in equal amounts of air and water. If he had tried to come up where he had jumped, he would have been directly under the fierce cascade and probably drowned--the water pushing him under until he died.

He floated to calmer water and looked back at the top of the falls. No one. *That was not my imagination--this pursuit?* He must not rely on that possibility. He was afraid to get out of the river, afraid to stay in. Floating in the dark was not something he relished. Walking in the dark, *or running, more like,* was not a pleasant option either. Manō's men would not give up. Even now, they would be scrambling around the falls, staying as close to the water as possible.

Tutu. Where are you now? What am I to do? Silence.

He pulled himself from the water, clear sky now lighting the river. Dense jungle rose on either side and a narrow path paralleled the shore. He began to walk, sure that his pursuers would use the same path as soon as they found it. No time or energy to cover his tracks. *Just keep moving. Follow the water.*

He concentrated on putting one foot in front of the other. He could see his feet as he placed them. Dawn. La would soon rise in the sky. Light. Warmth. Sleepy birds rustled in the forest, ready for the day. The water still pulsed by, muted but comforting. Vines and lavender-pink flowers grew in profusion. He stopped. Could it be *'uala?* He stepped off the path and dug at the base of a plant. The root was large and familiar. Sweet potato. Delicious cooked, and could also be eaten raw. In his starving state, he began to gnaw. He felt a little ray of hope, like La's light, enter him. He stuffed several potatoes into his *malo* and continued on the trail. Still no sounds of pursuit, but that meant nothing. *For all I know, they are already there, at the gates of the* heiau, *spears at the ready, waiting. This thinking is not helpful. Keep stepping. Keep eating. You have light and warmth and water. You will do this. Lono will help you. You have not come this far for Manō to win. Ha. That is what he thinks as well.*

This discussion with himself carried him to the mouth of the river. The shore spread out to sandy beaches and trickled into rock strewn shallows. He stopped at the edge of the forest. The beach showed no footprints as far as he could see. Caution made his heart pound and the *'uala* dry in his mouth.

His exhaustion disoriented him. How close was the refuge? In that direction, a point of land obscured his view. Perhaps it was just around the point? He did not know. He would be more in the open now. If he went inland--*mauka*--he could lose track of the *heiau* altogether. He was unwilling to do that, so close to sanctuary.

Cautiously he stepped onto the beach, hugging the tree line. As he approached the point of land, the forest thinned, leaving him exposed. He hurried over sharp *a'a* lava rocks, his tough feet nevertheless registering pain.

He stopped in the shadow of the point. He could climb it, not a difficult ascent, but that would leave him exposed. He could walk, wade, or swim around in the sea, depending on the depth just off the beach. Not good. Or, he could turn inland, where again, forest would conceal him but he had no idea where to find a path that would take him to the refuge.

He carefully scanned the forest. All seemed quiet. He checked for an opening, a path, something to suggest he should go that way. A wall of green. The ocean was unacceptable. *I have spent enough time in the water in the last two days to last a lifetime.*

The point. He forged his own path, scrambling up, seeking handholds, feeling his feet slip. The sun, although new on its journey, struck fiercely on this shard of black rock. Sweat rolled into his eyes and reflection off the lava strained his already taxed vision. He felt a sweet potato slither out of his *malo* as his foot slipped. He held on with straining arms and one foot as his other foot struggled for a hold. A sharp pain told him he'd cut his leg on the lava. Warriors sliced pieces of this lava to stud their war clubs with cutting blades.

He found a hold. Through his sweat and hair he spied the top. He lay draped over the apex and regained his breath. Not even enough energy to pull himself upright. His skin dried in the wind and sun, his breath slowed as he lay face down in the dust, his panting making little holes in the dirt. The smell of it filling his nostrils, earthy and oppressive.

He sat up. The point was a rounded knoll, the *mauka* side leading to a cliff top and a trail entering the forest. The far side of the point he had climbed led to a steep but established path to the beach far below. The edge of the knoll cut away directly to the ocean, the water a dark blue with surf pulsing against the rocks at the base. *I'm glad I didn't go that way after all.*

The beach sheared sharply away from the point, taking the trail and any access with it. He saw no cliff access, once he reached the beach. He would be trapped there, until he could find his way up. Or, again, swim. *Always that. Swim.*

The knoll path led back the way he had come, but atop the cliffs, so he began the steep descent. The wound in his leg had stopped bleeding, but still ached. Lava cuts often hurt for a long while.

He reached the beach and walked. No shade. No food. No water. The day progressed. *I could use one of my hats right now.* He recalled his first meeting with Kaleo. Kaleo had liked his hat. *I must make Kaleo his hat when I return. Yes, you must.* The voice was Kaleo's in his head. Like Tutu's, not his own thoughts. *I guess I should be getting used to this.*

Yes, you should. Kaleo's unmistakable laughter.

I could use the company.

Yes, you could. The belly laugh.

Coconut Man shook his head to dispel the laughter. Another point rose before him. He scanned the cliffs. Something moved far above him. Too far to identify, but he knew. They had found him. He spun around, seeking escape. What he saw almost dropped him to his knees. A small group, far behind, walked toward him on the shore. Too far to see how many, but it didn't matter. One warrior with a spear could finish him now. The beach was a trap. Warriors behind him. The cliff, where he now knew more men hunted. The ocean, wild and hungry. And ahead another point. He ran toward the point.

This second point had an easy path, and he thanked Lono for that. When he reached the top, he froze. No beach on the other side. A long trail on the top followed the spines of rocks and would lead him directly into the arms of the cliff top pursuers. He turned back. The beach warriors still walked, inexorably. They knew to save their strength. He had nowhere to go.

He swiveled again to search for a path on the other side. Nothing. No beach met his eye. The water was deep directly under the cliffs. The warriors moved forward. Two groups, trapping him like an animal between them and the sea.

Maybe he could climb down to the ocean and find a path to the cliff side. *Maybe I just can't see one from here.*

His pounding heart felt as if it would explode. The sound filled his ears. *They won't have to kill me, I will die of fear.*

Look. Tutu's voice. *See.*

"What!" he shouted into the sky.

See what is there. Really look.

He whirled. "Warriors! More warriors! The sea--should I just drown myself now, or struggle until the sharks eat me?"

A sigh of exasperation from Tutu. He

squinted in the direction of the *heiau*. And there it was. Spread from the beach to lava outcrops, its magnificent walls rose two men high, *ki`i*--wooden carvings-- adorning them. It blended perfectly with the landscape, but now he wondered how he could have missed it.

A huge, blue bay separated him from his goal. One last look at the men pursuing him from two directions--no escape. *Once again, I am faced with a choice between certain death, and likely death. I am cursed.* He backed up, took three running steps, closed his eyes, and threw himself off the cliff. *Twice in two days, I am throwing myself off the earth into the water to drown. What is the matter with me?*

Chapter 27

Icy water closed over his head. The surf pushed him to and fro along the cliff. He surfaced and flipped his hair from his face, to clear his vision. *Good.* He scanned the cliffs. No pursuit. Yet. He turned toward the *heiau.* From the bay, he could barely see the tops of the trees at the site. He began to swim; an inefficient paddling and scrabbling against the swell which quickly tired him. He prayed to Kanaloa, god of the ocean, to help him. *So tired.*

His eyes closed, even while his arms and legs kicked like a newborn. He stayed afloat. His eyes flew open and he saw he was in the center of the bay. He had made progress. Here the water was deep and dark and terrifying. He pushed down panic, but could not control the thoughts of what might come for him from below. He struggled again.

His flailing drained him quickly and he began to sink.

Stop. Relax. A voice he did not know. It startled him enough that he did in fact stop kicking. He continued to sink. *The water will hold you if you let it.* He stopped sinking and floated, half a man's height, below the surface. He could see the sun through the blue. *Quite pretty. I am probably dying and do not know it.*

A chuckle. *You are not dying. Far from it. I have sent someone to help you. Float up and breathe, and wait.*

Coconut Man was sure he was dying, but it was not unpleasant. *Compared to being speared and tortured, drowning is wonderful.* He swished his hands until he surfaced and inhaled. The bay was quite calm in the center, and his muscles had stopped complaining. He scanned the cliffs and beach for pursuers. Nothing. *That means they are going around the bay to meet me when I get out. If I get out.* Getting out seemed a real possibility now. Until he saw a large, dark shape approaching. Several shapes. They moved slowly, but steadily toward him, and he would have tried to escape, futile as that would be, but his muscles, overtired from his journey, refused to move. He stayed at the surface, with plenty of air, while his legs dangled enticingly. He could not feel his heartbeat in his terror, and was sure it had stopped. Though surrounded by air, he could not breathe. He waited for that first bump, the first bite tearing his legs away, or perhaps just ripping him in two. With no defense, he closed his eyes and waited.

Open your eyes, Coconut Man. Pay attention! Tutu's voice, scolding. *You ask for help, you receive help, and now you close your eyes to it!*

Coconut Man did as he was bid. Instead of a fin, he saw a flipper. A huge turtle surfaced and inhaled. The shell was a man's height across, the flippers as long as his arms. A placid, wise eye watched him. The turtle turned and swam in the direction of the *heiau* just out of reach. *I suppose I am not getting a ride.* Coconut Man followed. When it floated, its giant body hovered just under the surface. Coconut Man did the same. He watched its flippers move, sweeping back water and moving it forward, with seemingly no effort. It did not fight the water, it used it. Coconut Man did the same. It did not need to breathe as often as Coconut Man did, but it floated next to him each time. By watching the *honu*, Coconut Man made steady progress across the bay. He was not tired. The air helped his muscles, and by mimicking the slow stroke of the turtle's flippers, he was propelled equally efficiently. *Odd. Perhaps I am a turtle?*

No, you are not a turtle, but if you pay attention even to those things that are far from your life, you can learn. The strange voice. Male, he thought. He did not recognize it as someone from the village. *A priest from the* heiau, *perhaps. That must mean I am going to make it.*

Coconut Man and the *honu* approached the far side of the bay. A rocky stretch of beach, where long ago lava spills here and there created pools and bumps, was the destination of the *honu.* Coconut Man reached the shallows, adjacent to the sandy access of the refuge. He was reluctant to leave the turtle. The *honu* began to eat the sea plants that grew along the rocks. Floating with the water's surge, it bobbed along, grazing. Coconut Man smiled as others joined it. More turtles than he had ever seen in one place fed on the bounty of the plants. His turtle was the largest. Others were nearly as big, and still others were only the size of one of his hats.

This *honu* was the *someone* sent to help him. And it had. Not only had the turtle been a companion in his fear, but it had taught him to swim. He paddled over and put his hand on the massive shell, opening himself to the *honu* the way he had to Kauila in her grief. The turtle did not move away, but turned and fixed his round black eye on Coconut Man. Coconut Man felt peace and neutrality from the *honu*. What kept it from being an alarming experience like his twining with Kauila, was that a large piece of kelp dangled from the *honu's* mouth, and it continued to chew, even as Coconut Man sent his spirit into the turtle.

It was time. He let go his connection and paddled toward the sandy crescent that allowed shore access. He stayed low in the water and remembered the turtle's lesson: body floating, flippers moving, no rush, gentle movement, the water is safe and protective.

The day had gone. It had taken him that long to cross the bay. La's chariot was low in the sky as he approached the canoe launch. He felt the warmth of La on the back of his head and the sea turned orange red in its last moments.

Smoke drifted up from cook or ceremonial fires. *Heiau* life was strange to him. He only knew what everyone knew. If you were accused of a crime and could get to the *heiau* ahead of the warriors, the priests there would protect you.

He was chilled now, and moved to the edge of the approach. Sandy bottom here, so canoes would not be damaged. He stayed close to the boundary wall. Voices drifted on the breeze. Not those of pursuing warriors, but of ritual, of the approaching evening, of life.

From being so long in the water, his legs did not want to cooperate. He squatted in the shadow of the wall. Warm and dry, he drew strength from the massive blocks carefully constructed and prayed upon by some long ago builder.

Although he had heard all his life of this type of refuge, he had no idea what to do next. Crawl over the wall? Look for an opening? Call out and ask for sanctuary? Wait to be discovered?

He walked along the wall until it turned, edged by the sea. The ancient lava made a foundation for the wall, and the ocean met it here. The high tide left little room to walk. It was nearly dark and the only illumination came from reflected light of torches inside the wall.

Retreating, he continued past the canoe launch and was gratified to see a canoe *hale* high on the beach he had not noticed from the ocean. *At least in that respect it is like a village.*

More carvings of the gods here. Of both stone and wood, they were sentries guarding the sanctity of the refuge. The stone wall had a gate of sharp spikes bound with cord, woven tightly enough to prevent peering in. Closed.

Now that I am here, what do I do? How do I get in?

"Aloha." Panic seeped into his call.

"So, you did find it. We had doubts." The voice came from shadows, from trees across a clearing behind him. He knew it well.

He spun to face the clearing. "Sanctuary! I seek refuge!"

Manō stepped out, laughing. "We caught you!" It was a game to him. From that one phrase, Coconut Man knew they had allowed him to come this far. Like children playing the hiding game, they had let him suffer through all of that, only to kill him at the last.

"You cannot hurt me. I am here, at the *heiau*! This is a refuge."

Manō took a few steps and several dark shapes followed. "You see, you are not *in* the refuge. You are out *here*. With us. Not in *there*."

"But," and that was all Coconut Man got out. Manō and his men lunged forward, spears dropped as one to impale him. He

250

pressed himself against the gate, knowing he was defenseless.

As the spears rushed toward him, the gate opened behind him and he was painfully yanked inside, dragged across the hard, pebbled ground. The gates slammed shut and the tips of spears pierced where he had stood.   He was dropped on his back by the two men who'd dragged him. Several more stood guard at the gate. Over him stood an immense man. Scars crisscrossed his countenance; tattoos covered his face and upper body. A long ago club blow had indented his skull slightly, pushing his features to one side and accentuating an old knife wound that pulled his mouth into a sneer.

I have been saved from Manō's spears, only to die in a more horrible way. Coconut Man fainted.

Chapter 28

I am not dead. Yet. Coconut Man woke in the middle of the *heiau*, on the ground, exactly where he had been dropped. Smoky torches lit the night sky, their smell mingled with cooking odors. His stomach flopped in protest. He sat up. Two men guarded the gate. He heard no sounds of argument from outside. Nothing from Manō. *Could he have gone? Have I won this battle?*

Carefully he rose to his feet. Sore, achy, hungry and thirsty, but whole and fairly undamaged. The men at the gate did not move. Did not acknowledge his presence. *Perhaps he was really dead? Maybe his spirit wandered the* heiau*? Manō and his men had broken in and killed him while he lay helpless, and now his ghost was here?*

Even if he was dead, he felt hungry, so he followed the smells. A group of men sat

252

near a fire. Calabashes gave off enticing smells. His jaw ached with the squirt of saliva, and his stomach wound upon itself like a sea snake.

Since he was dead, he could just help himself. Would they see the food rise in the air? He approached the group. They were the priests, he decided, from the bits of conversation. They probably saw ghosts all the time and would not be surprised. He picked up a bowl of poi and hungrily scooped with two fingers. It had been salted and was perfect. When the bowl was empty, he looked up and saw the ring of faces staring at him.

"If you are hungry, you are welcome to what we have. It is customary to ask, however," said a young man facing him across the fire.

"Because we grant you sanctuary, you are absolved, or will be, for your crimes, but you are not absolved from good manners," another added, this one older and heavier.

"You can see me?"

Degrees of confusion flitted over the five faces. The older one spoke. "Yes. Of course we can see you. Why would you think we could not? Sanctuary does not mean invisibility."

The young priest chuckled, and was joined by the others.

The bowl hung from Coconut Man's limp hand. Bits of poi still clung to his fingers. "I am not dead?"

More laughter, but the older priest spoke softly, one hand admonishing the others to be quiet. "No. You are not dead. You are safe. Why would you think you are dead?" He gently pulled Coconut Man to a place in the ring of men.

"They, the guards, did not see me when I stood. My body was. . . I was still on the ground where I fell. I passed out, and I thought perhaps my enemy had broken in and killed me, and I was left where I lay. In disgrace. Or dishonor."

"Ah. The guards are trained to focus all their sight, both internal and external, on the protection of the *heiau*. That is why they did not acknowledge you."

"But why do you not have guards outside, then?"

"What makes you think we do not?"

"When I sought help, no one came to my aid! I was outside your walls and in desperate need and I saw no one!"

"Then they did their job exactly the way they should. You were never alone. Did you not reach us in time? Now that you know you are not dead?" He smiled indulgently.

"Yes." Coconut Man pulled his feet up

254

and rested his face in his hands. "I am confused. If I was not in danger of dying at their hands, why did you wait so long to open the gate?"

"We opened the gate at exactly the correct time."

"But the outer guards. If they were there, why did they not assist me?"

"I will just say this. They are *heiau* guards, not your guards. They keep us safe in here, from attack, from invasion. They are not designated to aid those seeking refuge. It is up to *you,* to gain entry to *us.* You accomplished that. Now, you must eat to gain strength, to heal, to face your next ordeal."

Coconut Man dropped his hands. "Ordeal? What ordeal? Gods, help me."

"They already have. Now eat."

He was plied with many dishes, sweet fish, savory seaweed, juicy breadfruit. As the food replenished him, he became sleepy, his injuries and traumas pulsing and rising to the surface of his consciousness. He wondered if he should ask where he could sleep.

The older priest turned to him. "Now you must speak to Kahuiwi."

Keeper of the bones? "Who?"

"The one who granted you sanctuary. Our *kahuna pule heiau.*" Temple priest.

"Yes." Coconut Man's head was heavy,

his body exhausted. However, he could not show disrespect for the one who saved his life. "I need to thank him. And you. And to ask how I can be purified so I can return to my village." *My village.*

The priest nodded and rose, guiding Coconut Man to a large *hale* in darkness, under trees and apart from others. He gestured for Coconut Man to enter, and bobbed his head, leaving Coconut Man to open the *kapa* flap.

A large man, silhouetted by *kukui* oil lamps sat crosslegged on *hala* mats.

"*Mahalo, kahuna--*"

The man raised his head, his scarred, angry-looking face met Coconut Man's gaze. The warrior who had dragged him and dropped him in the clearing. The man who looked as if he could kill Coconut Man with no more regret than one stepping on a bug. Coconut Man's bowels turned to water and he backed up so suddenly that he smashed his head on the solid doorframe. He slithered to the floor, dazed. "I beg for sanctuary. Do not hurt me until I can explain." His head throbbed, his legs splayed ungracefully almost to the edge of Kahuiwi's mat.

"You have been granted sanctuary. You do not need to prostrate yourself for me." A slight smile. "Are you all right?"

I don't know. Am I all right? Coconut Man sat up, gingerly feeling the back of his head. A lump. *Well, that will go nicely with all the other lumps.*

"I think so." The *hale* bristled with weapons. *Why would a priest need weapons? And so many? Much I do not understand of the kāhuna.* He sighed.

"I see you have many questions. Many concerns. With La's return, we will begin your purification. I can forgive your crimes, but that does not mean you are out of danger. Do you understand that?" Coconut Man nodded. "Then, you should sleep. Rest is one of your best defenses. You will need them all before this is over, Coconut Man."

How does he know my name? The mysteries of the kāhuna are great.

"You will sleep in a separate *hale*. Go. Tomorrow we begin. The gods will forgive you. Some men will not." His eyes, though fiery, were not evil as Coconut Man had thought. He had seen much, suffered much, including the injuries that so deformed his features. The eyes, when he looked into them, were kind. Coconut Man determined he would ignore the scars that pulled and disfigured the kindness.

Coconut Man nodded, and crawled from the *hale*, showing the utmost deference and keeping his head below Kahuiwi's. Unnecessary perhaps, but he wished to show his gratitude, and respect and knew no other way.

The same priest met him outside and showed him to another darkened *hale*. Again, he gestured for Coconut Man to enter. This one unlit, Coconut Man had to feel for the sleeping mats and *kapa*. The bed was soft and warm, the ocean lulling, his full stomach and tired body dropped him off the edge into sleep.

He did not move until La's chariot filled the *hale* with heat and light.

The same older priest stood over him and his heart lurched in panic. *How long had he been there?* The priest gestured for him to follow. The ritual was beginning.

Chapter 29

Coconut Man was purified in salt water. *Kapu kai.* Then he was taken to a *hale* where Kahuiwi waited. His instruction was similar to *ho'opononpono*, and Coconut Man relaxed into a trance as the gods' assistance was requested. Aid from ancestors was also requested. Coconut Man's closed eyes saw the figures who came to help.

Kahuiwi had him relate his crime as he was accused. Coconut Man did not feel compelled to defend his actions, or pronounce his innocence, he simply related events as best he could. The shadow figures nodded and shifted, much as *kūpuna* and *kāhuna* would in a *real-life* council. *This was real. Wasn't it? It feels real. I smell the matting, earthy and musky. I feel the air moving on my face. I hear voices, mine, Kahuiwi's and others. Is that not* real? *Aī. Do not think so much.*

More prayers. More *mele*--chanting. This time ritual salt-water sprinkling--*pī kai.* Kahuiwi asked for absolution from the ancestors and the gods. It was granted. The priest thanked them, asked for their blessing and dismissed them. The gods vanished first. The ancestors milled about and hovered, much as the living do at a *makahiki* feast, Coconut Man felt very comforted. Very natural. Kahuiwi thanked them and dismissed them. Most of them faded away. Two remained.

"Why are you here?" Kahuiwi asked them.

"This one is still in danger," a spirit presented as an old man replied, pointing to Coconut Man.

"We are concerned and wish to offer protection," added a young woman.
"This man," Kahuiwi nodded at Coconut Man, "faces danger until the one who accuses him is removed. What can you do?"

"We are his guardians. Make sure he understands that we are with him on his return journey." The old man moved to Coconut Man's side.
Coconut Man looked up at him, eyes still closed, but clearly seeing. "I am right here. I can see and hear you."

260

The woman moved to his other side. "You have come a great distance in a short time, Coconut Man. Yes, you can see us now, but when you leave this place, our spirits will seem far away from you, and you perhaps, might attribute all of this to a dream."

The old man's features grew hard.

"The one who seeks to end your life has not given up just because you are in sanctuary."

Kahuiwi interjected. "I will offer further instruction. Know this, Coconut Man. Manō is waiting outside these walls, somewhere. Tutu tells me you hold the key to Manō's success or failure. Like the fronds in your baskets, your hands hold the weaving together. If you are no longer here to do that, the pattern will fall away and Manō will succeed with his own pattern."

"What can I do?"

"First, understand that all in your village know you reached *pu 'uhonua* and have been forgiven and cleansed."

"How?"

"The drums."

What drums? I heard no drums. Even a runner would take a full day. How long was I here?

"Five days. Look to your guardians. You may not see them for some time, but they will be with you. Listen to their advice. Now you must ready yourself for the journey back. We have food and weapons for you. Yes. You will need a weapon. The priests have prepared a safer route that will be revealed as you progress. You must be on your guard. Tutu is waiting for you."

"What of the village? Are they safe?"

"For now. Manō used all his resources hunting you. His plan to hurt the queen failed, so he sent a dark spirit to Puna to confuse him and Puna cannot leave his queen's side. This allows Manō to pull the village under his control."

"What of 'Umi?"

"'Umi is doing his best, but he is overwhelmed with the task of rebuilding the village. His duties as *konohiki* have taken his eyes and ears away from the danger. Since Manō is away from the *ahupua'a* seeking you, 'Umi feels safe. That is false. He is not safe at all."

Kahuiwi thanked the guardians. Coconut Man rose and thanked them as well. They nodded and vanished.

"Put your head down and hands on the matting," Kahuiwi instructed.

Coconut Man opened his eyes to find he was still seated. His aching joints told him that only his spirit body had stood. He did as

262

he was bid, head down, hands on the mat. He felt less dizzy and slowly raised up.

"I am ready."

Kahuiwi's eyes were open, flitting back and forth over Coconut Man, seeing something all around him that Coconut Man could neither see nor feel. He nodded once, his eyes returning to focus. "Manō is far. You are safe for now. Keep vigilant. We will prepare you, but the rest is up to you."

The older priest ducked inside the *kapa* and beckoned Coconut Man to follow. Creakily, Coconut Man rose. At the doorframe he turned to thank Kahuiwi. The priest was slumped, pale, and breathing shallowly.

"He has done much for you. The cleansing and preparation were more than he expected. He will be fine. He needs to rest. He has poured his energy into you, because you are the one who can stop a war. A war that would endanger all, even we who are protected here by the gods and ancestors. Even they cannot always stop the evil channeled through man."

A solid weight of responsibility settled on Coconut Man's shoulders. His usual fear and anxiety did not settle with it; instead it was contained by Kahuiwi's energy. Coconut Man followed the priest to a circle of other priests who silently handed him weapons, food, water, *kapa*. They followed him to the portal and flanked it. The two guards bowed their heads as they opened the gate. The priests bowed as well. No words. Nothing more to be said.

Coconut Man left the sanctuary. The night, rich and velvety, enveloped him. He inhaled deeply, closing his eyes. The gates shut behind him. He turned *mauka*, away from the sea, and opened his eyes to see a faint glowing line, like the *aka* threads from the *ho`oponono*. He began to walk the line.

Chapter 30

At first, Coconut Man leapt at every rustle in the shrubbery, startled at every crackle in the undergrowth. After many false alarms he grew annoyed with himself and concentrated on the glowing path.

His time at the refuge had prepared him well with excellent food and spiritual counsel. Even his stride was different, more confident. It helped that his body had healed. The temple priest had healed all his wounds the first day, even the deep gash he had received climbing the lava point. He had heard of such, instant healing, but had never seen it firsthand. Even a *kahuna* such as Tutu could not heal such wounds so quickly and thoroughly. He carried that sense of protection with him just as he carried a gourd full of fresh water.

The night was clear and lit with stars

and moon. No overcast marred his sight, and the route was a protected, dry stream bed with high banks, with clear sky above. He could not be seen except from directly overhead on the edge of the bank. The disadvantage was that it would be hard for him to escape. Every so often, he stopped, closed his eyes, and listened. The skill he had learned accidentally, of sending his spirit out to seek or twine with others, had been honed in the *pu'uhonua*. He sent it out to search for pursuit, and each time it returned alone. Safe. For now. At Kahuiwi's insistence, he carried a spear, the wooden tip sharpened and hardened by fire. A dagger was tucked into his *malo*, its obsidian blade sharp enough to shave hair with the barest pressure. The spear he used as a walking stick, but it was hard to convince himself that the dagger was only for eating. The thought of pushing that shard into human flesh terrified and nauseated him. *I am definitely not a warrior.*

The night passed and La began his ride. The little canyon became deeper as he continued. As the day reached its half, even La's rays barely touched him inside the depths of the ridges. By the priests' calculations, this path cut his journey in half, so he was nearing the village.

Coconut Man had traveled this island

for many years and had not known of this road. The runners apparently did not either, for they used the same paths that he and others had traveled. How was it that no one was aware of this special route? Perhaps the gods saved it for their own use and for their emissaries. *That could mean there are other secret paths, known only to the gods or their priests, on other parts of the island. And on the other islands. Perhaps these paths are also used by the spirits of slain warriors?* He glanced around, suddenly aware of his isolation. He swallowed. The canyon walls rose steeply above him. He could not climb them now if he had to. *At least the spirit warriors only march at night,* he consoled himself. He stopped. In his musings, he had not sent his spirit out for some time. He must be approaching the village, but did not know where this path ended. *Still clear. Hurry. You must reach the village before La completes his journey.*

He broke into a trot. The banks of the streambed lowered as he traveled. He heard voices and stopped abruptly, but couldn't concentrate over his own gasping for air. A pain pierced his side and he walked, trying to calm his spirit and body. The side pain diminished with his breathing. The voices continued in a barely audible mumble, but when Coconut Man stopped to listen, they neither quieted, amplified, nor became understandable. Puzzled, Coconut Man sent his spirit out and the voices instantly clarified.

They had been in his head, spirit voices, and only his spirit could help. Warriors. Waiting for him at the end of the path. How could that be, when this path was secret? Even sacred? He was close to the village now. Warriors waited for his return. Manō was not among them.

This close to the ahupua`a, Manō would make sure he had no connection to the discovery of my body. My body. Shock flooded through him, from the crown of his head to his toes.

They really plan to kill me. He sat on the ground with a bump. Gourds and weapons crashed around him in the dry bed. La was reaching the horizon now, and the bright orange rays poured down the path into his face, blinding him.

The old man and young woman stood before him, outlined in La's beams.

"We are still here. You will be safe if you do as we say. If you do not, we cannot protect you." They spoke with one voice

Confusing. His rush of alarm faded, leaving weakness in its wake.

"This path leads directly into their arms.

But, they do not know this."

"What?" More confusion. "If they are waiting for me, and I can hear them, how do they not know?"

"First you must feel the ground under you."

"What?"

"Feel the earth supporting you?" *Yes.* Suddenly a rock under his *'ōkole* announced itself. He shifted.

"Hear the earth speaking to you?" He listened and heard only birdsong and a gentle breeze rubbing branches together.

"What do you smell?" *Me. I am sweaty. And scared. What else? The sand in this old stream bed. A sweet smell of rotting jungle, comforting and pungent.*

"Now. You are back with us." True. His panic and fear had abated. "This *kapu*--sacred-- path is known to very few. It has been shown to you, and it is not for you to show to others. Do you understand?" *Yes.*

"It will be made clearer to you when you emerge. This stream bed vanishes in the forest around the next turning. You will know where to walk, and the forest will end in a clearing near a well-known village path. One branch of this comes from the direction of the refuge. It is part of the path system you used to escape. They think you must return the same way."

"I could have come back on the beach."

"They have men on all the known routes. You would be dead." It was the woman who stated this so frankly.

"Stop." The old man commanded sharply. Coconut Man stopped and once again, sat solidly, if shakily, on the ground.

"Are you listening to me?" The woman. *Yes.* "Can you stand? You must walk. You must reach your village before night."

La had dropped further into the sea, and now Coconut Man could see them both, although they seemed a little faded. Was that the bank he saw right through them? *Don't think about that. Just listen.*

She sounded a little frustrated with him. "When you get to the clearing they will be hiding, waiting to attack you when you come out of the path." She saw his alarm. "The *other* path. You must send your spirit out to that path. When they pursue it, you will cross the clearing safely to the entrance of the village."

"I cannot do that!"

"Then you are dead. And many of this village with you. Do you want that?"

"No! Of course not, but my spirit is a feeling. It is not a person. A thing! No one can do that."

She put her hands on her hips while the old man folded his across his chest.

"Well. Perhaps *you* can. But you are dead!"

"Are we?"

"What? You are ghosts and spirit matter can move wherever you want."

"We do not have time for this now." The woman gathered her patience. "Listen to me. You have abilities. One of these is sending your spirit out to help others. True, you have just learned this, and it can be a difficult skill. I wish I had time to teach you, but I don't."

The old man interrupted. "Do as we say or many lives will be lost and it will be on your head. Your fear is your greatest enemy. If we told you to walk across the clearing, could you?"

"Yes. Of course I could."

"Could you always have walked across that clearing?"

"Yes. What do you mean?"

"When you were first born to this world, could you have walked across the clearing?"

"No, I was a baby. I didn't know how to walk."

"But you learned, correct?"

"Yes. I see now." Coconut Man did see.

The woman's touch on his hand was like warmth from morning sun. "You must trust yourself and us, that you can do this. Remember the feeling of Kauila. How her pain brought you to her, and how you soothed her. It is the same. The pain of the *ahupua‘a's* death will be your guide now, not your own. Remember that."

"Will you help me?"

"We cannot, more than we have."

"Will you go with me?"

"We will be there, but again, you must trust our presence. You will not see, hear, or feel us on this part of your journey. Perhaps. . .?"

She turned to the old man and he nodded. "This will help you. Remember these things. Do not rush. Give your spirit body time to manifest. You are not powerful enough for them to see it, but they will hear it. That must be enough to draw them to the other path. While you run to the village, your spirit will lead them away and that can be dangerous for you. Find Tutu first and then recall your spirit. She has been making what preparations she can in your absence, but protecting Kehau and Puna has been her foremost task." She inhaled deeply and went on. "When you are divided, you may forget your instructions. You may panic and forget we have been here, and that we *are* here. This might help to remind you." She touched the back of his hand and her touch seared his flesh to a bright mahogany. He pulled back, gasped and cradled his hand with the other. Eyes closed, the pain ebbed to a manageable throb. When the pulsing of the injury waned, he was aware of only the birds, the breeze, and a sense of aloneness in the streambed.

He gathered his fallen things and rose. Only one direction to go. He headed down the path, each step making little puffs of dirt, until around the next turning, as promised, the path stopped at a solid wall of forest. He scanned it for an opening and finally plunged in, fighting his way through the undergrowth. The pulsing in his hand accelerated and he slowed. The pain lessened. He pressed on and the throbbing increased. He slowed and it was less. *Hmmm.* A few more experimental steps assured him his pace and his wound were connected.

He proceeded cautiously, each step calculated for the least noise. Eventually, the throbbing increased and would not be assuaged no matter how careful he was. *That must mean I am close.* He heard nothing, saw nothing until a few more paces brought him to the edge of the forest. He lay flat and saw the path he had taken the night of his escape, across the clearing and to his left. He looked for the warriors he knew waited. Nothing.

Across and to the right, was the way to the village. La's journey was nearly over.

I must hurry. Even as that thought entered his brain, the burn flared up in protest. He nearly cried out. He remembered the words, *do not rush.*

La is nearly done. I will wait until dark. At that thought, the burn spoke once again. *I must be in the village by dark. I must not rush. How am I to do this?*

Eyes closed in thought, he heard rustling around him, far too close for comfort. Without moving his body, he opened his eyes. Warriors moved in the forest near the path. By quietly waiting, he had discovered their positions. He closed his eyes and sank into his trance state, his body growing limp, blending with the surrounding brush, protected by the trees. He floated, sank, floated, sank, until he was deeper than he had ever been. The thread between his spirit body and his *kū* body stretched long and thin. He was not afraid. He sent the spirit body across the clearing and onto the path. It identified the armed men under Manō's control. It was time to make some noise.

Chapter 31

Coconut Man's spirit body walked through the bushes along the path, back toward the clearing. He was nearly there when the scramble of the warriors told him they had started down the path. He turned and ran away from the village, making as much noise as possible. It took great concentration for his spirit body to do this, and Coconut Man experienced exhaustion, not from running, but from the effort to make the spirit body pant as though running--an effect he created to lure the pursuers. The fatigue stemmed from his head, where enormous amounts of energy swirled and pulsed. He so concentrated on the chase, he was nearly unable to pull himself back toward his body to allow his real escape. He opened his eyes, feeling as though he had been tossed about in the ocean.

He keenly felt the division of his spirit's split from his body as he pushed to his feet and staggered out of hiding. Running into the village, as he had optimistically envisioned, was possible.

His ability to move his body forward and manifest his spirit's noise grew increasingly difficult as he neared the *hale*. As usual, the *keiki*, more specifically Kaleo, were the first to note his return.

"You look terrible. Where have you been?"

"Tutu. Take me."

Kaleo looked about to protest, but didn't. He took Coconut Man's hand and led him to the *ali'i's* hale. His small-boy energy, pulling him along, spurred Coconut Man to continue his duality. He wanted to drop his far-flung energy like a useless pack at his feet, but was afraid to lose contact with his spirit body.

Kaleo, still holding his hand, called to a retainer. "Tutu? I need her."

The retainer nodded and ducked inside, reappearing moments later with Tutu.
"Coconut Man. You are here. Good. Come to my *hale*. You, boy, bring him." Now at his journey's end, Coconut Man could only follow where he was led. Kaleo's hand was like a life-thread, keeping him moving. His own

life-thread felt very long, thin, and weak. *Surely it will snap soon.* He found he didn't care. He only wanted rest.

Tutu and Kaleo helped him lie on the matting, clean *kapa* under his head. Gourds of all sizes and shapes filled the *hale*, hung from ridgepoles and stands. Pouches lay everywhere, looking identical to Coconut Man's weary eye. *How can she tell what she needs?* That thought swirled away and was replaced by Tutu's instructions.

"Kaleo, sit next to him. Keep holding on. He needs your *mana* now. He has traveled too far and needs our help to return." She pulled gourds and pouches to her. "I was afraid of this." Kaleo obeyed, his slightly moist hand holding tight to Coconut Man's.

Tutu began to pray. She *pikai'd* with salt water. She asked for the gods and ancestors to help guide Coconut Man's spirit back to his body. She told Kaleo's spirit body to stand at the edge of the village to add *mana* and act as a beacon.

Coconut Man's eyes remained closed, his body pale and limp. In his head, he floated, indifferent to the activity around him. His spirit body was far away and weak, but that did not bother him much. Kaleo's spirit poked him with its finger. *Hey. Come on. Come back.* The chubby hands, just like his real hands, tugged at the life-thread. Coconut Man's spirit body, tethered to the life-thread, floated like a kite, bobbing and unresisting to Kaleo.

Warmth pulsed along the life-thread where Kaleo grasped it. When Coconut Man's spirit body reached Kaleo's, it floated there in a sleep-like state. Kaleo stuck his lower lip out in a familiar display of stubbornness. *I said, come on. Stand up straight.* He tugged Coconut Man's floating hand and gently the spirit body set its feet on the path. *Walk. I can't carry you, and you are not a kite I can fly back to the village.* Kaleo's words gave comfort and familiarity. His hands, one on the life-thread and one tightly grasping Coconut Man's, gave *mana*—power—to move back to his *kū* body lying in Tutu's *hale*.

Reluctantly at first, Coconut Man's spirit followed the trail. Yanked and chastened by Kaleo, his own strength gained with each pace, his life-thread thickening and shortening as the distance closed. The pallor of the thread reversed, and with it, Coconut Man's body regained its vitality.

With a plop, Coconut Man's spirit body returned, the life-thread intact, glowing and resilient, coiled within him. He opened his eyes.

Kaleo still sat next to him, their hands

entwined. Coconut Man smiled.

"*Mahalo.*" He twisted to see Tutu. "*Mahalo* as well."

"How are you?" She busied herself putting away her materials.

"I am a little tired, but fine, I think. What of this one?"

"He is a boy. An extremely special boy, and his youth repairs him quickly. He will be fine."

"I am here with you. I am not asleep." Kaleo was indignant.

Coconut Man sat up. "We know. I am grateful to you for bringing me back. I have much to do. Where is Manō?"

"I don't know." Tutu shifted to face him. "I have not seen him. His plot to kill 'Umi failed, but that one always has more than one path to his destination. I know he counted on your death to put an end to the speculation around Kaiki's murder. That did not happen. You returned from *pu'uhonua*, but do not think you are safe."

"I know. The priests made that clear."
"I have been safeguarding my daughter and her husband as best I can, but I think they are his direct targets. Kehau is weak, not well. Puna is so distracted he is not listening to 'Umi about the safety of the village."

Coconut Man drank from a water

gourd. "Manō has allied himself with another district to overthrow this one. The temple priest told me that much."

"Who purified you?"

"Kahuiwi."

Tutu's eyebrows flew up. "You are honored indeed. He is the most sacred, has the most *mana*. He walks among *ali`i* as one of them. You must be more special than you look."

Coconut Man knew she was teasing, but the serious note in her words alerted him.

She added, "Did he also tell you what might come?"

"He is concerned that Manō will bring war to the *ahupua`a*, and that war will defile the refuge and his people will be hurt as well as ours. He knows Manō is evil."

Tutu grunted. "It is good to have a friend as powerful as Kahuiwi. All is not lost, then. We have work to do. Take this little one to his mother. He will be fine. You must eat and rest. Use this *hale*. I don't know where Manō is and I think he is desperate enough to kill you as you sleep, but he will not come here. His spirit is dark and cannot enter this *hale*."

"Where will you sleep?"

"I will stay with my daughter. She is past the danger of death I think, but another attack could finish her. Puna is lost. He cannot care for the village while his spirit twines with Kehau's. I have begun to suspect Manō's dark hand in this, too. Puna is under a sorcerer's spell, placed by Manō. He will not leave Kehau's side, will not eat or drink. It is like my brother. I did not suspect sorcery then, but I see the parallels, too great to push aside."

"Come, Kaleo." Coconut Man felt good. Wonderful, in fact. He pulled Kaleo to his feet and put his arm around him. "Tomorrow will be busy, I think. You need your rest."

"Coconut Man." Tutu had more to say. "You have done well. This village has much to be grateful for in this visit from the frond-weaver."

Coconut Man smiled. "Every day I think it is all over, and then I realize it is just beginning."

"Wise, too." She turned her back. He was dismissed. He slowly walked Kaleo to his mother's *hale,* arm still about his shoulders, comforting and being comforted.

At the *kapa,* he knelt before the little boy, making them eye to eye. "You have done a man's work. You brought me back. I am grateful."

Kaleo's brown eyes were huge, and dirt smudged one rounded cheek. "We are partners now, right?"

281

Coconut Man nodded.

"Forever, right?"

"Forever."

Chapter 32

Morning found Coconut Man in a strange place. *Where am I? This is not my* hale *at the refuge, nor my mat outside the men's sleeping* hale. He was not alarmed, but lay relaxed as the village sounds seeped into his consciousness. *Ah. I am back in my own village, in Tutu's* hale. He sat up.

All his limbs appeared to be working properly and he felt completely recovered from his spirit-walk of yesterday. He rose and left the *hale,* headed to the Wai for his morning ritual.

La's light glowed among the leaves and fronds, glinting off the rippling Wai. Relieved and washed, Coconut Man sat on his log to think of all that had happened. While at this moment, he could deny all that had gone before, he knew that it was not over.

Hunger wormed through him and he

283

made his way back to the village, prioritizing his tasks. Tutu. 'Umi. The *ali'i*. Perhaps another village meeting. *That is a wonderful idea, given how well the last one went. I am no better off than I was before. It is still my word against Manō's, who still has much more favor in village politics than I. Tutu has nothing tangible to show, just her words, too. As powerful as they are, they are not enough. The poison is long gone, I am sure, and even that did me no good. He says I supplied it, then hid it. It is half true, so in the eyes of the elders, it could be all true.* He sighed. Eat first.

Tutu squatted outside her *hale,* mixing food. Kaleo trotted from the opposite end of the village, and they met by Tutu.

"*Aloha,* Tutu." Coconut Man sat before her.

"*Aloha* Tutu," Kaleo echoed and also sat, his small brown body mirroring Coconut Man's flanking Tutu. She looked at them, her silver head bobbing back and forth like an *'ō'ō* on a branch.

"*Aloha,* Coconut Man. Kaleo. Have you eaten?"

"No," said Coconut Man.

"Yes," said Kaleo, but his eyes fastened on the bowl.

"Would you like to eat again?" Tutu's

284

eyes crinkled in amusement.

"Yes, thank you."

She offered a prayer, scooped out chunks of various raw fruits and they ate hungrily. She unwrapped steamed breadfruit and they continued.

"How is your daughter this day?" Coconut Man folded his feet and rested his forearms on his knees.

"She is better. Puna wants to return to his village as soon as she is well enough to travel. That will be soon. We still have Manō to deal with. It will be safer for our *ali`i* to return home, but not safer for us. This war you spoke of. Have you any proof, besides the strands you have woven together from Manō and the others? And Kahuiwi's words?"

"No. I have been running for my life. Are Kahuiwi's words enough?"

"If he were to tell the *ali`i* directly, but he will not leave *pu`uhonua*, and Puna cannot leave Kehau."

"So Manō is safe." Kaleo folded his legs like Coconut Man and his little arms rested just so.

"It would seem so."

"I have an idea." Both adults looked to Kaleo.

"We need a person on our side, who knows what Manō has planned, is that right?"

"Go on." Tutu's attention was full.

"That person has to tell one of us, or 'Umi or even the *ali'i* so Manō can be stopped? Is that also correct?"

"Yes. What are you thinking?" Tutu asked.

"I know someone who might tell a child his problems. A child because he is not so *akamai* himself, and thinks children are stupid, too."

"What?" Coconut Man almost shouted.

Kaleo scooted closer. "Lako."

"What do you have in mind?" Coconut Man whispered.

"I have been thinking, all the time you were gone. Manō is too strong to oppose alone, as you found out." Coconut Man remembered vividly.

"So, I have made friends with Lako. He did not go on the hunt for you with Palani and the others. Manō has stayed far away from the village. Lako feels alone. He has few allies anyway, and most of them were chasing you. I took advantage of his solitude."

"What did you do?" Tutu smiled with pride.

"I kept him company, gave him food, told him he was a fine, good man, asked many childish questions. He thinks I admire him. I have told him I can't understand how his skills have been overlooked by Manō."

"Well done, Kaleo." Coconut Man's grin was huge. "What can we do?" This he put to Tutu.

"Kaleo, can you get him to admit Manō's plan? He must be aware of it. Perhaps not all, but enough to convince the chief that our safety is in jeopardy."

Coconut Man shook his head. "I doubt he will confess the plot. It could mean his death."

"We must trick him into admitting this knowledge before witnesses. If you and I and 'Umi were to approach the *ali'i* together, along with Lako's words, Manō would be banished."

"If Manō had no standing here, perhaps the rival *ali*'*i* would not attack?"

Tutu was troubled. "I think Manō has done an excellent job of encouraging that chief to take over our peaceful *ahupua'a.* I fear we cannot stop an invasion. But we can prepare for it."

"What has Manō to gain by destroying his own family?" Kaleo's question reminded Coconut Man that he was still a child.

Tutu put a wrinkled brown hand on Kaleo's smooth, plump one. "Manō would be chief and headman of this *ahupua'a.* He would help his ally become *ali*'*i ai moku,* district chief, of combined districts. I think he would, by war, try to become high chief. I do not know their agreement, but this other chief may not know how ruthless and cunning Manō is. Manō has probably told him he just wants to run the *ahupua`a*, and then perhaps the district when his 'friend' becomes high chief. An agreement without honor is no agreement at all, and this chief may not be aware of the depth of Manō's treachery."

"Yes." Coconut Man nodded.

"We must stop him!"

"Yes, Kaleo, we must. Not only would he be a terrible leader, the kind whose own greed is always the foremost motive, but he would put our people in grave danger. This would not be the last battle our men would fight." Tutu patted his hand. "Now. This is what we must do." Her head bent in prayer, her chant asked for assistance from the gods and ancestors, and a special request for Kahuiwi's aid, until the sun was directly overhead.

"Coconut Man, you find 'Umi. Kaleo, you find Lako. We must get him to. . . where? Where is a place he will talk freely, and we can hide safely to overhear?"

"He has been spending much time near the *imu*. I usually find him there. He just sits."

"Excellent." Coconut man clapped his

288

hands. "The clearing is not too large, and there are many trees to hide us. Let us meet there near dark? Will he feel safe then, Kaleo?"

"I think so. I will spend the day with him and get him ready to tell me how he could be of use to Manō. We will work back to the *imu*."

"Good." Tutu was pleased. "You're sure you can get him to reveal the plot?"

"Not absolutely, but most likely. He thinks I need a father." His eyes rolled. "He has even spoken of spending time with my mother." He stuck out his lip. "I do not like that at all."

Coconut Man felt a pang of what? Jealousy at Kaleo's paternal needs? Sadness for fatherless Kaleo? He was not sure. He focused again. "You do not have a father?"

Kaleo glared at him. "I don't need a father."

"I know. I see what a strong person you are. Your mother is fortunate that you are there to care for her."

Kaleo scrutinized him for signs of teasing. Satisfied, he turned back to Tutu. "I will spend the day with Lako."

"Kaleo, if something changes, come back and spill this water gourd over the doorway of the *hale*. Leave the gourd upside down. Coconut Man and I will know to find you, that something is different."

"I will not need you."

"Do you understand?" Tutu looked fierce.

"I understand!" Kaleo jumped up and ran toward the ocean.

"He is still so small," Coconut Man said.

"Yes, but so strong. He will make an excellent chief one day."

Coconut Man's eyebrows flew up.

"Yes, a chief. Now. Go to Io. He has things to tell you." At Coconut Man's startled look, she added. "Yes, your friend will play a part in this, too."

Coconut Man rose and helped Tutu up. Her spirit was strong, but her body was bent and frail. He left her at her daughter's *hale* and went in search of Io.

Chapter 33

Coconut Man wandered the village looking for Io, without success. This did not bother him since the day was warm and he received no bad feelings from the people he encountered. Perhaps not all were aware of his 'crime?' And those who were, had been informed of his absolution.

He continued to the beach and the canoe *hale*. The shoreline had changed a little from the storm, but was still useable for village purposes. Io sat before the canoe *hale,* a mound of netting nearby. He did look like his namesake, the hawk, sitting in a nest.

Coconut Man smiled, pleased that Io looked fully recovered. His skin glowed and his frame had filled out to its old muscle tone. "*Aloha*, Io."

Io continued to mend a net. "*Aloha*, Coconut Man. Sit." Coconut Man sat while Io tied off one of countless knots in the sea of mesh.

"Ah." Io stretched his fingers, opening and clenching his fists. "I am out of practice."

"How are you? I am a little surprised to see you back at your duties."

"I am well, thank you. I had excellent care, Tutu sent the best medicines, and my need to get away from my women's fussing sped my recovery." The smile belied his words.

"How is the wound?"

"See for yourself." Io moved the net aside to reveal a bright pink circle of flesh where the spear had entered. It was not much indented, and the hole had almost healed.

"That looks very good. Does it hurt much?"

"A little. I keep moving. I sit for awhile and work, and then I take a short walk. I should do that now. Would you like to come with me?"

"Yes. Infection?"

"Not at all. Thanks to my wife, if you ask her." Again, the warmth in his eyes told Coconut Man how difficult the healing truly had been.

"I would like to tell you, Coconut Man, that I am grateful for your part in my recovery during and after the storm. Others were preoccupied with their own tasks, and you cared for me."

Coconut Man felt he had done nothing extraordinary. "You are welcome, my friend." Their eyes met, and Io nodded once. It would not be mentioned again, but the bond was sealed.

"I have something I wish to discuss with you." Coconut Man continued past the canoe *hale* to firmer ground, following a path that led away from the men at work.

"Have you heard I was accused in Kaiki's death?"

"Yes. You sought refuge and were granted forgiveness."

"I only ran because I was chased. My only hope was sanctuary before Manō caught me. Had I not, I stood no chance of righting this, one of many wrongs done to this village."

Io turned to him, eye brows raised.

"I did not kill Kaiki, nor was it an accident; either theory Manō would like the village to swallow."

"I did not think you did. However, during *ho'oponopono*, I heard tell of many threads pointing to you."

"I had nothing to gain from killing Kaiki. Manō had much to gain."

"What did Manō gain from Kaiki's death?"

"First, that was a mistake. He intended to kill 'Umi."

"What do you mean? Why?"

293

Coconut Man inhaled deeply. This was harder than he thought. Io's steps were labored, and Coconut Man turned back to the beach where a graveyard of driftwood provided seating.

"Io. You are a good man and well regarded in the *ahupua`a*. What I need to say may be difficult to believe, but please let me finish before you decide."

Io nodded, eyes fixed on the ocean, and massaged his thigh.

"I am not sure where to begin, so this may sound a little confusing. It is to me, too. Manō's power is great. It goes back to his childhood. Do you know his relationship with Tutu?" Io nodded. "Then you know how Tutu's brother, Manō's father, died?" Another nod. "You know his death was like Kaiki's? That Manō was under suspicion for his father's death?" Shrug. "You also know that Manō stood to succeed for *konohiki* and perhaps an *ali'i ai moku*?" Head shake. "Yes. And the reason he did not advance was Tutu. She stopped him then. He has never forgotten or forgiven. He has waited all these years, and forged dark alliances, to exact revenge and take control."

Io scooted on the log so he could look at Coconut Man. "You are sure of this?"

"Are you sure of Tutu?" Nod. "I know I am new here, and have no standing, but can you

294

see any gain for me in any of these actions?"

"You could be a spy."

"I could. But why come to you, and Tutu? Why would I return here, after being absolved of the crime of murder, if I didn't have to?"

Io grunted assent. "Why would Manō accuse you, then? Go on."

"The plot he works now is different from the plot he forged. And it is because of me. I came here, learned things, heard things, and found the correct person, Tutu, to confide in. Manō's path now is two-fold. To destroy the current *ali`i*, and to make me responsible, not only because I am new and the logical stranger, but in revenge for my foiling his original plan. Io, listen." Coconut Man grabbed Io's shoulder. "If I had not come when I did, our chiefess undoubtedly, and perhaps even our chief, would be dead!" Coconut Man pushed his energy into Io.

Io gasped. "*Aī*"

"I'm sorry. I have strong feelings and you felt my worry. Do you see the urgency?"

"Yes. The storm and my injury have distanced me from the workings of the village. Usually I am involved in all, but with my wound, I was unable."

"That is it, then."

"What?"

"I wondered why you had been targeted,

and now I see it was to keep you out of such councils. You are strong and highly respected. If you were killed in the storm, no one would suspect."

"Killed!"

"It could have happened. But wounding you was just as effective. Hmmm. Probably Palani, but we may never know."

"What are you talking about?" Io's eyes were wide.

"Also, your friendship with me had to be severed."

"You had better explain it all."

Coconut Man told him everything that had transpired since the storm. All his conversations with Tutu, Kaleo, and the priests, especially Kahuiwi.

"Do you see? This village is running out of time, because Manō is running out of time. He has set a course involving a war with an opportunistic chief. That chief will not wait, therefore Manō cannot wait. His first plan failed and he is scrambling to tie another together strong enough to destroy us."

"A war?" The color had drained from Io's face.

"Yes. A war."

"We are not ready for a war. We are at peace. No one wishes to harm us."

"You could not be more wrong my friend,

and Manō counts on the entire village to feel as you do. Until it is too late and spears are at our throats."

"But, *ali`i* Kona would come to our aid."

"Yes. If he knew. He is far away. Too far to help without advance warning. I do not know the other *moku* as well as I know Puna's and Kona's. It is my guess that the district of *Ko'olau* is the one allied with Manō. That district is isolated by the wet mountains and I do not trade there. Others who do, say the people are not friendly."

"But you do not know?"

"No. I am guessing. In the end, it does not matter who, but everyone *must* believe it is coming."

Io nodded. "What can I do?"

"When Kaleo gets Lako to admit his part in the plan, we are going to Tutu and the *ali'i*. We hope Lako will go with us, to confess. Will you accompany us to the *imu*? The more who are respected by the *kāhuna* and *kūpuna* and who hear Lako's words, the more chance we have to prepare. Manō must be destroyed or he will destroy us all."

"Why have you not gone to the chief before this?"

"Tutu says he is under a sorcerer's spell. He will not leave Kehau's side until she is well. She has not had his ear, and Kehau's recovery

297

has been slow. Tutu has reversed the sorcery as best she can, but it is strong. All our words and speculation have not been strong enough to pierce the shield around Puna. We hope that Lako's words will."

"I will help."

"*Mahalo*. I am worried that Manō is working faster than we are."

"What do we do next?"

"'Umi. Come with me to see 'Umi. He was Manō's intended victim, and it is vital to convince him of that. Our success depends on his joining our fight."

Chapter 34

Coconut Man and Io found 'Umi at the fishpond supervising a small repair crew.

"*Aloha*, 'Umi," Io called.

'Umi waved from his position atop the wall. Several men, 'Ehu and Nuu included, attended to various tasks.

'Ehu called to 'Umi. "I think the gate is ready. Will you check it?"

'Umi worked his way to the sluice at the center. He opened and shut it several times and nodded at 'Ehu who waited in the deeper water.

'Ehu waded to the shore while 'Umi walked along the top of the seawall toward them.

"That is done." 'Umi gazed at the repaired pond with satisfaction. The other men gathered gourds and materials and returned toward the village, leaving them alone.

"'Umi," Io began, "we have come to

discuss Kaiki, among other things."

'Umi grunted. "Come." He led them to the trees where he and Coconut Man had had their earlier conversation. "Sit." Silently, he handed out food and water.

"*Mahalo.*" Coconut Man hadn't realized how hungry he was. After the prayer and food, he began. "'Umi, the village is in danger."

"You, who killed Kaiki, tell me this? He was my friend. And my cousin."

"I did not kill Kaiki."

"So you say."

"I do." Coconut Man sighed. "If I did, I sought refuge and was purified and absolved. So my crime is erased."

"Not to me."

Io interrupted. "'Umi, this gets us nowhere. We can prove it, but we need your help. This crime is tied to the safety of the village."

"Go on. If you did not kill Kaiki, who did? And why?"

Coconut Man let Io answer the question. He added details of his flight, but otherwise did not comment.

Finally 'Umi said, "I did not understand why you would kill someone who had done you no harm. In fact, I was beginning to like your presence in the *ahupua'a.* I felt no bad *mana* from you. If what you say is true, I will help."

"*Mahalo,*" Coconut Man smiled.

"But," 'Umi held up a finger, "if it turns out that you have some dark purpose, I will never stop seeking you. There will be no place for you to hide, and that includes *pu `uhonua.*"

A trickle of fear ran through Coconut Man. "I speak the truth. I only wish to help."

Io said, "Do you not see, 'Umi, your feelings are exactly why he could not tell anyone before? Even I had my doubts, when all he has done has helped us."

"Perhaps. We shall see. I will wait until you have met with Lako. If I am displeased with what I see and hear, I will confront Manō and see what he says about this."

"No!" both Coconut Man and Io said. Io continued. "If you do, Manō will know how much of his plot has been revealed. He will change his methods. No one will be safe. It will be too late. As it is, we have no time to waste."

"I am not entirely convinced Manō is as bad as you say. True, he is rash and bold, but both are excellent traits in a warrior. I have never seen him do anything to endanger our village."

"That is just it! He is a spider, working and weaving in the dark, waiting for our *ali `i* to step into the web."

"Perhaps. But I stand by my words. I will not take part in the loss of another good man. I will be there when Lako speaks. If I do not like

301

what I hear, you know what I will do."

'Umi gathered his water gourd and the remaining food. He strode onto the forest path without another word.

Io shook his head. "I hope Kaleo succeeds. Without 'Umi's support, we cannot hope to convince Puna."

"I know. I would hate to be proved right by the war cries of invading men and the screams of our unprotected and unwitting people."

"Then we must be sure that does not happen. Let us go to the *imu* and see where we might hide tonight."

The men stopped just outside the *imu* clearing, in case Kaleo had beaten them there. All was quiet.

"Let us circle the clearing, back here in the trees and find the best place," Io whispered.

"We should choose several, in case Lako doesn't stop where it is best for us."

"True."

As quietly as possible, they circled the clearing. For the most part, they were able to stay hidden. The shrubbery was thin in several areas and they would try to avoid those. Io began to pick up sticks and rocks along the way.

"What are you doing?"

"It will be near dark when Kaleo brings

Lako. We will not be able to see well, and I don't want to make any noise. It is important that he feel alone to confide in Kaleo. Then we can step out and circle him and show how futile escape and lies would be."

"Yes. Very good." Coconut Man helped to clear the way.

When they had done all they could, they returned to the village.

"I must work on my nets. It will give me something else to think about."

Coconut Man nodded. "I will find Tutu and apprise her of our plans. I will meet you at the clearing when La is finishing his journey. I wish to arrive before Lako."

"Good. Aloha."

Coconut Man stopped at Tutu's *hale*. The water gourd was not upended. He heard movement from inside.

"Aloha, Tutu."

Tutu ducked out and sat in the shade of the wall. Coconut Man told her of his discussions with Io and 'Umi.

"I think the tide is turns in our favor," she mused. "Kehau is much better. She and Puna plan to leave tomorrow. Whatever happens here, will happen tonight. Manō's sorcery has lost its hold and Puna is willing to be addressed. I have mentioned my concerns, but I do not think he agrees about their gravity. He still believes Kehau became ill naturally, and that Manō's accusation of you was a logical result of a tragedy at a difficult time. Since you sought refuge and were blessed, he sees no reason to interfere."

"What of the alliance with another district? Manō's treason?"

"He feels that is unfounded, and there is no proof. I even reminded him of my brother Kai's similar death, but he does not see the danger. He has been out of his head so long he is not taking even the most basic precautions. We must get Lako's confession and bring all the *aka*--threads--to Puna."

"I understand his desire to return to his home village, but he must be made to see that a war would involve the entire district, and possibly Kona's *moku*, too."

"I agree."

"What of our own warriors? Are all the men followers of Manō?"

"No. That is why we need 'Umi on our side. We have many warriors but we must also turn the ones who are undecided. Manō has great strength of will. When I began to listen to the rumblings in the *ahupua'a*, I realized how many men do follow him. If 'Umi and Puna decry Manō, then we have a chance. The village can prepare for war, but no one will make a move without Puna, especially now that our *ahupua`a* houses him, however temporarily."

"I wish I had never come. I am to blame for much." Coconut Man dropped his head in his hands.

"Listen to me. None of this is your doing. Rather than a bringer of death, you are a bringer of salvation. You have suffered as much already as anyone in this village. If we are invaded, you will die along with the rest of us. Remember that." Her brown eyes bored into him.

"I don't know if that makes me feel any better, Tutu."

She gave her gap-toothed grin. "It was not supposed to. Eat. Take this."

She shoved food at him and struggled to her feet, waving off his attempt at assistance. "Go." She walked firmly but slowly to the *ali`i hale* and entered. The *kapa* curtain slapped as it closed behind her.

Coconut Man set off for the *imu*. The sun rode low and a brisk breeze picked up, shattering bands of sunlight on the path. On silent feet, he reached the trees surrounding the *imu*. In the chill, the birds had quieted, roosting with feet tucked under breasts for warmth. Coconut Man settled across from the main opening, behind the *imu* and the firewood pile. He tucked his feet under him too, breathed deeply and slowly, and waited.

Chapter 35

Silence pressed in upon Coconut Man and he became concerned that their plan would fail for lack of witnesses. *Perhaps I should return and find 'Umi and Io? Did they forget? A worsening of Io's wound? 'Umi decided I am lying?*

He was about to run back to find the others, when Kaleo's strident voice floated to him.

"Come, Lako. It is not that bad. I'm tired. Let's sit a while and rest. You can tell me a story?" This last was said with just right amount of childish worship.

"Yes. I'm tired, too. Tired of all this waiting," grumbled Lako. "Do you have anything to eat?"

"I have a little breadfruit my mother prepared."

"Your mother. She is pretty. And an

excellent cook."

Coconut Man could not see from his position behind the woodpile, but smiled as he imagined Kaleo's scowl and stubborn outthrust lip.

"Sit." Kaleo was brusque and Coconut Man almost laughed, understanding the waterfall of words Kaleo must have held back.

"Lako, you said you were tired of waiting. What are you waiting for?" Silence.

"I am just tired of not knowing anything."

"What do you mean?"

"Nothing. Do you have any more breadfruit?"

"Here is the last. Where are your friends? I used to see you together all the time, but now I only see you in the village."

"Friends." Silence.

"I guess," Kaleo's voice was probing, and Coconut Man hoped he would not alert Lako. "that with the storm, everyone's tasks have changed?"

"That is right."

"You said you had big plans. You were going to have a new job in the village? What will that be?" Again, childish admiration.

"Yes. I suppose I can tell you. The chiefess is very ill."

"She is? I did not know that."

"It is important to keep it a secret."

"Why?"

"Well, you know the people. They will worry and be afraid." Pompous now.

"Yes."

"And when she dies, the chief will die of grief."

"How do you know? That is terrible!"

"Yes, but we have to think of the entire district, not just of the *ali`i.* We must plan for the future."

Coconut Man was shocked that Lako would speak so openly and falsely. Everyone knew the district's wealth and success was directly tied to the *ali`i's* health and well-being. Only a child or a simpleton could possibly think differently. *Well, there it is.*

"But, how do you *know?*"

"I am one of those helping to look to the *moku's* future," Lako said with pride. "When the new *ali`i* come into power, I will be among those appointed to safeguard it."

"Safeguard from what?"

"Those who would oppose us."

"I don't understand."

Lako heaved a sigh. "It is like this. Our chief and chiefess are not well and cannot rule much longer. When the new *ali`i* take over, there are those who will spout falsehoods about the right to rule of those in power. It is always so."

"Well, who will be the new *ali'i*? How are they chosen?"

"You are so young. I will explain to you. We have friends in another district. You know that Puna and Kona are close--allies?" Kaleo must have nodded. "Well, when Puna dies, Kona will not be our friend anymore. It is important to have friends in other districts to help us. Manō," he stopped. *Probably realizing he should not mention names.*

"Go on!"

"Manō has friends in another district who have agreed to help us."

"But I thought the chiefess was better. That they were going home?"

"That is what they want you to think."

"When will Manō's friends come to help us?"

"Soon."

"So, Manō will be the new chief?"

"Oh, no. He says he does not want that. He says the people from the other district will rule for a while, until we are organized. Manō has said he will be *konohiki* and I will be head of the fish pond."

Oh, no.

"But 'Umi is *konohiki*. Why won't he still be headman?"

"He is going away. He is one who will not like the new chief and so will move to another *ahupua `a.*"

Does he really believe that? 'Umi will be dead along with most of us.

"No he won't. He would never leave us. He is like a father to this village." Kaleo sounded upset.

Careful, do not reveal your true concern, little one. Coconut Man prayed he would be able to convince the others of Lako's words. His concern was unfounded. The next voice he heard was 'Umi's. "Enough of this."

Uh, oh. Coconut Man rose and peered out. Over Kaleo's head he saw 'Umi standing before them. Io came out of the bushes on the other side. Tutu's brown face appeared more slowly, as she too made her way into the clearing. Coconut Man stepped out to join them.

Lako's mouth hung open. Kaleo looked startled, too.

"You had better explain." 'Umi stood, arms folded, legs spread.

"I don't have to explain to you."

"You have to explain to all of us." Tutu sounded reasonable. "We have all heard your words and now, if you want to save yourself, you had better tell us everything."

Lako swallowed and looked from one grave face to the next. "I have done nothing wrong. The village is in danger, and I am helping."

"We all agree the village is in danger, but our opinions differ as to the source of that danger."

Lako's eyes were huge. The silence grew.

Tutu took advantage of his lack of wit. She stepped forward. "Must I force you to speak?" She stretched a hand to place it on his head. He shied back as if struck.

"No! Do not curse me! I meant no harm. I will tell you what I know. You cannot punish me for protecting the people. If you do, then I will know what Manō said is true."

"And what is that, Lako?"

"That you," he licked his lips, "are all. . . evil. That you wish to harm both the old *ali`i* and the new, to take over for your own ends."

"Enough of this," 'Umi repeated.

"No, 'Umi." Io stepped between them. "We know what Manō has said about us is not true. That it is poison. We must not show Lako that Manō is right."

"This is not the way to do this." Tutu sat on the ground. "All of you. Sit. Lako and Kaleo, come off that log and sit in circle with us." Reluctantly, all complied. Tutu chanted. Night had fallen, a rich blackness filled the clearing, lit with bright sparks of stars directly overhead. No moonrise yet. Tutu asked for help and guidance from Lono and Kū. She asked for help from the village ancestors and from the spirit

311

of Kaiki.

Oddly, the tension went out of the circle and Coconut Man felt safe and prepared. *Prepared for what, I don't know.*

"Now, Lako. You are safe. You must understand that perhaps Manō has not had your best interests in mind. Do you see that?"

"But he promised me."

"How could he fulfill that promise to you, and still be true to the *ali`i?* How could the village function under strangers? Do you truly think a chief from another village would let us live as we do?"

"I suppose not."

"How could you ever think that? Are you so gullible?" 'Umi was still angry.

"'Umi." Tutu's voice was gentle but firm.

"Do you not see? Manō put Lako under his spell. Lako is a good man, perhaps not as far-thinking as some, but he only wished to please his friend. Is that not so, Lako?"

"Yes. Manō is, was my friend."

Io asked, "But now he is not?"

"No." Lako's voice was dreamy. Coconut Man could not see him clearly, but he felt relaxed and thought Lako did too.

"Tell us from the beginning, Lako," Tutu said.

"Manō gave me a calabash and said to give it to the chief's retainer at the hula feast.

He said it was a gift, but a surprise, and so to tell no one."

Coconut Man remembered the drunken revelations on the beach, but said nothing.

"Manō said we must think of the whole village when the *ali`i* die, and only he was concerned enough to plan for the future. He said he had friends in another district who would help us."

"What about Kaiki?" 'Umi tried to soften the emotion in his voice, but Coconut Man felt his pain. "Kaiki never did anything to Manō or anyone else. He tended the fishpond and that was all."

"Kaiki was an accident." Coconut Man could not see the faces, but the energy in the circle shifted.

"Do you mean Manō did not mean to kill him or that his death was a true accident?"

"Kaiki was an accident," Lako repeated. "That is all he said."

Io shook his head. "That is sad."

Tutu said a prayer for Kaiki, then thanked his spirit for coming to the circle and let him go.

"Lako. We need your help." With Tutu's *mele* had come the moon. Although just a sliver, it was enough to light the circle. "It is time to reveal all of this to Puna. He is our chief and our connection to prosperity and the gods.

Do you see, he is the only one who can help us now."

"Manō will help us."

"No, Lako, he won't." Kaleo put his hand on Lako's. "Manō is bringing warriors. Manō brings war to the district."

"No." Lako did not sound strong as before.

"Yes," Kaleo said. All the heads in the circle nodded. The adults were silent to let Kaleo speak.

"Lako. I have been with you every day. I have been your friend, yes?" Lako nodded.

"Where has Manō been?"

"I don't want to say."

"Tell me. Just me. I am your friend."

"He has been over the wet mountains." The energy in the circle bumped up.

"Why?"

"To bring back his friends. His other friends." Lako's voice was smaller and quieter with each answer.

"When will he return with this 'help?'"

"Tomorrow."

"Lako. This is very important." Tutu's voice was a caress. "You only want the best for all of us, yourself included, yes?" Lako nodded.

"We will protect you, but you must tell us. When did Manō 'predict' the *ali`i* might die?"

The silence stretched. The air had

314

stopped moving or so it seemed to Coconut Man. The trees did not move, no one breathed or twitched.

"On their homeward journey."

"He told you this?" A nod. "And now that things have changed?"

"He said it was for the good of the village--if they were not strong enough to withstand. . ."

"They would die in the attack?" Another nod. Tutu shook herself like a dog coming out of the Wai. "It is time. We must go. All of you must come with me. It is unusual, but all of our energy is needed to convince Puna of the danger and the fate that awaits this village if another moment is lost."

"No, no, no, no," Lako repeated, a quiet whimper, as he pulled himself into a ball. "I will be killed. I will be punished."

"Lako!" Tutu scolded. "If you come with us now, I will do my best to protect you. You have done wrong, but your motives, for the most part, were good. Right now we have bigger problems than you. Puna will see that, but only if you come with us now. If you do not, I cannot help you, and no one else will either. Do you understand?"

"Yes."

Tutu closed the circle, the prayers and the spirits. She moved as a young woman and

Coconut Man was stunned to see her rise and trot toward the village with the same fluid energy Kaleo had.

Her words, speed, and the change in her body shocked the others into motion as well. All jogged after her, Lako in the middle, Kaleo ahead of him, Io and Coconut Man flanking, and 'Umi behind.

There was no mistaking their urgency as they ran through the torch lit village, straight to the *ali`i hale.* Evening routines dribbled to a halt as people watched the procession open-mouthed.

Tutu ran straight into the *hale* without waiting. Seconds later, Puna appeared in the doorway, huge and regal, even after days of strain and worry. Puna's hawk-like features were the last things Coconut Man saw as the group prostrated themselves at Puna's feet.

Chapter 36

"Explain." Puna's voice, rich and deep, commanded immediate response.

Coconut Man could not see with his face in the dirt, but Tutu's voice came from above him, so she had probably knelt, but was not flat on the ground.

"Puna. Grave danger has come while Kehau fought for her life. This village has been put under a dark spell. Through the good deeds of several, and Coconut Man especially, we have a chance to save our people."

"Why do you bring this *group* with you?" Puna sounded more curious than disdainful of the motley gathering. Coconut Man turned his head to breathe better and opened his eyes. Kaleo lay next to him, eyes wide, staring at Coconut Man.

"My words alone are not enough and each one here holds a cord to this plot."

"Plot? What plot?"

"You have been betrayed, my chief."

"That is a heavy accusation."

"I know. That is why I brought the ones who can explain each part of the puzzle."

"Who is behind the treason?"

"Manō."

"Your nephew?"

Tutu sounded her age. "Yes." Perhaps she felt responsible for Manō's behavior, merely by being related to him. He wanted to reach out to her, but was afraid. He felt a wave of anger from Puna and experienced the connection between *ali`i* and the gods. It was true, the gods smiled on the *ali`i* and worked with and through them.

"This plot will not happen."

"No, my chief. We will not let it. Can each of these, your loyal subjects, speak directly of his knowledge? It will save much time and we have none to waste."

"Yes." Coconut Man heard rustling and shifting, but dared not move. Puna's *mana* flowed freely and swirled among them, making him dizzy. He prayed that power would never be directed at him.

Puna's voice came from only a little above them. A servant must have brought a seat. "Who should begin, healer?"

Coconut Man understood the shift in

318

relationship. This was royal and political business. They had ceased to be mother-in-law and son-in-law. They were now *ali`i* and *kahuna.*

"The knowledge first came to me through a stranger to our village, the basket weaver. He learned of dangers to the people and did not know where to turn. The gods sent him to me. He will tell his part."

Coconut Man's pulse raced and he began. Puna stopped him. "You may sit up."

Coconut Man did, and saw that Puna was in fact, sitting on a stool. He felt reassured that his head remained lower than Puna's while he told his tale. Torchlight swayed and danced, and he adjusted himself so no part of his shadow would touch even the shadow of the chief. Puna's power was great, his anger held in check, and Coconut Man did not look at him, but gazed beyond him. He told all of his story, starting from his arrival in the village. Puna asked few questions.

Coconut Man dropped his head lower and lower as his story pointed more to Manō. Did it sound as if he was shifting blame from himself to Manō? Perhaps that was his fear talking.

Tutu said, "'Umi, tell your part."

'Umi was also allowed to sit up. He told of Kaiki, and then how Io and Coconut Man came to him. He made no assumptions, no accusations. Coconut Man kept his head down. 'Umi's story seemed to point to himself as much as to Manō. After all, he was a stranger.

Puna sat very still. "I would hear from Io. You may sit."

Io too, said only what he had been told to, citing who told him, and his own experience. He expressed trust in Coconut Man. 'Umi had not made such an endorsement.

"Why is the child here?" Puna was an excellent listener.

"He--"

Puna interrupted Tutu. "He may speak for himself."

Coconut Man looked at Kaleo. His eyes were huge, his chest rose and fell rapidly. He remained lying in the dirt.

"Speak!"

"I am a friend," Kaleo's usually strident voice was barely above a whisper.

"Go on. Of whom?"

Coconut Man felt great empathy for Kaleo. He had never seen the boy afraid to speak. Even Lako and Manō had not frightened him like this. Coconut Man sent a wave of energy to Kaleo and nodded encouragement.

"I have been a friend to many in the village. I know everyone." Kaleo recovered a little. "I know Coconut Man and he has helped all of us."

"It is nice that you have many friends. You are a kind child. But what does that have to do with treason?"

"I am a child. *Keiki* are not really, well. . ."

"Go on. Speak your mind. You are safe."

"Yes. Well. I watch and hear things that an adults do not, because I don't count."

"I see. Go on." Coconut Man detected the amusement in Puna's voice, but could not be sure without looking. He was unwilling to check.

"I know many things about the village. I know secret paths, I know places to go, I hear what people say. They think I am stupid because I am young. They are wrong."

"I recall similar feelings when I was a boy. Continue."

"Coconut Man was the first adult to treat me as if I was more than a child. He was kind and respectful to me. I was near him much more than he knew, because I liked him. He was kind and respectful to everyone he met, including Manō. He is gentle and patient. He harms no one and nothing. Even when provoked."

"Explain."

"I, uh, saw his burns when he bathed them in the Wai. He did not get them by accident. Someone hurt him on purpose."

Coconut Man looked at Kaleo, eyebrows raised, *yes?*

Kaleo's eyes were wet, from fear, memory or empathy he could not tell.

"I see."

"When he told me the village was in danger, I believed him. I wanted to help. He cared about me. About all of us. So, I began to listen. And watch. Manō, Lako and Palani were together most often. They talked in whispers while I watched from hiding, and when I walked past, they talked of fishing. They do not fish much, and yet it was always the same. Fishing."

"What bearing has this on the plot?"

"I was there when Manō declared 'Umi was dead and he would be headman."

"I have heard nothing of this! Why not?" Puna was thunderous.

Tutu's spoke gently. "A sorcerer's spell, my *ali`i*. You were tending to Kehau with such fervor, the spell that touched her, also encompassed you. I was unable to pierce that veil until Kehau began to recover."

"I see."

"So we all went to see who was really dead, and it was Kaiki."

"'*Ae.*" Puna sounded genuinely saddened. "A good man. An excellent caretaker. His death will not go unpunished." Coconut Man saw Lako squirming, still prone, the dirt around him damp with his sweat.   "What else?"

"Manō leaves the village a lot. I heard he goes to the wet district."

'Ko'olau? We are enemies! We are separated by the high mountains. That chief is in league with the chief from another island. What is going on? We must finish this."

Kaleo spoke quickly. "Palani was hunting Coconut Man so I made friends with Lako. He was left alone and I knew he could help. He did."

"You. Lako. Is it true, you are friends with one who may betray me?"

Lako stayed flat. "I *was* friends with Manō and Palani, my *ali'i*. But I did not know what he planned! He said you were dying and he was only looking out for the village!"

"I was dying!" Puna's anger rumbled through the very earth. "He would take *my ahupua'a? My moku?* I think not."

Tutu interrupted. "Chief, Lako has come to help. Without him, we cannot stop Manō. Consider mercy. He is not. . . complete in his mind."

Coconut Man admired her bravery on Lako's behalf. True, Puna could order Lako's death. Well, all of their deaths if he felt they were conspiring. Everything he had heard of Puna said he was just. He prayed for that now.

"Heed me well, you! Every word you say

compels your death or your freedom. Weigh that and speak only the truth. If you lie, I will know, and you will die at my feet. Do you understand?"

"Yes." A whisper.

"Begin."

Lako spoke. Coconut Man felt Lako's fear keenly. It laced every sentence, trembled through every word. Coconut Man also felt the truth. At last Lako was finished.

Puna turned to Tutu. "You have done well. We have no time. I cannot even send my family back to my village for safety. I will send a runner for more warriors. I will send another to Kona for help. He will not receive it in time, but he can send reinforcements. Our only hope is that Manō's surprise is gone." He turned to a servant. "Bring my guards."

Tutu shifted. "My *ali`i*. May I take the women and *keiki* to the caves for protection?"

"Yes. 'Umi. Alert your warriors. Have them meet here quickly. You and Io prepare the others for travel."

Panic swirled through the clearing as the word spread. Coconut Man helped Tutu up.

"You will get Kehau?"

"Yes. Manō is near. I feel him. There is no time to pack. You must run, do you hear me? Run and get the others to the caves. I fear the *kūpuna* will not make it."

"I will see to the old ones. I will do my best."

Coconut Man ran. He felt disembodied. Fear was contagious and the men, even those trained and prepared for war, were angry and agitated. He sensed that it was not just war, but the betrayal by one of their own that fueled their fight.

Shouting, running, panic, and screams barely penetrated his mind as he pulled sleepy children from *kapa*, urged tired women from their *hale*, and shoved, pushed, and herded them to the upland path. As promised, he arranged for the *kūpuna* himself. Old Kai, he picked up with 'Ehu's help, followed by Lehua, 'Ehu's woman.

The moon, in its whimsy, had hidden behind clouds. The people, terrified and off-balance, were afraid to light torches for fear of alerting the enemy to their escape. Stumbling and crying, the villagers clung to one another as they made their way up the steep path.

To add to the nightmare, someone fell off the narrow trail, the body sliding downward, the cries of the victim mingling with the cries of the escapees. No one stopped to help. No one could. Coconut Man shut his mind and stubbornly struggled with Old Kai.

He heard sounds of battle from far

below. It had begun.

Chapter 37

Coconut Man joined several armed men who accompanied the women, children and elderly to the relative safety of the caves. By necessity, the strongest warriors remained to defend the chief and the village. Coconut Man saw Tutu with Kehau and only a few guards. He understood Puna's feeling that to protect Kehau best, he had to save the *moku*. Puna was a true leader.

Coconut Man also knew that despite Puna's years, he would fight with his men. If Puna died, the *moku* would be unbalanced. A battle between Ko'olau and Kona would most likely result, with the weight of victory leaning toward the younger invading chief who had planned his attack.

Coconut Man found Kaleo with his mother in a cave. "Are you safe?"

Kaleo nodded. His mother looked at her

son enquiringly. "Mother, this is Coconut Man. He is saving us."

Coconut Man laughed aloud. An odd sound, but the whispers and shiftings of many others in the cave helped to mask it. "Kaleo has been a great help to me."

"I am Lea. I have heard much of you. You have the aspect of a legend in my son's eyes."

Named for Lea, goddess of canoe builders. Coconut Man felt himself darken with embarrassment. Kaleo scowled, his forehead pulled down practically over his eyes. It had not occurred to Coconut Man that Kaleo would discuss him at all, much less with his mother.

"I am sure he has exaggerated."

"I had thought so too, until we ran from our homes in the middle of the night to avoid death or capture. Now, I am not so sure." Despite the gravity of the situation, her eyes twinkled. *I guess you would have to have a sense of humor to raise that one.*

He gazed fondly at Kaleo. "I must check on the others. Kaleo, I must go see what is happening to the village. You will stay here and do what you do best. Listen."

Kaleo looked even more ominous and about to object.

"Please? *Kokua.*" Help.

"Yes. All right. But you must come back and tell us what is going on."

"The men will keep you safe. I must find Manō. His objective is Puna's death and that must not happen."

"Yes---"

Lea interrupted. "Kaleo. Let him go. He will do his best. You have a job here, too. There are others here who need you." She nodded to a family huddled nearby. Honu sat between who Coconut Man decided were her grandparents, eyes on Kaleo.

He nodded, small chest inflating. "Yes. I have work to do. Safe journey."

Coconut Man blinked. Kaleo sounded a thousand moons old.

Lea said, "*Mahalo*, Coconut Man. Safe journey."

Coconut Man nodded and searched the cave for Tutu. She sat in the back with Kehau and several retainers. Kehau's guards had been posted near the entrance.

"Tutu. I am going back to the *ahupua`a* to find out what is going on. What do you know?" Kehau sat silent, eyes on Coconut Man. He knelt to keep his head lower than hers. She was a striking woman, and Coconut Man realized this was as close as he would ever get to *ali`i*. War changed certain things he found, as they took stock of each other; Kehau directly, Coconut Man less so, in short glances. Her glossy hair was bound by a pick. She had regained her strength and coppery color, but she seemed thinner. Perhaps a little *mana* had been lost as well. Her eyes remained steady and he felt only support and pride from her.

Tutu placed one hand on her daughter's and the other on Coconut Man's. He immediately felt calmer. Tutu's eyes went blank, the pupils dilated and darted back and forth, scanning, seeing something not in the cave. "Manō's goal is Puna. Their relationship could allow one moment of hesitation on Puna's part and that is all Manō needs. Ko'olau is nearly here. He brings more warriors than we have, not even counting those Manō has turned from Puna. Puna pulls his men back to the mountain, away from the beach. He must not be surrounded. He does not have enough men for that. There may not be enough time. Tell him he is outnumbered. Tell him to pray. Go!"

Coconut Man plunged out of the cave, startling the guards. The moon, now free from the clouds, lit the mountain path like a silver stream. From this height, he could see the beach far below and the darkness where the ocean met the sand. He could not distinguish the *hale* or other buildings. He could not see men, although he knew they must be there. Halfway down, he stopped running to listen for any noise of advancing warriors.

Had he not overheard the threats of

treason, the village would have been asleep when it was attacked. That thought sent a river of fear through him. *What had been the noise he heard on their escape? If not warriors, what was it?* Clearly, he had been mistaken because all was silent as he approached the *ahupua`a.* He did not even hear any sounds from Puna's men. That frightened him, too.

He did not want to be attacked by his friends, or his enemies if it came to that. He froze, barely breathing. No sound. He felt exposed and vulnerable on the path. He crouched and crawled into the bushes. It would do no good to get killed, his task to warn Puna unfinished. His legs would not support him. His muscles began to shake and he forced himself to breathe deeply as his dizziness increased. What caused the sounds he had heard as the group had approached the cave? *Perhaps his spirit body heard the warriors. It had happened before, perhaps it had happened again. It would be nice to be able to tell the difference.* He thought back to the exact nature of the sounds. Were they attack sounds? Or merely approach? He let his body relax on the hard ground, the bumpy stones reminding him he was indeed sitting. He leaned back, melding with a tree trunk, his hands relaxed at his sides. He inhaled. Flowers. Night air. His own sweat.

Back to the sounds. *Definitely warriors. Not attacking after all. Approaching, but far enough away they felt they didn't need stealth. Yet. How long ago was that? Where would they be now?*

He sent his spirit body out along the path to the *ahupua'a*. Quiet. He found the path toward La's beginning, toward the refuge. It too was quiet. Where was the wet district? How would one get to the wet district? He had never been there himself. Too far.

His spirit body was able to find Puna's men, well hidden and silent. Many men. This made him feel much safer. But still. He should be able to sense Ko'olau's men, too. Something was wrong.

He had his spirit run now, through the village, along the beach, even for a bit along the secret path to *pu'uhonua*. Nothing. Maybe he had made a terrible mistake? Maybe he had endangered himself and everyone else on some dream? *Some days I do not know what is real anymore. Perhaps I am living a dream?*

He brought his spirit body back. Perhaps Tutu knows. He sent his spirit body along the upland path to the caves. Tired now, he let it float rather than walk. *This is quite pleasant. Like a bird flies. The moonlight is bright and beautiful. Can I go higher? It is a little like when my life-thread grew thin and Kaleo pulled me like a kite. I floated then. It is not so hard. Higher. Relax. Above the trees! There is the cave. I can see the guards at the mouth.*

What he saw next caused his spirit body to fall out of the sky with a crash. His *kū* body was bound close enough with it to feel pain when it met the earth. That pain was nothing compared to its cause. The mountain above the caves crawled with hundreds of warriors. They did not use the paths, but slithered silently like sea snakes down the mountain. The ridge line was filled with shapes, sinewy and unstoppable. The lack of noise was the most unnerving. *Perhaps Ko`olau has found night marchers to fight for him?* Terror split Coconut Man in two. He sent his spirit body to Tutu to warn her while his real body scrambled out of hiding and began to run. He shouted as he ran.

"Ko`olau warriors! On the ridge. They are not coming to the *makai* village! They are attacking from the uplands. The caves! All are in danger!"

He must sound completely crazy, but he did not know what else to do. He ran through the village shouting for Puna. He heard the rustle of startled warriors, but he needed Puna. Where was Puna?

"Puna! My *ali`i!* You must hurry. The warriors are near the caves. If you all run, you will meet them there. If you delay, all might

333

perish!"

A large shape separated from the forest. Puna. Coconut Man threw himself down at Puna's feet. "My chief. You must believe me. No warriors come this way. The attack comes from above. Any hesitation could mean the loss of the entire village."

"How do you know? Why should I believe you?"

"You believed the *ahupua`a* was in enough danger to prepare for war, did you not?" Puna nodded. "I was the one to bring that knowledge here. I have no reason to lie. Respected members of your community trust me. Please, if I am lying, you may kill me."

"I will."

"But I am not. You must go now!"

"I am not fond of being told what I must do."

A man stepped out of the darkness. "My *ali`i.*" He knelt. "I believe him."

Another stepped out and knelt. "I, too."

Man after man followed suit until Coconut Man was surrounded. He felt his life-thread thinning and weak. He had done all he could. He must pull his spirit body back to his own body so he could accompany the men. He hoped it had been enough. He prayed Tutu had understood his message. He realized he was staring directly into Puna's face. Men had died for less than that. He collapsed once again.

"I will permit this." Coconut Man had no idea if Puna referred to the insult or his plea that his words be heeded. "Because of Kehau. For Kehau. And for Tutu, I will permit this. We go."

As one, the warriors pulled out of position and streamed up the mountain. Coconut Man struggled to his feet to follow. He could not run. If a Ko`olau jumped out of the bushes right now, he would just have to be killed.

With each step up the mountain, he pulled his spirit body to him. The life-thread was worn, and seemed to meet opposition. After far too few steps, Coconut Man heard the sounds of war. This time he knew they were real.

Chapter 38

Moonlight bright as day lit the mountain from the ridge to the clearing fronting the cave.

Coconut Man stood in the trees and watched, untrained and afraid. No weapon. The sounds were terrifying. Shrieks of wounded men combined with war cries. Already the clearing was slick with blood. A group of Ko`olau had reached the clearing and had attacked the few men guarding the cave. When Puna's men arrived, those in the center were trapped. At first, Puna's men took losses, now the Ko`olau were being eliminated. The rough terrain above the cave kept the Ko`olau from advancing quickly, but they came like the tide, constant, unstoppable.

Sling stones flew unceasingly and in the dense fighting, hit a target more often than not. Spears flew occasionally, but the distances were too short and many used them as lances, stabbing those around them and deflecting attacks. The spear shaft reached farther than the shark-tooth club or dagger.

Puna's men had engaged as soon as the first ones had reached the cave, and now Ko`olau held them at bay down the trail. When Puna's men attempted to swarm the clearing, several were picked off before they could retreat and flank the area. The sheer numbers of the Ko`olau frightened Coconut Man. From his vantage point, he saw Puna in the thick of the fray, and searched for Manō. The moon played hide and seek in the clouds and visibility was poor. The smell of blood and entrails was pervasive. Coconut Man could not tell which side took the most casualties. Both appeared to suffer heavily.

Men began to throw the dead off the mountain, just so they could have room to fight. *At least I hope they are dead*.

The site for the battle was poor, but was most to Puna's advantage, since only a few Ko`olau could enter the clearing at a time. The element of surprise had been lost and for now, Puna's women and children were safe in the cave. Coconut Man saw Puna's men regroup before the cave and attack the Ko`olau as they dropped into the clearing.

Coconut Man recognized almost no one. The battle was so fast and intense, the men covered in tattoos, blood, and dirt, were unrecognizable. Puna's helmet was the only beacon. The sounds were unbearable: the chop of shark-toothed clubs, the swish of spear or lance, the thud as it entered soft flesh, the screams of pain and fear, the falling of many men, the crash as they fell or were thrown from the mountain.

The numbers of the Ko`olau began to have effect. Puna's men were tired, and fresh men kept pouring from the ridge. As fast as Puna's warriors dispatched them, more spilled from above.

Tutu's voice entered his head. *Go now. Kona is here. Find him. Lead him to Puna.*

Happy to leave the battle, Coconut Man did not question the voice. He ran through the bushes, avoiding the trail, then he cut over when the mountain's tapering stopped at a cliff. The moonlight still came and went, oblivious to the war taking place below.

He skittered into the village. Still quiet. He sent his spirit body out. Yes. Kona was approaching from the beach. He had paddled in the dark, around the island. Coconut Man shuddered, the courage of that beyond his comprehension. And then to face a battle with unknown enemies. Kona was a great man. And a great friend.

Coconut Man ran to the beach to meet

338

the first canoe.

"*Aloha*. I have come to guide you."

"Who are you and why are you here?"

"The battle is. . . the other chief. . . Puna needs you."

The warriors facing him were huge. Sixty piled out of the giant canoe, with more canoes behind them.

"You are not making sense, man! Speak!"

Coconut Man backed up as more and more men filled the beach. Their energy and *mana* were overwhelming.

"Where is Puna? Why is it quiet? We are not too late?" This was asked by Kona himself. Coconut Man dropped to his knees. Kona was a larger version of Puna. If Puna was powerful, Kona was unstoppable.

"Chief. The Ko`olau have invaded by stealth and treachery. I was sent to guide you. The battle is up the mountain, just under the ridge. Puna is outnumbered and we are lost without your aid."

"Then lead!"

Coconut Man scrambled to his feet and ran. *I can't believe I am running. Again. I have never run so much in my life as I have this last moon cycle. If I live through this, I will never run anywhere again.*

He led them through the *makai* village to the upland path. He was keenly aware of the hundreds of men running behind him and wondered what would happen if he fell. *Probably be trampled to death like a bug under a boar's feet.* He ran first on the trail, higher than the *ali'i,* breaking *kapu. Just another thing to be punished for later.*

His breath came in painful spurts, but he heard almost nothing from the men following. When he heard the sounds of battle, he veered into the forest, allowing the warriors to flow past him like the Wai, silent and comforting in its power.

Tutu. They are here. Be strong. Kona is here. Coconut Man worked his way painfully back to his vantage point.

The additional men cheered Puna's warriors. They were no longer fighting alone. With renewed vigor, they fought side by side, colors of cloaks and headpieces the only difference.

The Ko`olau sensed the battle had turned, but it was too late for many of them.

Coconut Man saw a man he thought was the Ko`olau chief from his headpiece and cloak. Manō fought near that chief and they realized the influx of fresh men at the same time. The chief shouted something and his men began to work their way to the upper trail. Retreat? Escape? Coconut Man could not tell.

Manō did not want to go. His angry

shouts, too far to be understood, suggested he did not want to give up the chance at his new kingdom. The chief was not pleased to be argued with. They fought off Puna's men and continued their own disagreement.

The clearing became easier to see. Moon? No, La. More Ko'olau were above the cave. They had spears and seemed to seek specific targets. No one threw. Sling stones still flew, but less frequently as the battle shifted to exhausted hand to hand combat.

Weapons littered the clearing. Dead and wounded lay scattered like a child's toys, making the footing more perilous as men stood on bodies to fight.

Puna's men fought valiantly but were clearly at the end of their strength. Even Kona's men, relatively fresh, were now struggling. The Ko'olau, having had the advantage of rest before the attack, plus a downhill assault, fared better.

The Ko'olau chief shouted again and Coconut Man heard the retreat this time. The Ko'olau shifted toward escape. Manō refused and came into the clearing, slashing and stabbing. Kona's men kept him at bay, barely. Enough Ko'olau filled the clearing to make it hard for Coconut Man to see what happened. The spear throwers above the cave received their signal, and darkened the sky with *kauila* shafts. Not one, but many flights of spears shadowed the dawn sky.

La rose higher on his journey and Coconut Man saw most of the men in the clearing had been hit by spears--men on both sides in the last effort to destroy the *moku*--the district. The Ko`olau streamed away from the cave. Wounded men groaned and writhed. Coconut Man searched for Kona. He was near the cave mouth. *Puna? Where was Puna?*

Coconut Man saw Manō, wounded but moving, struggling toward a prone figure with a protruding spear.

Oh, no. No. No. No. Not Puna. Coconut Man dashed into the clearing. He closed his mind to the broken, bloody bodies he stepped on, trying to get to Manō's target before Manō. Manō held a shark's tooth club in one hand. A broken spear shaft pierced his other shoulder and that arm hung limply.

Coconut Man picked up a shark's tooth club. He knew nothing of weapons, but he had to do something.

He tried to shut out the sounds of the wounded and dying, but could not silence them completely. He had never seen such carnage. He knew that many of his fellow villagers would not return after this day.

Manō was having as much trouble

walking over human bodies as Coconut Man. Manō was intent on his victim.

Coconut Man saw that indeed, it was Puna who lay there. A spear had entered his leg with such force that when he fell, it speared him to the ground. No weapons lay within his reach and the crush of warriors around him made a nest, impossible to escape. Coconut Man was still several bodies away when Manō reached Puna.

"It is time, old man, to give up your reign."

Puna was conscious, but said nothing. Manō worked his way toward Puna's head to crush his skull.

"Manō! Don't!" Coconut Man struggled over limbs.

Manō halted, club raised. "You again. After I am finished with him, you are next." He lowered the club and squatted near Puna's face.

"Do you see? Even now, Coconut Man thinks he can win. But, as in all games, Manō always wins."

Coconut Man lunged and raised his club and brought it down with all his strength on the back of Manō's head. Manō fell sideways, into the pile of men surrounding Puna.   Another twig in the nest.

Puna's eyes met Coconut Man's and that was all he knew. He fainted.

Chapter 39

Coconut Man awoke to bright sun in his face and many men moving about the clearing. Puna had been removed and efforts were underway to aid the wounded. He sat up cautiously. The smell of death in the hot sun was overwhelming. In the morning light, the damage was worse than he could have imagined. He felt his mind retreat as his eyes took in the destruction.

He struggled to his feet, trying unsuccessfully not to step on anyone. He made his way to the cave, now empty save for the things people had left behind.

He felt his brain sliding away from the battle and circled the clearing, looking to the trees until he found the lower path. He refused to look for Manō, and could not bear to see the faces of those he knew. He gazed upward, and felt for the path with his feet, as some of the

Ko'olau had met their ends here, too.

At least the battle left the village whole, even though its inhabitants are terribly damaged.

Indeed the structures were sound, but the people, even those who escaped injury, were far from sound. He knew Tutu would be helping Kehau tend to Puna. He did not know where to look for 'Umi. He sought Kaleo's *hale*.

Kaleo and his mother sat before the doorway, he picking listlessly at some food, and she roasting sweet potatoes in a small, smoky fire.

"*Aloha*, Lea, Kaleo."

Kaleo looked up. "*Aloha.*"

"Sit, Coconut Man, join us," Lea invited.

"*Mahalo*. Kaleo, have you seen Honu this morning?"

"Not since we came down from the cave together."

"What happened at the cave last night?"

"Where were you? You did not come back."

"I watched from the other side. I guided Kona's men to the clearing. Was anyone hurt in the cave?"

"A few, but not too badly. The Ko`olau tried to enter at first, before Puna's men arrived, but Lele, and my mother, the other women and the guards fought them off." His voice was filled with pride.

Coconut Man looked at Lea. "Are you all right?"

"A few scratches. It is nothing."

"The others. Are they all right, too?"

"Lele was pushed by a Ko`olau and hit her head on a rock. He tried to stab her when she fell, but we took care of him." Her smile was grim. "Lele is fine today." She looked at Coconut Man. "The Ko`olau saw that we were not easy victims. Then Puna's men arrived, and they had to give up on us. Sometimes, one of them got near the mouth of the cave, and then," she clapped her hands, "he was no longer a threat."

Coconut Man was surprised at this core of hardness in the women of the *ahupua`a*. He supposed he should not have been, for he had heard of women who would fight along side their men, but he had difficulty picturing Lele of the kapa dyes and wise, gentle Tutu suddenly taking arms and attacking a muscular male warrior. He shook his head in amazement.

"What?" Kaleo had begun to eat.

"I am just impressed, that is all. Impressed by your mother. And impressed by this village. I have not experienced this kind of caring before."

"Where have you been?" Lea's voice held a hint of amusement. "Surely, wherever you are from, people care about each other?"

"I suppose. I just have never seen it before." His mind went back to the many villages he had visited. They were only stops on his quest to make baskets and trade, eat and survive. *What a way to live. How did I do it all those years? And why? All that travel without seeing. Talking without listening. Touching without feeling.*

Lea patted his hand and brought him back. "Well, this is your home now. Whatever you decide to do." She smiled.

Coconut Man smiled at Kaleo, who scowled in return. "So, the women and children are safe. What of the men?"

Lea shook her head. "That I do not know. The men are dealing with the dead. Most of the women are taking care of the injured. I am going to help. I just needed to check on this one. Make sure he ate. You know."

Coconut Man did not know, but he could guess. The terrible night had frightened everyone, and Lea needed to be with her child, doing something normal like preparing food, before she once again faced the pain of loss. He did not know, but assumed she had lost her husband in some other battle, and facing the loss of others was akin to her own.

"I should go." Lea brushed off her hands. "Kaleo, you either stay here, or find Honu and the others. I want you in the village, not on the beach. Do you understand?"

A reluctant nod. "And you are not to go to the cave. For any reason." The scowl, but another nod.

"I want to help. Will you take me with you?" Coconut Man stood.

"Yes. Come."

Lea led them to a group of *hale* that now housed the injured. First the sound then the smell struck him. Lea entered without hesitation and Coconut Man tried to emulate her confidence. Two steps inside and he froze. Broken men lay everywhere on *kapa* pallets. Both men and women tended the wounded. It looked hopeless to Coconut Man. Even the *kūpuna* were there to assist.

Lea headed for a woman bent over a warrior with a shoulder wound. They conferred and Lea then went to a corner and sat to pull pieces of *kapa* and wrap the bloody arm of the man lying there.

Coconut Man followed and sat, too. "What can I do?" The man, eyes closed, moaned.

"Hand me that calabash." She pointed. He did. She swiveled to the next man and assessed his leg. Filthy and bloody. She dipped *kapa* into the gourd and began to clean the wound. "This will help prevent infection. These stab wounds are deep. Some of them will fester. It will be difficult."

Coconut Man looked into the face of the man. He looked flushed, the skin tight and reddish. Lea nodded. "Yes, he is already infected. The wound is deep, the muscle damaged."

Coconut Man scanned the *hale* and saw similar scenes in every corner. It would be like this all over the village. Was anyone undamaged? Even Kona and Puna were hurt. How gravely, was the question. The entire *moku's* well-being hung on that question.

The day passed with Coconut Man no wiser. All worked feverishly to help the wounded. The dead. The lost. The afraid. Coconut Man wandered from group to group, not quite able to fit in, to render aid or comfort. He recognized the feeling. He was still a stranger. In his previous life, it had not bothered him. Now, it did.

He would find the children and see if that helped. The *keiki* had brought him into this village, and perhaps they could do it again. He returned to Kaleo's *hale*.

The boy was there, as he had been that morning. The sun was completing his journey, but the day still held heat.

"Kaleo. Let us walk."

Kaleo glanced up. He said nothing, but

got to his feet.

Coconut Man set out, Kaleo a pace behind. "Where is Honu?" Coconut Man asked.

"I have not seen her."

"We'll go to her *hale* and ask."

Honu's mother met them at the doorway. "Aloha," Coconut Man called. "How are you?"

"We are well, and give thanks for that."

"Where is Io?"

"He is tending his nets. He helped with the dead for a while, then needed to cleanse himself. The village needs food. He has gone with some men to fish for the village."

Coconut Man remembered the shark fishing. All the men who worked under 'Umi, as *konohiki* and head fisherman.

"What of 'Umi? Do you know?" Coconut Man did not want to hear, but had to know.

"His wounds were small. He is not fishing. His role as *konohiki* takes precedence now. Others must fish."

"Where is he?"

"I do not know now, but he has spent the day with the dead and wounded. He will get the village running, you will see!"

"Yes. I am sure of that. Have you heard how Puna or Kona are?"

"No. Their condition is secret."

"Where are they?"

"Look for the guards. I must go." She

strode past them.

"Honu?" Kaleo shouted after her, his first words to her.

"The Wai," she called back.

Coconut Man and Kaleo found Honu filling gourds at the river bank. Her hair pulled back from her face with a pick, she looked older now.

"Honu!" Kaleo ran to her. She turned and they stared at each other, inches apart. Then Kaleo leaned in until their foreheads touched.

Coconut Man sensed such a wave of affection flowing between them, he felt almost embarrassed. They were children, but already their love exceeded anything he had felt. They would bond in marriage when the time came, although they had no such thoughts. Yet. He smiled.

"Come on you two. Honu, please catch me up on what is happening. What have you heard?"

They sat on the log and watched the river flow, and Honu spoke. "Father is well. His leg prevented him from moving quickly and I was worried. But he managed and is now fishing. I sat in the *hale* most of the day. I was sad. But now I am better. She smiled at them both.

"Do you know how many are injured or dead?"

"No. Most of the men are in the uplands

clearing. The *kāhuna* have been praying and blessing, as have we all."

"What of Puna or Kona?"

"I don't know."

"Have the other children heard anything?"

"I have seen no one today, but you." She looked at Kaleo. "My mother told me to stay near the *hale*, so I did."

"Mine, too."

"I think all the mothers did," Honu continued. "So we have not seen each other."

"Let us see what we can find out." Kaleo's spirit was back.

"I must take this water back."

Coconut Man and Kaleo carried the water for Honu. They left it at Io's *hale* and looked for a *hale* surrounded by armed guards. The *ali`i.*

"No one is going to let us in, or tell us anything." Coconut Man stopped across from the *hale.* They sat. A man came and lit torches throughout the village. La had finished his ride. Clouds sat over the village like a lid on a gourd. The night was still and close. Perhaps more rain.

Retainers came and went, but Tutu did not appear.

"All *seems* well within," Coconut Man whispered.

"My mother will want me back," Honu said.

"Mine, too. Besides, I am hungry."

"Me, too. Let us go back." Coconut Man rose and walked the children home. He did not have to, the *hale* were close, and nothing would happen. He wanted to. The children seemed to want it, too.

Alone and at a loss, Coconut Man was unsure where to go. Village life was not what it had been and would be again someday, but he did not want to sleep outside. He also did not feel he could sleep at Tutu's *hale* based solely on her earlier invitation. He was hungry. Eat first. Would there be food at the men's eating *hale*?

He found the *hale* lit and active, and felt grateful for that discovery. It seemed that the *hale* was a stop for all who needed food or rest during their horrible labors. The men were subdued, talk limited to passing bowls back and forth or discussing still-needed tasks. Coconut Man sat and helped himself. Several men nodded to him in greeting. As he ate, his own exhaustion settled in.

'Umi entered and sat near Coconut Man, grabbing the closest food with a mumbled prayer of thanks, eating it hungrily.

"'Umi. 'Umi. Can you tell me what is going on?"

Mouth full, 'Umi turned to look at him. "What do you mean?"

Under his fierce scrutiny, Coconut Man's courage wavered. "Have we lost many men?"

"We have lost enough." Fatigue ringed his eyes and grayed his skin. His voice softened. "Not as many as we could have. Not as many as I feared."

Coconut Man nodded. "The *ali'i?*"

"I don't know. No one is talking."

"What will happen in the village?"

"I don't know that either. My job is to keep it running. We will fish. We will farm. We will build our canoes and grow our kalo and raise our children. That will never stop." 'Umi pushed in a last mouthful and rose someone unsteadily. He addressed all in the *hale.* "We are finished for the night. Guards are posted. You will sleep. You will eat. Tomorrow, we take care of the dead. We pray, we grieve, we cleanse. We finish this! Tell the others."

His words, like commandments, hung in the air after he left the eating house. No one spoke. Silently, each man got up and went out. Presumably to follow 'Umi's directions. Coconut Man knew no one to tell. He went to the men's sleeping *hale.* Instead of going behind it as he had in the past, he entered, found a pile of *kapa,* and fell into an exhausted, dreamless sleep. Others came and went, but he heard none of it. The sound of running feet awoke him. He knew La's journey was well underway from the stifling heat in the *hale*. He was alone, and plunged out into fresh air and clear skies.

People ran by he joined them. "What is going on?"

"Puna is going to speak. To all of us!"

Puna! Puna is well enough to speak. This is a grand day indeed.

Chapter 40

Puna sat on a stool padded with *kapa.* He leaned against a *hale* pole for support. He looked very chiefly to Coconut Man. Despite all he had been through, the devastation of his village, and the betrayal by not only one of his subjects but a relative, he still looked ready and capable of ruling.

Coconut Man smiled. All would be well.

Puna addressed them. "*Mahalo* my people, for your support in this time of war and treason." The people lay in the dirt, all castes, showing the highest honor and obeisance for their king. "I have seen much and discovered some unpleasant truths. Many good men have died for you. For me. I will not forget that. I will continue to bestow prosperity and joy here. Today we inter and pray for the dead. Ko`olau's warriors fought well, too. They have died with honor. I do not deny them this simply because one of my own betrayed me.

"You will live with honor as well. I wish to leave you a gift. That gift is men. You have lost many in your village, and I will leave men--guards, farmers, fishermen. Their families will join them and your prosperity will grow. The gods have seen to our victory. I am doubly blessed that my brother-in-spirit Kona came to our aid." A cheer went up. "And, that Kona is healing well and will join me when I return to my *ahupua`a*." Another cheer. "My queen joins us." Kehau appeared in the doorway behind Puna, with Tutu's brown face behind her. A huge cheer.

Kehau looked fully recovered. Coconut Man saw her beauty as Puna saw it. She absolutely glowed. She knelt next to her husband and they shared a look as bright as a life-thread.

Puna continued. "As I said, many fought for us, many died for us. But I wish to discuss certain crimes." The crowd quieted. "Kaiki was murdered and one was accused of that crime. He is still among us and I wish to address that now."

Coconut Man wanted to throw up. He had all but forgotten Manō's manipulation of the *ho`oponopono* and his own flight to the *heiau*. In the context of war, that experience seemed minor. But apparently not to Puna. He would die now. He had not the strength to make it to the refuge a second time, even if he could escape the hundreds of loyal subjects lying between himself and the trail.

"Coconut Man!" Puna's voice was thunder. All strength left Coconut Man's limbs. "Coconut Man! Come before me. Now."

Coconut Man crawled between bodies to lie at Puna's feet, waiting for the death pronouncement. It would not be pretty. It would be slow and painful.

"Coconut Man. Kneel before me."

He rose to his knees, head down. *Odd. Better to cut my head off? A quick death, perhaps?*

"This man. This stranger who came to our village with his baskets, who took nothing and gave much, saved us."

What? The crowd murmured in confusion.

"He discovered the plot against me. He could have done nothing. He could have run before the battle, but he did not. He fought his own battle and saved us. He was accused of a murder he did not commit. He was in fact, punished for that crime, but that did not stop him from continuing to seek help from the gods on our behalf. He is the reason most of you are alive right now. We would have been attacked while asleep, under cover of darkness. We have much to be thankful for. He is to be honored in this village forever. If he wishes to make it his home. he will always be welcome. After the way he was treated, he may not want to stay. But if he does, he is in the *ali`i's* favor." The crowd roared and clapped. Coconut Man was glad he knelt with his head down, because he could not stop his tears.

When the cheering waned, he was allowed to crawl a bit away. He heard Puna also honoring and thanking his brother, Kona, for his aid, but could not fully focus on that, still reeling from his own experience. A feast was announced, with hula and music and games to be held three days from now.

The village was cleansed. The dead honored, purified and stripped to bone as ritual demanded. Prayers said. Widows knocked out their teeth and grieved. All wept. All comforted. All rebuilt.

Fires stayed lit and enormous amounts of food were prepared. Kona had recovered enough to participate. Some of his warriors opted to stay and rebuilt the village along with Puna's men. With so many working together, the physical aspects of damage from the storm and the battle were quickly erased.

The emotional damage would take longer. Coconut Man felt fortunate that he had not known many who had died. Nuu, 'Ehu's friend, had perished at the clearing. Old Kai's heart could not take the strain. Palani was also dead, but it was unclear at whose hand. Coconut Man sighed. Everywhere he looked, someone he did know in the village was touched by grief. It would take time. Many of the women were widows now, and that made him sad, too. Perhaps the new warriors would help ease that darkness.

He sat on the rocks at the beach, his beach, with a partial basket between his knees. It felt like years since he had woven anything. His hands were a little stiff, but still remembered their task. Done. A simple basket, not too big, good for holding shells, leaves, coconuts, any small or medium-sized things. The wedding basket was long gone in the storm, as well as the one for the *ali`i*. Almost all the baskets in the village had been destroyed or swept away in the winds.

He would make more. He had time. He put the basket in the salt-water to cure and pulled more fronds to him to start a new one.

A shadow fell over him and sand sprayed into his lap. Brown feet stood next to the fronds.

"Hey, wanna come with us?" Kaleo stood above him, all respect for his elders evaporated. His usual companions straggled beyond him and Honu was at his side. "We're going to the tide pools and then we're going to

360

swim. Wanna come?"

"I should finish. . ." Coconut Man started. But, he didn't want to finish. In fact, he wanted to go to the tide pools and then swim. "Yes, I do."

*   *   *   *   *

The day of the wedding dawned clear and bright. The *kāhuna* had chosen an auspicious day to unite 'Ehu and Lehua. The village was happy to celebrate again, and all joined in the preparations. The wedding *hale* had been rebuilt. The *imu* had been prepared and flower leis festooned the site and the people. The day waned and torches were lit. The wedding was about to begin.

Coconut Man settled on a mat adjacent to Kaleo and Lea. Honu and her family were near. The deep mournful sound of the conch shells floated out of the night. The *kahuna* sprinkled salt water and blessed the union. 'Ehu and Lehua stood radiant. A new beginning. For everyone.

Glossary–many Hawai'ian words have more than one meaning. I chose the one which best applies to the story. Hawai'ian does not use the letter s, and plural nouns are indicated by a change in spelling, punctuation or context. I have taken liberties when combining Hawai'ian and English in this regard.

Handy Hawaiian Dictionary
Judd, Henry P.
Pukui, Mary Kawena
Stokes, John F. G.
Mutual Publishing
9th Edition 2004

The Ahupua`a
Kamehameha Schools Press
Third edition, 1994

Ahupua'a	land division from mountains to sea
akamai	skillful
'ākia	false `ōhelo (a tree)*
Ali'i	chief, king
Aloha	greeting, affection, sympathy
'aumakua	ancestral spirit
'awa	kawa root, often fermented into a drink
'Ehu	reddish, light-colored natives

hale	house, home
he'e	octopus
heiau	large place of worship
Honu	turtle
Hōlua	sled used on grassy slopes
Ho'oponopono	to superintend, make up deficit
hūnōwai	father or mother-in-law
'iliahi	sandalwood *
imu	ground oven
ipu	gourd
kahuna	expert practitioner
kāhili	feathered standard symbolic of royalty
kalo	(taro) a staple plant, can be made into poi
Kāne	god of creation, all living things
kanaka	a man
kapa	cloth, bedclothes
kī	(also ti) a woody plant of the lily family
kō	sugar cane
kōnane	Hawaiian checkers
konohiki	overseer of chief's estate
Kū	god of war
kukui	candle-nut
kūpuna	elders
limu	a genral name for underwater plants

lolo	idiot
Lono	god of peace, agriculture, games
lomi	to press, massage
mahalo	approve, praise, thank, wonder
malo	loincloth
mana	authority, power
Manō	shark
mele	chant, song
milo	Portia tree*
moku	district, land division
niu	coconut palm and fruit
noni	Indian mulberry
'ohana	family, clan
'ōkole	buttocks
olonā	fibrous shrub, cord*
'ō'ō	type of bird
'ōpae	shrimp
poke	to slice, cut, piece
'ulu	breadfruit
'Umi	to throttle, stifle, strangle
wana	sea urchin
wauke	paper mulberry tree*

In the Ahupua`a

Coconut Man	nomadic basket weaver
'Ehu	young man in the village
Nuu	'Ehu's friend
Kaleo	a loud, happy boy
Honu	a girl, Kaleo's friend and daughter of Io and Lea
Io	a net maker
Lea	his wife
Lele	a kapa maker
Tutu	a grandmother-figure
Manō	a bully and power-seeker
Palani	one of his sycophants
Lako	another, but not too bright
'Umi	konohiki, village headman
Puna	ali'i moku, chief of the district
Kona	chief of another district
Kahuiwi	priest at the refuge
Ko'olau	chief of the wet district, The wet district, or warriors in that district

Victoria Heckman is also the author of the K.O.'d in... Hawai'i mystery series, over 75 short stories and articles and the editor of four anthologies. She divides her time between Hawai'i and California. Visit her website at www.victoriaheckman.com

www.ingramcontent.com/pod-product-compliance
Lightning Source LLC
Chambersburg PA
CBHW050912250626
47155CB00001B/203